MW01614090

The Secret of a
Long Journey

Sandra Shwayder Sánchez

Floricanto ™ Press

Copyright © 2012 by Sandra Shwayder Sánchez

Copyright © 2012 of this edition by Floricanto™ Press and Berkeley Press

All rights reserved. No part of this publication may be stored in a retrieval system, transmitted or reproduced in any way, including but not limited to photocopy, photograph, magnetic, laser or other type of record, without prior agreement and written permission of the publisher.

Floricanto is a trademark of Floricanto Press.

Berkeley Press is an imprint of Inter American Development, Inc.

Floricanto™ Press
19043 Marilla St.
Northridge, California 91324
(415) 552-1879
www. floricantopress. com
ISBN: 978-1480285033
"Por nuestra cultura hablarán nuestros libros. Our books shall speak for our culture."
Roberto Cabello-Argandoña, Editor
Yasmeen Namazie, Co-Editor

THE SECRET OF A LONG JOURNEY

Acknowledgements and Special Thanks

I want to acknowledge and thank Orlando Mondragón for introducing me to the fascinating history of the descendants of Spanish *Conversos* in the new world, Gloria DeVidas Kirchheimer for her editorial help and for providing the Ladino proverbs, to Catherine Robles Shaw for graciously permitting us to use her artwork on the cover and to Matthew Bokovoy for his editorial assistance and encouragement in developing the manuscript. Also to editors of The Denver Journal of International Law and Policy, Carmi House, and the Texas Historical Society for graciously granting permission to include the quotes that introduce several chapters and to Floricanto Press for bringing this work into the light. Additionally, I owe many thanks to many people who nurtured the literary muse in my life: to my mother Jeanne for surrounding my childhood with literature, music and art, to my father Bud for reading to me at a very early age, setting an example of impeccable integrity with his word and sharing his love and knowledge of the night sky constellations, to my stepmother Carol whose quiet strength and vigilant love kept him among us longer than I could otherwise have hoped, to my friend and role model of half a century, Ita Willen who got me started writing stories, to my old friend Ugo Scotto whose enthusiasm kept me writing and to Jack Salamanca whose praise gave me confidence, to Susan Bright and Peter Burnham, who not only published early work but whose editorial feedback and example of social responsibility in literature was better than an MFA program for me, to my husband Ed Sánchez who graciously shared me with so many fictional characters, and to my daughters Rachel and Sara who learned a little from me but taught me so much more.

Dedication

"Life is a journey and death a destination"
This last book is dedicated to those who have arrived: Sol and
Ida Shwayder, Bernard and Lil Hershorn, Bud Shwayder and
Jeanne Segal, and to brother Dougie whose journey was short but
left the world an infinitely better place.

Chapter One
The Woman Who Talked To Birds
Flanders 1566

"My generation has seen all of this: how the sons of Essau exiled us and imprisoned us and destroyed us, and told us: 'flee to the hills, lest the pursuers find you." First it was Spain and then Portugal and they did everything to consume us alive. Yet, they have not vented all their anger and they still seek to harm us. They have stood on the road to plunder and loot us, leaving us naked to the elements . . . there wasn't a single beastly thing which they did not inflict on Israel, killing them by the sword, by starvation, or by the plague; selling into captivity and forcing them to convert. Thus, when a man fled from the lion, he was confronted by a bear, and when he came home and rested his hand against the wall, he was bitten by a snake."

From the medieval account by Elijah Capsali within The Expulsion 1492 Chronicles, David T. Raphael (Ed), Carmi House Press, 1992.

It was the far off cry of a single crow that always woke Mayken at the nighttime edge of dawn. In the old days, in the countryside of Brabant before she married and moved to town, she would get up and run to watch the morning mist lift from the hills, magically unveiling the landscape. Whether green and gold or snow white with touches of amber and auburn, it always took her breath away, the exquisite valley seen from above, the winding glittering creek, the intricacy and mystery of the filigreed trees and even the people, as they rose and went about the mundane tasks of the morning, a part of the natural world around them like the crows and the geese that flew here and there, waking the world. Even the people in the very early morning were so exquisite to Mayken that she felt compelled to try to paint them. She had grown up with her father's art and met her husband when he came to live with, assist and study with her father. Pieter was now himself a successful painter and member of the guild. Painting the world around her and sometimes the world inside her was as much a part of her life as drawing breath.

Mayken painted her landscapes from memory but peopled them with the faces and figures she'd drawn from the town and her paintings were full of small oddities for the keen observer: a man slit the throat of another in the midst of harvest, lovers embraced in the midst of holocaust. There was no detail in reality or in dream that she did not closely observe and long remember and sooner or later everything she ever saw, or dreamed, or envisioned as she listened to stories, found its way into some crowded painting. Her husband kept Mayken's work stored in his own studio and occasionally found a buyer for one of them but it was not commonly known that she was an artist.

Now she watched the world from the tower of a house in the central square of the town where she could see the Cathedral and the market place. Sometimes she went out and about, but often her husband, for her own safety, kept her locked in the house. He was not a cruel man but worried for good reason. Mayken had succumbed to those same symptoms of madness that had overtaken her own mother, during pregnancy and seeing the change in her, Pieter was relieved that their daughter was stillborn. Mayken would often forget where and when and who she was. She would converse, and not so quietly, with voices only she could hear. She would become alternately sad or enraged or sometimes, not often, joyous, and Pieter would stroke her arm, try to hold her although she would immediately squirm out of his embrace, and when he spoke softly to her, his was the only voice she seemed not to hear. Then as suddenly as she descended into this other world where he could not follow, she would emerge quiet and calm and sorry and there was no regular season to her madness, and no reason he could discern or foresee for the sudden storms. Like the weather she was, closer to god, the housekeeper told him. Blessed or cursed, he mourned for her each time it happened. When she would wander about, lost in her interior world of fantasy that did not connect to any real road home, Pieter decided to lock her inside the house. He knew that a woman lost and rambling in her mind was likely to be picked up as a witch and burned. It was happening all around them in those times:

witches, heretics, *Marranos*. It was a time of well kept secrets and hidden lives.

Thus, when Mayken watched the morning sunrise, she watched discreetly, standing behind the wall and peering out the window opening from the side observing her world from a secret space. The first to move about the streets were the cripples who positioned themselves by the entrance to the Cathedral in order to catch and coax alms from the people entering there for morning mass. Mayken was fascinated by the combination of the grotesque and the ordinary and the way it all blended into the music from the Cathedral: the voices of the nuns and the voices of the bells, and whatever was immediately awkward or abrupt became ultimately part of the overall choreography of the town and ultimately graceful, as if the people only moved to the rhythm of the bells and stood still, interrupted mid stride, when the bells and the voices were silent. After watching a while and humming with the chanting nuns, perhaps taking a few steps as if shadowing some figure down below, Mayken would begin the work of her day.

Holding a piece of charcoal loosely in her hand and facing a piece of precious paper set on a smooth wooden board on an easel, she would begin to move her arm. She would do it with the same rhythms she had observed in the movement of the people below, the farmer leading a beast burdened with the produce of his garden, the rapid stride of the tall laundress delivering her basket of clean sheets to some wealthy family, and the running and darting of children. She did not miss the trip and lurch of the one legged man leaning on a rough cut crutch until she was able to reproduce not only their faces and figures but the special ways in which they moved. Later she would incorporate these figures into her paintings on canvas. The one legged man was often accompanied by a hunchback who would leer up at her from a greasy grey, hooded cowl, toothless, and with keen eyes that frightened her. Even from such a great distance she feared he could see her, perhaps even deep into her own eyes, and she wondered if by observing him, she had angered him for he would pucker his lips at her as if scolding or perhaps she only imagined it.

Many of the beggars below her window were blind, but one among them seemed to see nonetheless, focused inward into a world that Mayken thought she could understand. She only knew he was blind because he felt out each step with a stick, then stumbled and fell over something that a mischievous boy had put in front of him.

She saw him once and then not again for a long time and by then he had a companion who helped him to find his way through the street and prompted him when to put forth his hand toward some potentially generous individual. Mayken was always glad when people stopped to give a gift of coins and receive a blessing. There were some people who rushed by, oblivious or perhaps offended, by such a state of destitution and toward these she felt a momentary anger for didn't they understand that anyone could be toppled by unforeseen disaster into a similar state? Her heart ached for these men and women, so poor already and suffering physical deprivations as well. She painted them more often than the handsome, whole and richly dressed citizens of the town because she could not give the poor ones justice or mercy, sight or straightness or return lost limbs, but she could notice and acknowledge their existence and that was something she knew everyone longed for.

Sometimes there were scuffles among the beggars and one night she heard angry grunts and cries but could not make out the words nor how many voices were involved nor if they were the voices of men or women or both. In the morning two vultures had joined the birds that flew over the town and some large men carried a body out to the fields around the town to bury the unknown body, man or woman, she didn't know, couldn't tell. Later she heard rumors that it had been an old woman and that she had been defiled in cruel ways. Mayken's imagination was so vivid that she trembled and felt chilled just hearing about it.

Balancing precariously on the edge between two worlds, each its own kind of dark abyss, the world that was supposed to be real and the world that existed only her own mind, Mayken lived her life carefully and vicariously. Being confined, she watched the movements of the people below her window with great interest. Being childless, she especially loved to watch the children and, as she aged, the young men and women who might have been her children now grown. She took too much interest in these people who passed through her field of vision sometimes daily, sometimes only once but they were part of both her worlds and she needed them and held on to them in her paintings.

One moonlit autumn night, Mayken saw a man come and go from the bell tower who interested her very much. She saw him again at dawn running as if pursued by dogs. His awkward movements and the way he always looked behind to see who was there, even when no one was there, made him seem childlike, even quite senseless, and she wondered where he was from and what he had done that he needed to hide. Sometimes she thought she heard him cry and try to speak but only grunts and whimpers came out. Perhaps she imagined it. He did not appear to have any money, she never saw him buy food and he did not join the group of morning beggars around the corner from his hiding place. In fact he ran inside to hide when they appeared. Mayken worried about this strange awkward young man and asked the housekeeper, who Pieter had hired to clean and cook and do errands, to take a fresh baked loaf of bread and leave it just inside the door to the bell tower. The woman who knew not to ask questions did as she was told. The bread was wrapped in a fine linen napkin with Mayken's embroidered initials on it.

Some days later Mayken saw with gladness and relief that the young man, with much frantic use of his hands and nodding vigorously and stuttering loudly, had made friends with the one legged man and the hunchback. She noticed as well that the one legged man had traded his rough crutch for a fancy wooden leg and a cane and that his companion's cloak was no longer greasy and threadbare but seemed new, made of thick warm black wool. She knew the wool of the black sheep was most dear and wondered what generous person had made such improvements possible for those poor men. She realized, as she watched the two coming and going and talking to a well-dressed man that they had had the good fortune to have attracted the beneficent attention of a newly-arrived priest to the town for she saw him give them alms, which made them laugh with delight. Mayken wondered about this priest who dressed in fine red silk and black wool and wore a large gold cross of intricate craftsmanship.

That autumn was brilliant with the warm colors of red, amber, rust and fiery orange, odd she thought that death should be presaged with such hot colors. Mayken longed to breath it all in. Pieter took her walking as often as he could or she would accompany the housekeeper on her errands. She would have slept outside if she could have, wanting that closeness to the colors of sky and leaves, the cleansing breezes, the full moon huge at dusk and again at dawn. She would wake in the night and walk to her window just to look at it, that huge full moon. In the bright moonlit nights a drama in four acts unfolded for her and she did not realize until the last act that it was a tragedy.

It began with dancing, the autumn leaves dancing on the air and the breeze blowing away the heat and dirt of summer, fresh. It was a fresh day and a happy one apparently for the timid senseless young man who always hid away in the bell tower was outside in the sunshine, dancing a little jig and laughing. The one legged man and his hunchbacked companion came around the corner and laughed with him and even tried a few dance steps, stumbling and strange. Mayken had no idea what it meant and couldn't hear them but she laughed too. She had begun to care so much about this young man and worried about his loneliness. Now he was out with friends, enjoying himself. They tired quickly and stood there, the three of them nodding and smiling and the two crippled fellows panting from their brief and awkward exertions. Then they all disappeared around a corner and Mayken went back to her charcoal and easel. She was working on the figures for yet another huge and crowded painting.

The next act transpired that same night. This time the young man had retreated into the bell tower which he clearly considered his home. The other two had walked him back and then met their friend the priest with the large fancy filigreed gold cross and wearing new silks, not red this time, but purple, absolutely magnificent beneath his auburn woolen robe. They whispered and money was passed and hidden and Mayken, observing this began to worry.

Act three took place a few days later; Mayken had lost count although she had been watching each day to see what would happen next. This time all the players arrived on the stone stage beneath her window at the same time. It appeared that the one legged man and the hunchback wanted to introduce their young friend to the priest and for a while it was a friendly meeting, all smiles and nods. It appeared that the two men had been teaching the young one who could barely speak to say things, and she watched him as he spoke, with difficulty, proud that he had learned some sentences. But they were not the right sentences or else he spoke them badly because the priest stopped smiling and became enraged at all of them, yelling and waving his arms. Not long thereafter two other very large men came wearing black with the sign of the Inquisition on the backs of their capes, and shackled the man who could barely speak and now wouldn't speak, and took him away. The other two had disappeared lest they be arrested as well, not at all concerned for their young friend, perhaps even enjoying his distress. Mayken knew there were people who derived pleasure from the misfortune of others, maybe even set them up just to watch them fall. She always felt stunned and outraged as human beings should simply not be like that. She related the series of incidents to Pieter who told her that the young man in the bell tower was not her responsibility. She could not worry about everyone, but of course she couldn't help it and she watched for the young man every day.

Then nothing happened for several weeks. Mayken watched from her window as fewer and fewer people scurried about, buffeted by cold winds and not wanting to be outside any longer than necessary. All the red and golden leaves blew off the trees leaving bare black branches to create a frenzy of design across her horizon, and then one morning he was there, the young man, and she wondered if she imagined him or if he really was hanging from a scaffold built in the night. In that last act, the man who couldn't talk squirmed on the gallows and cried and screamed making no sense, just noise, until death quieted him, and the only sound was the scurry and scuffle of dead leaves blowing along the street. A period of sadness overtook Mayken that lasted through the winter. She painted pictures of black birds against white snow and dreamed of flying. She wouldn't speak until spring.

Spring teased out the buds early that year only to yield to a last long snow storm that killed the early buds and flowers and discouraged the townspeople and the farmers just beyond the town. With that first early warming, came a strange old woman who stopped every person in the town that she passed and babbled incoherently in a rough country dialect so that the people became annoyed with her and hurried on their ways. The housekeeper found her near the Cathedral and brought her to the house, knowing Mayken would want to help her if she could.

At first the woman was overjoyed that Mayken seemed to understand her but she soon became dismayed as she watched Mayken's expression of concentration turn to pity. The woman was looking for her grown son, a big strong man with the mind of a small child who had run away and disappeared after the last harvest. As if afraid to allow Mayken to break in with bad news, the woman talked on and on, explaining how he'd been god's gift to her, a barren woman already old, not grown in her belly, but left in the hay like Moses for her to find and already big enough to be talking. But he'd never learned more than a few words that he combined with gestures and grunts to communicate. He could draw quite well, she told Mayken, imitating the way her son would draw in the dirt with a stick for hours and hours. When he had attained his full growth and considerable strength he would have fits of wildness when he would try to hurt himself, banging his head against a wall, or attack strangers who might be passing by. Sometimes he would run off and they would spend entire days searching for him. That was when her husband fashioned a halter for him like a beast of the fields and they kept him tied to a stout post set deep in the ground behind their cottage.

At harvest time he was set free to help in the fields which he loved to do. His job was to carry the heavy baskets filled with the colorful fruits of the earth to the stone building where everything was sorted, piled, hung in the sun to dry or set to ferment in barrels. He would be so exhausted at the end of the day that he slept soundly until dawn and didn't try to run off. His mother hoped he had learned to stay home and perhaps they could stop tethering him like an animal. But the first day he went to the field and found it bare with nothing left for him to do, he wandered off and was not seen again.

As the cold winter set in, her husband fell ill and she nursed him until he died one night and then she waited alone for the spring so she could venture forth to find her son.

Mayken listened carefully to the story, imagining the young man she remembered working in golden fields, how much he must have enjoyed that. She had no idea what to tell this woman about the young man who had wandered into her heart and out of her life in a less than a month's time. Had she really seen him die? Or had he been just another of her many hallucinations?

Mayken stopped listening to the woman who was so eager for a happy ending to her search, and looked up at the bare trees, winter coming again briefly to the land, and birds gathering into flocks swirling around the city preparing to migrate and confused by that last unseasonable storm. But the countrywoman was still talking to Mayken expecting somehow that if she talked long enough her search could end joyfully. Mayken was finding it harder and harder to concentrate on the woman's story; her thoughts went more easily with the birds. Then the woman stopped. She had run out of things to say.

Mayken knew the woman would never stop searching for her son, so she told the woman that she had seen him, had given him bread, had tried to converse with him and had even danced with him once. Finally she told the woman that her son had died before the harsh winter in the shelter of the Cathedral, a fact that seemed to give the woman some comfort. Illness, Mayken told her, perhaps the same illness that had taken the woman's husband. The woman thanked Mayken for befriending her poor son, she was grateful to think that he had not been alone or afraid during his last days.

Mayken fed the weary old woman and invited her to rest her body and grieve in the comfort of her townhouse. Weeks went by. The old mother spent that early part of spring in Mayken's home until the days grew longer and she began to talk of planting and was anxious to get back to her home. Then she would remember that there was no one left at home and she would fall quiet, trying to envision a future for herself. She would cry quietly then at a vision of her son working the hoe vigorously through the black loam and kneeling to plant the seeds so carefully, patting the earth lovingly over them as if putting a baby to sleep. And then she would remember her husband, the man had been so harsh in life, so purely practical, but when he knew he was dying he was afraid and looked to her for help, and looked at her with such a sweet gratitude when she stayed and held his hand. He might even have whispered that he loved her had he lived a bit longer. But then he was gone, peaceful and she was left alone with her worries. "Why do they all die?" she asked Mayken over and again and Mayken, who had no answer, cried with her.

One night Pieter brought home one of the Anabaptist preachers that had begun to roam the countryside at that time. Pieter did not explain this strange guest, but Mayken thought she recognized a cousin of Pieter's whom she had met during their courtship long ago and had not seen since. After supper the animated preacher talked to them about his visions of the creator and explained how man could only know God and become one with God through these revelations. Such teachings were heresy and soon these visionary preachers would be tortured and burned like the *Marranos* in the south but that night the old mother found her future and left the next morning to follow this preacher with a religious fervor that obliterated her loneliness and her grief forever. Pieter had been kind enough to offer the visitor a brief night's respite on his travels but was glad to see him on his way again and glad as well that he took the strange old woman with him, for it was becoming ever more dangerous to even listen to such thoughts as the preacher expressed with such enthusiasm and he'd been worried about that odd woman for a while. Mayken was not surprised that her husband did not acknowledge any familial relationship with the man. She herself would adopt every sufferer she encountered or observed but in her heart she was grateful for Pieter's caution.

Flocks of geese and crows followed them out of the town, past a lake and then swirled back screeching and barking, the geese arrowing down on the lake, the crows landing on the rooftops. Mayken listened to the squabbles of the birds and fell asleep for a mid-morning nap. She dreamed a dream so real she thought she'd awakened in the country in a large rambling house built like a covered bridge over a stream. She was alone in the house and walked out the back door to the garden. She noticed the gate to the street was open and some people walked through: two men and two women. They were wanderers looking for a place to rest. As she walked with them back into her house the house was different, made of wood, not stone, and there was a stream running beneath it and dense trees all around. Mayken could smell the damp matted leaves that covered the earth beneath the trees and the soft lichens on the rocks in the stream. She stood and sniffed the air while the cries of the geese and the flocks of crows became distant and the voices of her strange guests were muffled and soft in the deep dark quiet of the woods. They climbed the wooden steps into the house and walked through many rooms. The rooms grew larger to make room for the people, and the people multiplied to fill the rooms. There were children among them and they ate and found beds with soft quilts and prepared to sleep in comfort in Mayken's endless house in the woods.

Mayken awoke feeling happy and still remembering the sweet smell of the forest until the loud close call of the crows, reminded her she was still in the town in the cold stone house built of immovable walls. She felt a longing to be somewhere but couldn't remember the place and she couldn't fall back to sleep. She went to her painting and she studied the landscape, the figures of people playing on the lake frozen amidst the snow and she added the crows that flew back and forth from country fields to the eaves of townhouses as if carrying messages for her. These messengers inhabited every one of her paintings. Then she stared the rest of the day at the painted landscape imagining herself struggling through snowdrifts to climb the painted ragged peaks beyond the town, climbing higher and higher to see as far as the birds, feeling the cold sting her cheeks, feeling the air grow lighter as she breathed deeply and deliriously, *remembering* this mountain where the crows and other huge birds flew at a level with her own shoulders and her own blood warmed her as she worked her arms forward and back, propelling herself through the deepening snow. She pulled herself out of her wintry painting in time for the evening meal which she ate alone with Pieter. She was distant, he was worried. They talked about the weather, about the last late spring storm, followed by such unusually dry spring weather. He didn't dare ask her how she felt.

The dry weather continued without respite for many weeks and gardens turned brown and shriveled and animals died. People waited for a rain, complained, prayed, cursed and were afraid. Mayken dreamed of wandering, her legs grown long and she herself so tall that she walked over the tops of houses and across fields in a few long strides and everywhere she stopped and looked at the earth, a well of water opened up and seeped into rivulets in the field grasses, along the stone walkways of the town. Wherever she walked, the well followed her and when she woke from this dream she knew she had to go to find it: the wandering well of endless water and the house of endless rooms. Mayken wanted to shelter the wandering people and quench the thirst of the land. Night after night in her dreams, the people had told her their stories, some so grim that she had awakened crying. They told her in their multitude of voices, of being lost around the shores of a sea so huge they couldn't see its end, and of being imprisoned on dank boats crowded together and starving, and of going ashore, only to be set upon by robbers and rapists.

They told about being stripped naked so that they had to hide for shame in the sea until nightfall to go ashore, and then climbing the ragged cliffs there only to be eaten by lions and bears.

They told her of children, hundreds of children, taken from their parents and sent to an island where lived only lizards and scorpions, snakes and crocodiles. They told of false friends who took their money and fine clothes in exchange for safe passage to some promised land that they believed in because they had no choice, only to find themselves abandoned, naked and in abject poverty. Some had swallowed gold coins, thinking to excrete these later and have something with which to purchase food and shelter, with which to bribe the tolerance of strangers, but these people were cut open by thieves who spread their entrails about on the ground searching for the gold and leaving the people to die horrible deaths in the desert.

No matter how many people came to fill the expanding rooms of her dream house, each one could tell Mayken of hundreds, thousands of others who had died, drowned, been tortured or burned, or had jumped from the tops of buildings to save themselves from worse.

Mayken told Pieter about her recurring nightmares and he remembered the stories about the persecution of the Jews in the south, in Spain and Portugal at the end of the last century. He thought that Mayken must have heard some of these horrifying stories as a child, as the people still talked of them for years and even wrote them down, rabbis did and priests did and some Jews from Amsterdam and the land of the Turks where they had found safe haven, those of them that could make the journey, who had been able to leave in time. So the stories were spread as a warning and in memorial. But for Mayken to hear them was to live them as these voices joined an already crowded chorus of voices from a past beyond her memory, from inside a mind that blocked out nothing, every passing word, every outcry, every whispered supplication and mournful prayer, was woven into the complex tapestry of her visions, tormenting her sleep, and interrupting her waking consciousness, so when she moaned in sympathy, he begged her to try to forget these terrible images, even knowing that was impossible, and warned her to talk to no one else about them for now that the inquisition had come to their own land, even to discuss such things could bring suspicion and tragedy to their family.

It was a hot, dry summer night when Mayken eluded her husband's loving but exhausted watchfulness. She had lain awake all night waiting for him to fall asleep, sometimes fighting off sleep herself, but she was desperate to get out and search the countryside for the miraculous things from her fantastic dreams. No one would believe that such things were out there but she had to seek for herself. As soon as she heard him snoring regularly, she got up softly, slowly, quietly and crept to the kitchen where she found the key to the smaller and quieter door from the kitchen the housemaid used when bringing the food from the market. She turned the key slowly, carefully, quietly and didn't breathe deeply until she was outside without waking Pieter. She loved him dearly; she knew he loved her dearly. She hoped she would find something to satisfy her in time to be back before he woke up and worried.

Mayken walked out in the direction of her old country home, looking for water. It was dusky when Mayken left her town and it never did get quite dark, the moon being full and bright. She walked what seemed many hours but she stopped when she heard a woman singing a song fraught with bitterness. By the moonlight Mayken could see that the woman was covered with oozing sores on her face and her arms which she raised to the heavens with the question why had she been so afflicted? As she approached more closely and heard more clearly, Mayken realized that the woman's song consisted of only one word, why? Sung quietly with grief, sung loudly with anger, sung over and over. At the woman's feet was a large smooth stone and as she sang the stone shimmered and reflected the moonlight as it turned to water, warm with summer, dark with night, a soothing oily substance and as the woman watched and saw what was happening she became quiet and she used the warm oily water to wash her face and arms and the sores began right then and there to heal. Mayken realized this was the miracle she had come to find.

Mayken heard the sky growl as though to thunder and she crouched expecting lightning but no thunder and lightning came that night, only a low crackling growl of tension in the sky. Mayken went to the strange woman who looked neither very old nor yet young. She could be close to forty like Mayken or she could be older. Mayken thought she seemed older, and wiser, or perhaps Mayken imagined it. She asked the woman to help her find her way home for she was lost and suddenly afraid. The woman spoke to God then, thankful, and then to Mayken to ask her name and the name of her people. But Mayken couldn't remember which people she should tell about and could only repeat her name, like music she had learned it so as never to forget.

Mayken, enthralled by the miracle and by Miriam, forgot that Pieter would be worried about her. For two more days and nights the women wandered about together and everywhere the stone followed them, turning to water at night, sweet tasting to drink and with a miraculous curative power, for soon the woman's sores were all gone. Miriam knew of wild herbs and plants they could eat and Mayken trusted her instinctively. Sometimes they took some cultivated vegetables withered and small, and Miriam paid for these by giving the gardens much needed irrigation.

Then Mayken heard Pieter, overwrought with fear for his wife, himself calling upon God, crying and railing, angry, guilty, angry, grieving, and she ran after his real voice and found him. He crumpled down inside her embrace but was thankful that she knew him and that she spoke reasonably to him. She wasn't that far from home, they had been wandering in circles, just missing each other. Mayken introduced him to Miriam and he, being now a completely desperate man, realized it would be good to invite Miriam to live with them and help him watch over his wife in these frightening times. Miriam accepted his invitation and then wondered how to hide her wandering well. Mayken, thinking Miriam's thought, brought her some rope from Pieter's wagon and they tied the rope around the stone so that Miriam could appear to drag it behind her, claiming she wished to study its alchemical properties and not realizing that, to a man, a woman having the uncommon strength necessary to drag such a stone was no less a miracle than the stone following her on its own. Of course, for that man to love a woman who lived in a world he could not know was to need and wish for miracles, and to need and wish for miracles is to believe in them whenever the opportunity arises, that has never changed.

When they arrived home, the two women lifted the stone and threw it down the well where it worked its magic and they always had water to spare thereafter. Then it rained. The people watched the sky in gratitude and felt relieved and forgiven.

When Miriam moved into the townhouse the weather improved, the flower gardens all around the neighborhood grew lush with the largest most richly colored roses anyone had seen in years, brilliant yellows, blood red and a hue of orange no one had ever seen before. The fruit trees grew taller and fuller and bore more fruit until even the birds were satiated and left plenty of cherries, plums and apples for the women to pick. And she took good care of Mayken, made sure she ate well and slept soundly and got out to walk in the sunshine more often. Mayken was healthier and happier than she had been since her youth and fell in love with Pieter all over again. She was past forty when she became pregnant a second time, a worry in itself, but Pieter was all the more worried because he had accepted a commission that required him to travel to another town and work on a large family portrait in the home of the mayor of that town. Mayken assured her husband that she would be fine with Miriam to help her and urged him to make the trip. He would be well paid for this large work and it could result in yet other lucrative commissions. He would not have left her but he trusted Miriam completely.

By now, they knew that Miriam was an unconverted Jewess, and Mayken understood that they had to be careful to keep the secret of Miriam's adherence to the Jewish faith. Had her companionship not been so beneficial to Mayken, Pieter would not have allowed her to remain with them. As the century progressed, the stench of death and burnt human flesh polluted the air more and more from Seville to Antwerp. First the *Marranos*, then Moors and Protestant heretics provided fuel for this constant flame and, more and more often, the hysterical women who claimed to hear God, as Mayken herself heard voices, and the lone country women who could heal with plants and special powers, witches because they were old or witches because they were mad, mad perhaps because they were old women alone in those times. Failure to confess was taken for further disobedience to the church and such impenitence was punished by live burning, for the Inquisitors were prohibited by the strictures of their religion from the shedding of blood. The poor souls who confessed might be rewarded with a more humane death by strangulation. Even after confession, the accused heretic might yet be tortured to reveal the names of other heretics or Judaizers, those Jews who accepted Christianity but still adhered to the Law of Moses. If they revealed enough names they might be spared their lives but were still made to parade the streets half naked and struggling under the weight of heavy crosses to be an example to the populace. Pieter had heard all about these events in whispers and did not tell Mayken but he couldn't protect her from seeing and smelling and hearing the burnings that took place from time to time in the Town Square.

Mayken watched as Miriam, in a closet away from any outside windows, lit candles at dusk and whispered words in a strange language, *Baruch ata adonay, eloheinu melech O'olam*, to Mayken it sounded ancient, primitive. Sometimes Mayken would begin to wander in her mind and the flame of the ritual, the small harmless flame lit in tribute to a god Miriam believed had not yet forsaken her as she would not forsake him, this small flame became confused in Mayken's mind with the flames that killed, the bonfires of human flesh and bone that she could smell in the air and see outside the tower window and she cried in panic. Then Miriam would have to attend to her before even finishing her prayers. Miriam was strong and loving and would carry Mayken to her bed whispering all the while words of comfort and reassurance and she would coax Mayken to lie still while she prepared an herbal infusion that made her sleep, deeply and quietly and, Miriam hoped, dreamlessly.

One Sabbath night toward the end of Mayken's pregnancy, Miriam gave her the infusion that would help her rest until daylight, finished her prayers and then went out into the night and found her way to the woods at the edge of the town. Whispering directions to herself, so many steps from this tree, so many steps from that spring, she walked on for several miles until she found the hill with a small cave that sheltered a young couple. The man still wore his priest's robes and the woman was dressed in the voluminous clothing of a nun to hide her huge belly.

Miguel, a young priest, had fallen in love with the Jewess Susanna. Being young and passionate, he had converted to her religion, determined to share her faith. But it was she who was doomed to share his punishment. When they realized she would have a child, they had escaped their town in northern Spain intending to go north to safety. Walking at night and sleeping in hidden places during the days, they had made their way as far as Mayken's old village when they had to stop. Susanna had become ill during the trek over the mountains but tried to hide her weakness from Miguel. When she began to cough up blood she realized it would be all she could do to stay alive long enough to deliver their child. Warily seeking friends who then sent them on to other friends along their journey, they had found Miriam and she had promised to help the young woman deliver and find a safe home for their child. Miriam had also hoped she could nurse Susanna back to health but when she saw that the young woman's disease was so far advanced she realized that would be asking too much, so she prayed instead that Susanna would live long enough to give life to the child inside her and that Miguel could ease his beloved out of this life before they were discovered by the Inquisitors. She had been visiting them more and more often as the time for the birth drew near, always bringing food and, of course water, a small spring that she left with them. When Susanna's labor began, Miriam wanted to stay with her but Mayken's labor had begun that same afternoon so Miriam had to go back to her. By dusk Mayken's labor had become painful but the child was not progressing naturally and Miriam was afraid for her. She sent for a woman named Martha who often assisted at births. Together they worked through the night, Miriam manipulating the tiny body into position but it was taking too long and she knew that something was wrong. When she finally pulled the boy child from his mother's womb he was blue, the umbilical cord tied tightly around his neck, but mercifully, for he was so malformed that Miriam knew he would not have survived more than a few days, weeks at most. She did not tell the exhausted mother the news but gave her the infusion again to numb her pain and let her sleep. Mayken had barely survived herself, but was all right once the child's festering body was pulled out of her.

While Miriam and Martha labored in the townhouse over

Mayken, Susanna stifled her own screams and, with muffled grunts, pushed forth a healthy boy child whose cries were covered by the first morning crow of a nearby rooster, which roused the dogs to bark and then the geese flying over the fields and woods into the town as the sky burst into a brilliant warm day. The young and grateful Miguel enjoyed the few moments of peace before allowing himself to think about the future. He laid his son upon his beloved's breast to nurse and as they fell into a sweet sleep he lay down beside them and sheltered them beneath his strong arm and warm cloak. When they awoke at midday, Miguel took his tiny son outside to feel the warmth of the sun. Susanna tried to follow but was dizzy and weak when she stood and Miguel was sorry he had no food to give her, only water to drink. He knew Miriam would bring bread for them soon.

When Miriam arrived under the stars, she carried a bundle as well as her usual basket of bread and wine. The bundle was wrapped in a table cloth which she carefully unwrapped to reveal to Miguel, not to Susanna, a dead and deformed boy child. While Susanna slept, Miguel gave Miriam his son who she wrapped in the cloth and he laid the dead baby beside his beloved. He kissed Miriam in blessing and she hurried off, trying to focus on the living and the possible.

Miguel waited for her to disappear in the darkness and then returned to the cave. He had kept the long sharp knife Miriam had brought him to cut the umbilical cord of his son. He cleaned it and blessed it and carefully slit Susanna's throat. The dead baby still lay in the crook of her arm. Then Miguel kneeled beside them and watched them through the night, sometimes going out to look up at the cloudless sky. He gazed at the myriad stars, some bright and large as though close enough to touch, others dim and distant and once or twice he thought he saw one fall to earth far away. Looking at the stars he felt serene, he felt happy, ready, hopeful that he and his beloved would be able to gaze at that beauty for eternity. It had been a sweet idyllic day and a perfect night. His body slept even while his eyes would not close against the soothing starlight. He waited for the dawn, glorious as it came in on high clouds of color. He went inside the cave and, kneeling, he said a morning prayer, followed by the *Kaddish* over his wife and the stranger's baby boy and then, reverently, he fell on the knife that was their salvation.

They were found later that day by a farmer who followed his dogs attracted by the smell of blood. It would not be long before the local inquisitor would report to the community that the man was a priest who had erred egregiously for love of a Jewess and tried to escape and the monster that she had delivered was God's sign and punishment. All three bodies were burned at an Auto de Fe which included some Protestant heretics. The ceremony was not well attended as the northerners of Charles' realm did not enjoy these events the way his Spanish subjects did. More people turned out afterward to watch the parade as Charles V, with a long and colorful retinue, was carried through the town to the Cathedral to preside over the baptism of several Indians who had been brought from the New World, not as slaves he proclaimed righteously, but to learn Christian ways and serve the emperor as free retainers.

The cries of the morning birds, usually so purposeful and positive, were sorrowful on the dawn of the two births, and distant, as if the birds themselves were in another world, mourning a loss. When Mayken was awakened thus she could be sad all day. And then the birds called again at high noon, unusual to hear them at all at high noon, and their calls sounded a reproach, Mayken didn't know for whom but felt it for all humankind. She first thought she no longer wanted to be human partaking unwittingly in some cruelty to the earth, but then she knew it would be worse to be a bird, all seeing, and all knowing, yet still powerless.

When Miriam brought the baby to Mayken to nurse, she expected a joyful response, but Mayken ignored the infant and Miriam realized she'd have to find some poor woman in the town to nurse him along with one of her own. Martha sent Marguerite, a woman she had recently helped in childbirth to Miriam. Pieter had finished his painting and come home just in time to find he had a healthy living son, but, being resigned to another period of Mayken's madness and feeling guilty for his part in bringing another innocent child into such a cruel world, he also ignored the infant. Miriam named him Jacob and loved him as her own, for it had always been her portion to care for other women's sons.

One night Mayken dreamed a dream that seemed to last for many days, even weeks. In this dream that felt like another life lived fully somewhere else, Mayken realized that she had had a child, a second child, but someone had taken this child from her and she knew she had to find and care for this child. She wandered in her sleep, until she found the sleeping Jacob. With great relief she picked him up in his swaddling clothes and carried him out to her garden.

It was spring and the roses were still tightly wrapped buds.

Without waking, Mayken stroked her child's cheek and thought she had never felt anything so soft. Cradling him in one arm, she picked one bud. Then she set the child down on the soft soil beside the rose bed, kneeled beside him and, with both hands freed, carefully, in her sleep, in her dream, she un-wrapped the petals of the rosebud and stroked her child's cheek with a single delicate rose petal as if to consecrate him to her world, so sweet with sounds and scents and softness when it wasn't terrifying. Then Mayken picked up Jacob from the sweet damp soil that clung to his blanket and carried him back to his bed. He made no sound and did not wake his mother Mayken who moved so surely and steadily in her sleep in the dark of the pre-dawn morning. When Mayken awoke and went to the kitchen to eat her breakfast, her hands were damp and a wilted rose petal stuck to her palm still.

The boy, Jacob spent his infancy and early childhood surrounded by the women who adopted him and the ghosts of both his mothers, the one a spirit in the candlelight, the other a solid pale woman who conversed with birds. Marguerite nursed him, Miriam raised him, Mayken fascinated him and Susanna haunted him.

Chapter Two
Lois Gold, Esq.
Denver, Colorado 1989

It is difficult for U.S. law makers who conceive of land as "real estate" or "property" to truly understand the relationship of the traditional Native Americans to their homeland... Their relationship is custodial rather than one of ownership and the land is not "property" but spirit, the place from which they came and to which they will return. It cannot be sold or exploited for its resources. The land gives life and in return they protect the life of the land: this is their sacred obligation which they abandon at their spiritual, psychological and physical peril (as the results of relocation indicate). In recognition of the rights of assimilated Hopi and Navajo who prefer to abandon the old ways and adopt the new (as is their right) there is always the solution of monetary compensation. That land is unique. Monetary compensation, on the other hand, deals with the easy universal of the dollar and would cost no more than the escalating costs of compliance with Pub. L. No. 93-531 by the U.S. government.

In view of these considerations, we recommend that the Court declare Pub. L No. 93-531 and Pub. L. No. 96-305 unconstitutional due to international human rights violations and order the cessation of all forced relocation efforts and allow those relocates currently living away from their homes to return.

Human Rights Violations by the U.S. Government Against Native Americans in the Passage and Enforcement of Pub. L. No. 93-531 Prepared by Lucy Hawley, Todd Howland, Ved P. Nanda, Judith Rhedin, and Sandra Shwayder for the Denver Journal of International Law, Vol. 15, winter/spring 1987

When the judge walked in and the bailiff called out in sonorous tones "All Rise," Lois could feel the cocky buoyancy of her client dissipate in a long apprehensive sigh. It happened all the time. There was something about a real courtroom that was simply intimidating no matter how many times a person had watched Judge Judy. Lois herself felt intimidated, even more so because dressing up as a lawyer and speaking on behalf of clients was basically an undercover act for her. She would have felt more natural shouting obscene epithets during a belligerent march on the building than walking inside to argue legal artifice in polite tones.

Annie Bonet was a tiny streetwise young lady who didn't take any shit from anyone and was proud of it. When the manager of the Twin Castles bar had decided to cut her off, she told him to fuck off and a few other things and then, when he told her to leave the bar, she huffed back to her bar stool to retrieve her backpack, and her boyfriend, muttering loudly all the way. The strap from the pack was caught under the leg of the stool and Annie didn't mind one bit when it went banging over on its loud metallic side as she yanked her pack away (or maybe she just gave it a push to emphasize her point).

Be that as it may, when she didn't hustle her butt out of there fast enough for the manager, he decided to give *her* a little push and then, of course, all hell broke loose, the upshot of which was Annie gave him the good swift kick in the balls he deserved. When the cops arrived on the scene it was Annie, bleeding head and all, who was charged with trespass, disturbing the peace and assault.

Misdemeanors in municipal courts were Lois' idea of a good time once she got over that initial rush of panic at entering all the way inside the halls of enemy territory. They weren't attended by the heavy consequences of murder or rape trials but still involved the serious social issues of racism, sexism and classism that motivated her to do three years of brain damage in law school right smack in the middle of her life. They also didn't drag on for years like her cases in Juvenile Court and the Mental Health cases which involved more on the order of social work than flashy trial techniques. What really turned her on were the cases with obvious political overtones, when protesters were arrested or the cops had it out for some poor black, brown or red guy or women in general because no one was more downtrodden than black, brown and red women. They got it from their own men who were getting it from the Anglo judges, police, employers and general hecklers and then, as if that wasn't enough, those poor women got it from the same cast of characters their men got it from . . .

"What?" Lois might ask rhetorically to anyone who had the time to listen to her harangues in the courthouse cafeteria. . . "What do these folks get at some level or other every goddamn day of their lives?" . . . why a major screwing of course, what else would she be talking about?

"It's backlash" she would say.

Annie Bonet didn't really want to hear it though, since she lived it daily and had found ways to deal. Now she was looking at a fine she couldn't afford and maybe even jail time if Lois didn't just shut up and win her case.

Annie's boyfriend was paying the legal fee which was OK with Annie because otherwise he'd just drink up the money anyway. He felt bad because he was quickly dispatched to detox and didn't get arrested with his girl. He didn't exactly regret what he did when that asshole Kevin Ruckaus pushed Annie, but he thought it was a shame that she had to take the rap. In fact he had threatened to kill the sonovabitch and had just begun to make good on his promise when he was jumped by about half a dozen bouncers who were in the bar on the pretext of watching a football game. They were all employed at other bars but hung out on their off-hours with Kevin, the manager, and, to a man, seemed to think Kevin needed protection, which image he was not too proud to maintain during the trial. Annie's boyfriend was not a whole lot bigger than she was but he was Mexican which made all the difference to some folks who knew for an irrefutable fact that all Mexicans carry knives and are born with an uncanny ability to kill, or at least maim, all comers in a fight. The six to one odds seemed fair, especially given that he was one extremely drunk and therefore even more dangerous Mexican.

"I don't like Black folks and I don't like Mexicans, and I don't like cops either." Lois actually wanted that renegade character on her jury but the prosecutor got him excused for cause and they went on to the next one.

Anybody with relatives on the police force could be excused for cause but she had more trouble with the folks who simply believed in the cops, respected them, generally would believe them whatever they said regardless of what they told her about not automatically believing a cop was automatically more credible than someone charged with a crime, or someone who had been drinking in a bar, or someone who associated with someone who was charged with a crime, or drinking in a bar.

She could only get three of those types excused on her peremptory challenges. So she had to settle for keeping one intelligent young woman, who appeared to be able to think for herself, even though her husband often played guitar on open mike nights at the Twin Castles. After all it was the town of Thornton and nearly everyone who lived and voted there would have had *something* to do with the place, there not being that many night spots in Thornton.

The others were nice earnest and honest young people who would understand that it was OK in this day and age for a young woman to talk like the proverbial sailor (Lois couldn't believe the prosecutor had actually said that). Despite the rising pseudo-science of jury selection based on factors ranging from dress styles to mini psych-evals, Lois always felt best going with plain old fashioned intelligence whenever she could find it. She had learned that it was a quality that sometimes got buried under too much of the wrong kind of education, that kind being what she liked to call bullshit and more of the same. So Lois wasn't impressed with degrees or what a potential juror did for a living but simply with what they said and how they said it. People who gave a straight answer to a direct question with heads held high and no apologies were her favorites and it helped if the potential juror went to the movies and was up on what was going down these days.

Lois loved debunking the pompous, the pretentious and the flat out, in- your- face liars that plagued the lives of her clients. The clients loved it too. Word of mouth got her more broke clients than any do-gooder lawyer could possibly want. She was thankful that the state paid for her indigent lunatics, unfit parents and juvenile delinquents, all of whom she liked and respected a hell of lot more than the too young, uptight and overly ferocious prosecutors or three piece suitors from her own profession.

Cross examining the Twin Castles waitress was easy. She arrived to testify in short shorts and some kind of halter top. No one seemed to notice, which said something; she wasn't sure what, about the town of Thornton.

"Miss Barber, you stated in direct examination that Mr. Ruckaus had walked behind Ms. Bonet to escort her out the door. Didn't he in fact push her toward the door?"

"No he never pushed her. He did kind of touch her back, you know, just gently. I wouldn't say he pushed her though."

"You said it in your statement to the police that night."

"I did not."

"Miss Barber, I have the statement right here. Would you like to read it? Your honor, may I approach the witness?"

Lois walked up to the witness stand and handed the written statement to the waitress. She had stumbled over her own handwriting and finally admitted that she had indeed characterized her employer's action as a push. She was under a lot of stress at the time and didn't remember things exactly as they happened.

"And do you remember events more exactly today, a year later and in this far less stressful situation?" A smile here that she could feel the jurors return. "We took a lunch break before you were called. Did you happen to have lunch with your boss?"

"Yes, of course."

"And did you discuss what you would say on the stand after lunch?"

"No, of course not."

"Of course not." and this time Lois had to look down at her notes to keep from smiling broadly at the jurors who were each and every one grinning. If she could keep them grinning she'd win.

The manager himself had been more difficult to ruffle. The young prosecutor, who had to be particularly hard on criminals because Thornton was not exactly a front running spot from which to start a successful career in law and politics, was a friend of Kevin Ruckhaus and knew the man had a temper, so he had taken pains to coach him and role play and generally prepare Kevin to remain seated and quiet during his cross examination.

Lois knew better than to argue with witnesses even when they drove her up the wall with deceit or amnesia, one, but she did manage to get Mr. Ruckaus to explain that he had seen Annie pick up the metal bar stool which was a little more than two and half feet high and fling it across the room four to six feet in his direction with her left hand while she picked up her purse with her right. He never seemed to quite get it that these minute details, so well-remembered, made a point. The Jury got it and she would remind them during her closing argument that he had testified in such careful detail to a physical impossibility.

Then there was the friendly bouncer Karl "Butch" Wilder who found reason to tell the court that he liked the ballet as much as wrestling and played the piano. He couldn't emphasize enough what a gentle man he was, how truly he disliked a good fight. Mr. Wilder even offered to draw a diagram of the bar and where everyone was during the fight that broke out after the bar stool had gone flying through the air, by his account, a good eight to ten feet, yes he was sure of that.

"I must commend you Mr. Wilder, on the record, for your incredible memory. It had to be phenomenally difficult to know which parties to this fray to observe, so you apparently decided to keep tabs on all of them even while you were holding two individuals in half nelsons, you did say half nelsons? Or was it full nelsons? I am not familiar with wrestling terms so I may have gotten that part wrong. And then to be able to recall in such extraordinary detail who and where everyone was in just the precise order of events. I am impressed. In fact I am so impressed that if I didn't know you are under oath and said you didn't, I could easily have concluded that you had rehearsed the choreography of this fight with your friend Mr. Ruckaus."

"Objection, Counsel is arguing!"

"Objection sustained. Ms. Gold please limit yourself to asking questions."

"I apologize, your honor."

At this point Lois had to put her head down in a pretense of reviewing her non-existent notes to avoid making eye contact with the jurors who weren't even trying to maintain impassive expressions. A couple of them had that kind of smile she had learned to love, the kind of smile that lights up the faces of people who have just been given permission to recognize the obvious.

But the good part was yet to come when her client would take the stand, admit honestly that she had indeed kicked the manager in the crotch and explain that she did that after he had kicked her in the head as she was trying to get up after being knocked down by that selfsame Mr. Ruckaus when she jumped on him to try to get him off her boyfriend who was under a pile of guys, how many she didn't know exactly because there was just too much going on to count, and she didn't even know if he was alive or dead.

And it wasn't just revenge for knocking her down and kicking her in the head either. It was SELF-DEFENSE because for all she knew when she tried to get up the second time he might have kicked her a second time so that second time she got up swinging and kicking just to be sure he kept his distance.

Lois had taken pains with her client too. Even though no one would blame her for kicking the sonovabitch in the balls after what he did to her, revenge was not an affirmative defense. Self Defense was and there were rules about how much force could be used in what circumstances to qualify for legal self-defense. Lois had these little maxims she impressed upon her clients in criminal cases like: "it's not enough to tell the truth; you have to look like you are telling the truth." And how it was a short step from innocent to guilty in American courtrooms so forget that shit about innocent until proven guilty and make sure the judge and the jury understand beyond a shadow of a doubt that you are a saint or at least a candid and well intentioned individual who would never break the law or intentionally cause anyone any harm, which in this day and age could qualify a person for sainthood, because, even though the prosecution has the burden of proving guilt, it's the defendant's burden to go to jail if she doesn't stand up for herself in no uncertain terms. Unless of course you happened to be a rich celebrity, or at least a middle class white, which Annie was not.

The Jury came back within minutes and acquitted Annie Bonet of the charge of assault because of her successful claim of self-defense and they acquitted her on the charge of disturbing the peace on the grounds that, at the Twin Castles Bar, there was no peace to disturb, but, perhaps in a misguided attempt to be even handed, they found her guilty of trespass which gave the judge the opportunity to tell her that if a manager of a bar, however rude he might be, however unnecessary and unfair the request, did in fact ask her to leave the premises she should probably leave them quickly and probably take her business elsewhere because it didn't take much for the manager to charge her with trespass if she didn't obey his command. It was at this point that Lois realized they might have been better off with a trial to the judge.

The prosecutor made the most of what the jury had given him and asked for the maximum penalty and a drug and alcohol evaluation which meant the defendant would have to obtain, at her own expense, whatever rehab services the evaluator deemed necessary, whereupon the judge had the further opportunity to tell the prosecutor that he was not about to order an alcohol evaluation just because a young woman had a little too much to drink at happy hour and the Court sometimes had a few drinks at happy hour and that didn't make a person an alcoholic, and then apologetically ordered Ms. Bonet to pay the minimum fine which was mandated by the municipal code and not within his discretion to abate.

Lois was devastated by the trespass conviction but Annie Bonet just waltzed into the clerk's office and paid the fine, which was less than she had expected in spite of Lois assuring her that for a first time offense she would only get the minimum, and asked Lois if she could pay her next month to which Lois just said "sure" like she always did and they all waved good-bye and got on with their lives. For Annie that meant going out and celebrating, hopefully not within the Thornton city limits, and for Lois it meant preparing for another trial the following week in Denver County Court. Same charges, different place and time, and radically different facts. The trial was scheduled to start the following Tuesday and Lois would work from dawn to midnight all weekend making sure every foreseeable aspect of the trial was perfectly scripted in a trial notebook so that she could spend Monday letting her brain rest. She appeared easygoing and funny in front of a jury but was meticulous in her preparation, like an actress rehearsing, analyzing and re-hashing her lines.

The geese woke her early Monday morning and she watched the sun rise through her special leaded glass window, set just so the morning sun would cast rainbows all around her living room, while she sipped her coffee and felt good to be alive. The thought that she only had to be in Denver that day was exhilarating because it meant that she could walk to her office in the brisk early morning chill and take the bus home later. Lois hated driving in the city traffic. She showered and dressed quickly, wasting no time. Her professional wardrobe consisted of several white button-down shirts, winter and summer weight black jackets with black slacks and a couple of skirts for those courtrooms where older male judges still frowned upon women wearing pants. She got her skirts long enough to go with the sturdy lace up boots that combined the barest nod to respectability with comfort. She was only 5'4" but always felt tall for some reason, weighed 110 pounds, had light brown hair which she kept cut short and neat, had hazel eyes which could be quite piercing when she removed her glasses but she had never been interested in contact lenses, makeup or any other such vanity that she considered a waste of time. Her one weakness in that regard was a love of long dangly earrings made of silver with a touch of turquoise, lapis or malachite. She admired hand crafted bracelets also but found them a nuisance to wear and anyway needed her wrist for a watch. It was always an amazement to her when men found her attractive until she figured out it was her gift of gab, her way with words, what had driven her to law in the first place, that and the sense of humor.

By 6:30am she was on her way, her files in her backpack and her Walkman firmly attached to her belt and her earphones in place. First she headed for the Seventeenth Ave Parkway so she could pretend she was walking in the woods and not in the middle of town and then she crossed over to City Park and walked along the lake, stopping to watch the geese, deliberately stirring them up sometimes just to hear them squawk, or walking beneath trees where she knew the loud mouthed crows and magpies nested, just to hear their scolding. Mixed up with the Brandenburg Concertos or Vivaldi's Four Seasons, no sound was more glorious to her ear than the far reaching cries of geese, magpies and crows. Sometimes she was so overwhelmed with the beauty of it she would sit on a bench by the lake and jot down some poems which she later tore up, she never could get it right, and she wished that she had learned the language of music well enough to think and write it instead of merely listening to it.

Then she would walk the last couple of miles downtown. If she hadn't lingered too long, she might catch the old Indian woman who sat out on her porch in the morning listening to a tape of Dineh chants while the grandchildren played on a bit of grass between the stoop and the street. The children had a pair of crutches they had turned upside down and were using as stilts.

Lois never smiled at the old grandmother like she did to the workmen and joggers she met along her morning walk to town. The woman had the look of someone watching a memory and not wanting to be disturbed. Her vision was so strong that Lois could feel an icy wind when she passed and imagined a mountain in winter. The chant was a winter chant, sung to the sheep perhaps, sung to the mountain for sure, sung to warm the bones cold to the marrow. Sometimes as she passed the old Dineh woman, Lois closed her eyes as if walking through something frightful that could only be vanquished by faith. She wondered how the children could laugh and yell so oblivious to their grandmother's power. But, of course, the woman didn't appear powerful. She appeared old and poor and beyond despair. If she had power, it worked in some other time and place, not in Denver, Colorado in 1989.

Lois thought of Roberta Blackgoat, a small woman with an ancient brown leathery face and long gray hair braided and worn down her back, dressed in her fancy velvets and turquoise and silver jewelry to address the conference of lawyers in the glass and chrome ballroom of a downtown hotel. It wasn't the usual Continuing Legal Education seminar where bored attorneys surreptitiously made to-do notes in their calendars while a speaker gave them tips on writing catchy appellate briefs or trial tactics that imitated popular television programs. These were radical lawyers, some modest and probably experienced, others, mostly young, swashbuckling about in their shiny new cowboy boots, bolo ties and pony tails self-consciously inventing themselves and cutting their teeth on the causes of the day. One of the causes involved the forced relocation of Navajo Indians from an area they had shared with the Hopi until the U.S. government became involved in a dispute between the two tribal governments with disastrous results for the traditional Navajo.

Roberta Blackgoat spoke in a soft voice and required a microphone to be heard in the large room when she began simply telling the stories. People who had lived all their lives in hogans without running water or electricity were given money for their homes but they didn't know how to manage that money. They went to Gallup, the closest town, and in Gallup mortgage brokers were lined up to offer the relocatees mortgages on rows of little box houses that contractors were building as quickly as possible for the new business coming their way. All of a sudden there were bills to pay: not just the confusing mortgage payments but the water bills (imagine paying for water) and the electric and gas bills (and no fire pits or wood stoves to heat their homes) and it wasn't long before most of the relocatees found themselves evicted again, this time broke with nowhere to go but back to some other part of the reservation where perhaps family members could take them in. Many just stayed on the streets as so many of their brothers and sisters had over the years, drunk, homeless, disgraced and ashamed. Roberta's own son, in his despair had walked out on the highway in front of a semi leaving a wife and children. At this point Roberta Blackgoat would pause a moment, but, knowing how important it was that she tell it all and not get bogged down in her own personal tragedy, she soon regained her composure and continued. There were church groups raising awareness and funds and legal groups drafting amicus briefs and petitions and even a delegation prepared to go to the United Nations in Geneva to get relief. Lois had already found her own contribution to a law review article reprinted on leaflets at the Big Mountain Support Group table at the March Powwow in the Coliseum where she went to watch the dances and look at crafts. Not long after the Conference where Roberta Blackgoat spoke, Lois went once to the Sundance held near Big Mountain and met with elders there but she never saw Roberta Blackgoat again. She would just think about her whenever she passed the old grandmother in the city and wonder what circumstances had forced that woman from her home in that other world.

It was indeed another world and Lois felt changed forever by the journey she had taken across deserts to the Sun Dance. She had been invited by a woman who worked with the Big Mountain Support Group who assured her it was alright for her to go. Lois herself wondered if it might not be intrusive but allowed herself to be persuaded. As much as she disliked driving in cities, she loved road trips and she headed out toward the four corners on Highway 285, stopping after dark at Wolf Creek Pass where she spread her sleeping bag and slept under the stars, lulled to sleep by the sound of the creek below. At dawn she awoke and saw how close she had slept to the edge of a precipice overlooking the creek. Somehow in the dark she had thought it was only a few steps away, steps she was thankful she had been too tired to take. She ate some beef jerky and dried apples, drank some water and got back on the road. In Arizona she stopped to hike in the Petrified Forest and then drove on to the site of the Sun Dance.

When she arrived she realized the event was as much about politics as about spirituality. The drummers and dancers were men and women from all the largest southwest nations but there were representatives of tribes from all over the North American continent and Canada: Bloods, Blackfeet, Brule, Dakota, Lakota, Oglala, Pawnee, Cherokee, Cree and Cheyenne, Hopi and Dineh, Hualapai and Havasupai, Shoshone from Wind River, Zuni and Utes, even an Innuit who had come from up near the Arctic Circle. There were aboriginal people from Australia, Buddhist monks from Cambodia and Boulder, artists from New York and Taos, some tourists from Scandinavia, Chicano activists from Albuquerque, and several self-proclaimed revolutionaries who bragged that they would do whatever it took to regain the freedom of Aztlán. The leader, the man who welcomed everyone into the circle in the morning and led the chants to accompany the dancers was a Lakota Sioux originally from Pine Ridge but he traveled now all over the country and all over the world. He'd been to Washington D.C to speak to some congressional committees more times than he could count and twice to Geneva to address the United Nations. Before he became a world traveler he had lived for many years in a prison cell because he refused to kill his distant cousins in Viet Nam.

A breeze kicked up some trash in the street and Lois remembered the sound of the cleansing wind in that ancient land, the scent of the sage smoke, the sound of the singers and the hallucinatory vision of dancers dragging Buffalo skulls by leather thongs attached to sharp spikes sewn into the skin of their bare backs. She remembered the moment the first dancer's skin broke and his blood fertilized that dusty dry soil and the lead singer intoned words addressed to the creator "we have nothing of our own to offer you but our blood." Then he spoke about the tree that was cut and replanted in the middle of the sacred circle all leafed out with promises and prayers written on scraps of colored paper and how the writers of those prayers could come back throughout the coming year in times of trouble and sit beneath that tree and Lois realized as he spoke where they would come from. The would come from the impoverished outskirts and dangerous alleys of the cities where they lived hidden from the popular view, in these buildings she was passing on her way to work, all cut up into too many, too small, too dark apartments with the peeling paint and the crumbling walls and the little patches of dying grass out front. This was where they would come from.

By the time Lois had snapped back from her thoughts, she had walked another mile and was about to pass the apartment that always had the window open no matter the weather and the blues playing no matter the hour, today it was Taj Mahal. She could always count on that music wafting out to the street to accompany her for at least a couple of blocks and wake her from whatever dream or memory had distracted her. She never saw the people who lived there anymore than she saw the people who seemed to be perpetually moving, their front door always open to allow some piece of second-hand furniture to be carried in or out. Or the people who managed to keep one eternally scraggly plant at exactly the same edge of extinction in their basement window, that window with the crack covered in masking tape. As soon as Lois passed that apartment she began to brace herself for the faint acrid odor of escaping gas that always reminded her of urban communes in old Victorians, the same from Berkeley to Baltimore: that smell of cats and incense and the feel of fine dust that finds its way beneath the wallpaper, the crumbling plaster, the mice in the walls. It never failed to make her sad.

John Ghost had lived in one of those apartments with his grandmother when he moved to Denver from Rosebud. He was doing well in the city, had a decent job, and was looking forward to getting his own place. The woman across the hall seduced him one night, he had put his head down when telling Lois that part, shamed that he had been with that drunken old white woman. When he met her old man coming in as he was going out, he knew he was in for some trouble. Her old man would beat the woman when he was drunk and was almost always drunk so no wonder she told him that John had raped her. Even John understood that. The man called the police right then and there, and the next morning John was over at the County Jail meeting with Lois because his grandmother knew about her work for the Navajo. The dilemma for Lois was that while the woman's testimony would be easy to impeach, she felt sorry for the woman as did John himself for that matter. The woman, whose name no one could ever seem to remember, told John's grandmother that she wanted to ask the DA to drop the charges but she was afraid her old man would beat her again. Never mind he sold her whenever he needed cigarette and whiskey money. Even the grandmother, worried as she was about her grandson felt sorry for the woman, Susan maybe her name was, or maybe Sharon, or Sherry, something with an S, something simple, something common, a blur like the woman herself. Then grandma did a pipe ceremony and prayed to the creator to help her grandson. Too many sons of the reservation spent too many years of their lives in jail for crimes they didn't commit or for crimes that they did commit which, had they been committed by white men, would not have drawn such long sentences. It was definitely after the pipe ceremony that Susan, Sharon, whatshername's old man fell down the stairs, probably drunk, broke his neck and died. Grandma told Lois and they dared to laugh together, what will the DA think she wondered? "Murder by prayer?"

In fact a woman assistant DA hinted on the phone that perhaps John had something to do with it: actually said the words "witness tampering" which made it hard for Lois not to laugh out loud. Lois knew the woman's boss and he was a straight up guy, he'd met with the alleged victim, knew her testimony would be a liability as would have her old man's come to think of it, and he offered not only to let John plead to a lesser charge of misdemeanor sexual assault but offered a deferred judgment as well with only six-month probation. Of course it could backfire if John was arrested during the upcoming protest of the Columbus Day parade. Lois advised him to take the deal, go back to Rosebud for the six months of his probation and not involve himself in any political protests until the charge was safely expunged from his theretofore clean record. She figured, absent racial prejudice on the jury, they could have won at trial but there is always risk and helping the DA save face on this case made it more likely he'd work with her to the benefit of future clients.

The last leg of her walk was the entire length of the Sixteenth street mall, splendid with its sidewalk vendors and musicians and street preachers. Adam Starvinsky played his cool clarinet while a hotdog vendor had fixed up speakers from which he broadcast opera, year in year out from early morning until after lunch, a woman with long blonde hair played Celtic music on a harp, a tall, thin, bearded man played Texas hill-country tunes on a fiddle while a young black man showed off his perfect body in tights and ballet tutu as he roller-skated up and down the mall and performed cartwheels in front of the restaurant windows. One fellow who strummed guitar on the corner across from a bank (good thinking there) always wore a fat cheeked Mickey Mouse mask and costume which made Lois wonder if he was maybe wanted by the FBI. He played so badly that no one would linger long enough to figure him out.

Finally she reached the end of downtown where she maintained a closet sized office in an old renovated building across the street from the train station. Sometimes she went into the deserted Station for an egg-salad sandwich and a coke at the lunch counter and thought about history. This was the place her maternal grandfather, Isaac Mendoza, had last been seen back in 1931, when her mother was thirteen. In the train station Lois pretended she was Luisa Rosaria Mendoza Goldberg again just like she was born. Lois was not a woman to run from a fight or deny her background to avoid discrimination and repercussions. It was just that her mother had married a Jew from a tight knit family and her Jewish heritage seemed more important and immediate than her remote Mexican background. Or maybe it was that her Mexican grandfather had run out on their family, leaving a legacy of rejection and resentment that was passed on from mother to daughter.

From her paternal grandparents Lois had the memories of annual Passover celebrations, the longest running freedom celebration in the history of the world. From them, as well, she learned that socialist principles were acceptable even after forty. She had been proud of her radical grandparents and missed them sorely when they died within weeks of one another (one of a heart attack and the other of a lonely heart). Lois was too old and too busy to dwell on that now except on those leisurely days when she had her lunch in the train station and pretended she was a kid again just getting out and exploring the city on foot and by bus, a wanderer from the start.

Besides the usual bills, advertisements and solicitations pushed under the door of her tiny office, there was a newsletter stapled shut written in Spanish on one side and English on the other:

> CAZAMOS PARA COMER Y SOBREVIVIR
> LA COMISIÓN INDEPENDIENTE 6 de MARZO está organizando las familias, vecinos y amigos de los cazadores que están acusados de cazar ilegalmente . . . The background to this week's military raid and the court proceedings is the national oppression of the Mexican nation. Southern Colorado and Northern Nuevo Mexico have always been strongholds and pockets of resistance since the 1848 conquest. There have been repeated attempts to break the spirit and the backbone of the nation. The March 6 raid is only the latest incident. We will not be terrorized out of our homeland and into homelessness in the cities . . . " and so on and so forth, Lois skipped to the end to find out what exactly would be expected of her:

> "The COMISIÓN INDEPENDIENTE 6 de MARZO is being organized to offer legal, political and spiritual support to those people most in need of help because of the March 6 raid."

Lois had already heard from colleagues about the two year poaching sting that was staged by a Federal Wildlife agent in the San Luis Valley. His name was George and he had been befriended, accepted into the community, invited to dinner at people's homes, had probably eaten a fair share of "illegal" meat.

Most of the people in the Valley were poor regardless of whether they had managed to hold on to their ancestral lands and they hunted not only for food but for barter. Their hunting rights were supposed to have been protected by the treaty of Guadalupe Hidalgo but of course treaty rights were usually granted by victors in war for expediency and intended to be eroded over time if the vanquished did not continue to fight daily for what little remained to them.

Lois laughed to herself, thinking about her last poaching case.

She was going to represent a man near Aguilar, who had been given a citation for poaching when a state trooper caught him tossing a dead turkey into the back of his pickup truck. Of course he had guns in the cab. Everyone had guns in their cabs. The man, Alonso Fernandez, had claimed the turkey was already dead, road kill he was picking up for his dogs and he threw it back out into the field of tall grass. The trooper issued the poaching ticket anyway and not wanting to search for, or, for that matter, touch, the evidence himself, he ordered Alonso to find and pick up the turkey and put it into trooper's trunk. Alonso refused whereupon he was issued another ticket that claimed he refused to follow the lawful order of the police officer.

"What are you talking about? You give me a ticket for picking up a dead turkey from the side of the road and now you are giving me another ticket for not picking it up?"

Lois could just hear him sassing the trooper and she'd never actually met the guy. The story had made the rounds and been embellished for weeks. Alonso's case was discussed at a special meeting of the Lawyer's Guild and by the time Lois had volunteered to represent him, Alonso had already decided that he preferred not to enter the United States Court house and offer his plea of not guilty as by so doing he would be recognizing the legality of the United States Government and submitting to its authority, which he steadfastly refused to do. This was, after all, Occupied Mexico, sometimes romantically called Aztlán. Alonso preferred to gather some friends and take over the Aguilar Court House just as Reies Tijerina had occupied the Courthouse in Tierra Amarillo back in the sixties. As a compromise, Alonso was persuaded to call a press conference and make a speech on the courthouse steps, but before this event could take place, the DA in Aguilar quietly dropped the charges against Alonso for lack of evidence. Apparently no one had ever found that dead turkey in the grass. Lois often had to admit that her own practice of law, while not stereotypically lucrative had been quite unstereotypically fun.

There was a message on her answering machine telling her the time and place set for the meeting of defendants and lawyers in San Luis and Lois looked forward to another adventure with a mix of excitement and anxiety. She would be returning to the region where her mother had been born and her grandmother had met her grandfather. She often wondered about this part of her history, the bits of stories she had heard from her mother and grandmother had been shrouded in secrecy and sadness. She knew that her grandfather, Isaac Mendoza was a brilliant and introspective man, the only man from his town to graduate from college back then. He graduated with high hopes but too soon to be accepted by the then predominantly white professional class and the circumstances of his birth cut him off from any helpful connections among the Spanish elite. He took a job in a store owned by one of his half-brothers. He was good for business because the whites who didn't welcome him into their ranks, nonetheless were impressed by his sagacity and liked to hear him talk, even asked his advice and opinion on all kinds of matters. Of course they never would have dreamed of paying him for this advice as they would a white lawyer for instance, but in fact they did pay with their business and that was the way he lived, partaking only indirectly and haphazardly of respect.

Even within his own family, he was an outsider, being the only child of his father's first wife, a common law wife, a strange woman given to strange habits and rituals. She was too independent for Guillermo Mendoza to tolerate and he put her aside, as it was told among the gossips, and married a second wife who died shortly after the wedding, where after he married a third wife, who gave him four more sons before she, too, died. The last of Isaac's stepmother's was more of a nurse to the old man and Isaac left before she moved into his father's home.

Isaac, so named by his exiled mother, surprised his family and the town by capturing the heart of Dolores Vigil, the prettiest and brightest young woman in the county it was said. She had left the town for a while to work in Las Vegas, New Mexico, had received her degree from Highlands University and returned to teach school. She was strong and independent like Isaac's mother but without his mother's strangeness.

Isaac encouraged her endeavors to teach the local children to read and write their native Spanish, as well as English which they learned in school. Her efforts caused some controversy in the community as the government was very clear that the Spanish speaking children needed to learn English speech and ways. Her daughter, Lois's mother, Rose, remembered being punished in school for speaking Spanish and she broke her own mother's heart by refusing to speak it at home either, claiming the road to success in America was to speak only English and learn Anglo ways.

But then many people's dreams of success in America were dashed by the great depression. The store, that afforded Isaac his financial contribution to the family, went out of business when the bank foreclosed on the building. The couple moved to Denver where Dolores was able to get a job teaching on the West Side where the immigrant Jews and poor Mexicans lived. Had Isaac been willing to go back to school to get a teaching certificate he might have been able to work in the school system as well but he chose instead to wait for an opening at the Municipal Public Library. Every week he inquired and every week they told him as soon as there was an opening they would contact him. Isaac, depressed from childhood, grew even more so and his depression made him useless and his uselessness made him even more depressed. He tried his hand at a variety of menial jobs but found it hard to focus an imaginative and lively intellect on mundane tasks, failing at the kind of simple things that anyone could do.

His first job was a downtown office job. He worked in a stone building on 16th Street, with marble floors and brass elevators, lots of dark wood and glass, very elegant but dark. His first day there the doorman mistook him for a janitor. He worked there as a file clerk and finished his tasks quickly and efficiently enough but offended his boss by reading a book during his spare time. Dolores, who also loved to read, was sympathetic and encouraged him to seek other jobs he found advertised in the paper. It seemed he never lasted more than a couple weeks and Dolores became less and less sympathetic with his inability to hold down a simple job.

Finally Isaac was hired by a neighbor who ran the neighborhood grocery store and perhaps felt bad for Dolores. Stocking the shelves of a grocery store was the sort of thing you could only mess up if you paid no attention whatsoever, but Isaac's mind of course wandered and customers complained when they couldn't find their usual goods in the usual places. Sweeping up and washing the counters and windows should have been even easier but he rushed through these tasks so he could return to his books in the back and left the place a mess. Dolores was constantly apologizing to their neighbor who felt too guilty to fire Isaac. Isaac himself kept hoping to quit and move on to the library but the last time he went to the library to inquire about openings he observed a new person working there and realized they had been politely putting him off and had no intention of hiring him. It was not a good start to their new life. When his daughter Rosaria was thirteen, he gave up and left a home where he didn't feel needed and he never returned. That was all that his granddaughter knew of him and most of it was her own imagination filling in the blanks left by a few hard facts.

Chapter Three
Elijah
1580 Southern Rocky Mountains

" . . . The sea began to rise very high and the north wind was so violent that neither the boats dared come to land nor could the vessels be let drive on shore because of the head wind. . . . At this time, the rain and the tempest had increased to such a degree all the houses and churches fell, and it was necessary in order to move upright, that we should go seven or eight holding on to each other that the wind might not blow us away; and walking in the groves we had no less fear of the trees than of the houses, as they too were falling and might kill us under them. In this tempest and danger we wandered all night, without finding place or spot where we could remain a half hour in safety. During the time, particularly from midnight forward, we heard much tumult and great clamor of voices, the sound of timbrels, flutes and tambourines as well as other instruments which lasted until the morning, when the tempest ceased."
Excerpt from the narrative of Alvar Nuñez Cabeza De Vaca
Regarding the 1527 Expedition of Pánfilo De Narváez to the Florida Cape edited by Frederick W. Hodge
Spanish Explorers in the Southern United States 1528-1543
Charles Scribner's Sons, 1907
Reprinted by The Texas Historical Association in 1990

The morning Elijah Benveniste died was the morning after the winter solstice. The huge full moon disappeared behind a mist of cloud and distant snow. The sky lightened and the stars were obscured from Elijah's eyes. He could see the clouds drift over them and he waited for the snow. He had curled into a warm place beneath the roots of an ancient tree. In this spot, the river had risen each spring and carved out the soil beneath the roots and subsided each winter leaving a shelf of soft sand warmed by the water's steam. Elijah lay flat on his back wrapped in a Buffalo robe. It was his habit to open his eyes in the night to see the myriad stars through the black lace of tree branches and pungent pine needles until he dozed off for a while. He didn't mind that sleep was brief and the nights were long. He had learned to savor his rest.

Most mornings he'd be up at first light and well on his way by the time the sun was visible over the mountains. But that morning the sky had lightened early with clouds and soon a gentle rain fell making musical sounds on the river before it turned to snow and silence. Elijah watched, warm and weary. He could feel the blood in his veins slow to a stop and he knew he would not live 'til dawn.

Only the night before, he had prayed for more time. He had wanted more time to find the great northwestern ocean he'd been seeking for so many years, all his wandering and adventures directed to that end. But now it didn't matter to him. He felt peaceful, wanting nothing but a small gift from approaching death: peace of mind. He'd been trying to recollect his long life and all the places he'd been, focusing his mind on this during the days as he walked with the morning sun to his back and during the nights as he lay with his eyes on the stars, closing briefly and reluctantly to doze.

He thought of his youth in Spain. He could barely visualize the faces of his mothers and sisters. It was because of them he came to New Spain to find and accompany Coronado in his search for the fabled seven cities of gold. Elijah's family had converted from Judaism to Catholicism under duress at the end of the last century and he and his sisters had been duly raised in the Catholic Church for which he felt no particular love but merely an expedient and mechanical obedience. He seemed to remember that he had been suspicious that many of his family's friends and acquaintances still secretly practiced their ancient Jewish religion in spite of the dangers if they were caught. No one told him but he noticed little things, or overheard bits of whispered conversations that ceased abruptly when he made his presence known. It seemed this aura of conspiracy was everywhere around him among the people that he knew and it occurred to him that if he suspected these people, surely others more interested could find them out with diligent investigation. Elijah thought they were foolish to risk their property and their lives for any religion because he himself never felt convinced that god, if god in fact existed, would care what foolish rituals foolish men and women performed. Perhaps because he was too close and took them for granted, he didn't realize that his own mother and sisters were among the most fervent Judaizers, willing to become martyrs for their faith if need be. This in spite of the fact that their father had gone to great expense to purchase documentation that their family came from a line of pure blooded Spaniards, old Christians, not tainted by the blood of any inferior races such as the Jews or the Moors. The fact that his father was wealthy enough to afford this expense put the family at risk as much as the fact that they actually had Jewish ancestors, for envy and greed were motivators as powerful as religious fervor.

When Elijah was seventeen his youngest sister, a passionate girl of sixteen, decided she wanted him to share their faith and told him everything about their activities and feelings. He remembered her talking at him for a very long time, breathless, excited, alternately joyous and worried, as her eyes followed his in an effort to see his immediate reaction. He would have turned from her but she had taken hold of his hands and held them tightly as if begging him to share her feelings. What was she thinking? That he would be as joyful to hear this news as she was to tell it? She was young and foolish and Elijah was appalled and frightened because he realized then that his sense of being followed for the past several weeks was probably not just an overactive imagination. It didn't matter that he himself was innocent of the crimes of heresy because, once he was arrested, he would be tortured until he confessed and, having confessed, would be further tortured to give names of family or friends the Inquisition suspected of Judaizing. Elijah had heard descriptions of the diabolical machines invented to slowly and painfully dismember a body at the joints and break the bones. He'd heard about the caged throne carefully shaped to the contours of the seated human form up to and including the face, the mask itself a work of art, and all this lined with iron nails. He'd heard about the immersions in water, the rack, and the perverted uses of the wheel. He'd heard it whispered that the suffering of Jesus on the cross was as nothing compared to the suffering inflicted on hapless victims by the priests who did it all in his name and if Elijah were to point out that Christ himself preached mercy and love, that too would be heresy for it wasn't about Jesus really, it was really about the power of the universal, the most catholic church of Rome. And it was about wealth. Should one's neighbor covet one's house or lands, best not to let them see any suspicious behavior: excessive washing on Friday, the lighting of candles at the wrong time, an aversion for pork, a lack of activity on Saturday and by Monday morning a person could be seated on that artfully crafted throne with the sides of the clawed cage closing in. None of this was ever spoken above a whisper because everyone knew that the Inquisition had spies in the most unlikely places and even to be seen whispering at all could raise their suspicions. But the whisperers couldn't help themselves. They were fascinated by what was going on around them and only in their own most irrational moments, imagined it could happen to them. Anyone who really believed and feared they might be caught in this web of insanity wasted no time whispering but made arrangements to leave as soon as possible. And that was what Elijah did as soon as his sister confided the family's dangerous secret to him.

Elijah didn't know if he could withstand the diabolical sadism of the Inquisitors and refuse to implicate his family, or even if he was capable of heroism, if it would even matter. A failure to confess meant a failure to repent and unrepentant heretics were turned over to the secular government (headed by the most zealously Catholic of monarchs) for live burning or burial. If one confessed and was therefore shown mercy, which could mean a number of alternatives from a less horrific death by strangulation to a humiliating parade naked through the town, there still followed the requirement to give the names of other "heretics" as the Inquisition needed constant fuel to maintain itself, the Inquisitors being paid with the property confiscated from individuals under suspicion.

As a child, Elijah had heard the stories told by the survivors of the ill-fated voyage of Pánfilo de Narváez in 1527 to the Florida Cape and even without a need to leave Spain, he longed to explore the new world they described. Ten years later he sailed across the ocean to Vera Cruz and was there in time to join up with Coronado who was inspired by the same stories. Like many of the men on that expedition, Elijah was a romantic and had more courage to face the unknown dangers of new worlds than to risk the near certainties of the Inquisition. He left Spain to escape but also with dreams of glory.

He waited to announce his intention to his family until his sailing arrangements were already made and imminent so as not to allow his mother and sisters too much time to try to dissuade him.

His sisters cried and wailed when he told them, because so many men were lost on these expeditions and they couldn't get enough of holding him close and praying both Catholic and Jewish prayers right out loud without concern for servants hearing them and they were right to believe they would never see him again for they never did. His mother was angry with him and refused to speak to him at all, not understanding his heart, believing that he took himself from her out of spite and she stayed in her room, maintaining silence and eating nothing until he could no longer stay to beg her to forgive and bless him on his journey. He would feel guilty the rest of his life when he remembered his mother disappearing behind her door without a word.

His father alone blessed him and seemed to understand and went to the dock to see him off on his great adventure. His father told him if he was younger man and not a family man, he would go with him and Elijah took comfort from that. They embraced and Elijah asked his father "please make her eat something" and his father assured him that he would and perhaps he would also make her understand. When speaking to himself in the wilderness, Elijah always directed a few words to his father's spirit and worried about his mother: "please make her eat something, make her understand, keep her well." Later as he grew old, he would ask his father or god, by then he wasn't sure, to make sure his mother's death was painless and peaceful and that before she passed on she would forgive her only son.

Sometimes when Elijah remembered his youthful dreams he felt bitter that he would die alone and anonymous: no word of him in history. He thought of the woman he could have loved, a coyote with magical powers over horses. But he loved wandering more, though he dignified this wanderlust by calling it exploration. He left her with his baby in her belly and now his punishment would be that he would not live to tell the tale of his wandering. Sometimes he lied to himself and to God, when he was lonely enough to believe in God, and claimed that he had planned to return to the woman and the child. But he knew in his heart that what he would have returned for was the triumph, to be able to tell of the places he had found, an inland route to the western sea, difficult but beautiful and strewn with riches in lumber, gold and silver. And to say that he'd done it alone, living with different tribes, sometimes as a slave, then surviving alone with the skills that they taught him, covering hundreds of leagues in the directions they gave him, led on by the tales they told him of the great ocean, the trees so large a single one could be hollowed out to make a boat large enough for fifty men, and the men so regal and the fish so plentiful in that land of the raven and the whale. That was the land he sought and the tale he would tell. To whom would he tell of his exploits? The Buffalo hunt? The skills he had learned? The languages? The wonders? But he had not made it all the way to that great northwestern sea and never really knew how much farther he would have had to go, so perhaps it was just as well he had no one to tell and there was no one to question the veracity of his unfinished tale. Trapped by weakness beneath a tree, it was enough to simply remember.

He remembered waterfalls higher than a Cathedral and indeed the water sculpted the rocks of the mountains in shapes and forms as intricate and exquisite as the most marvelous stonework wrought by man for the glory of God. And mountains, the mountains had become for him a palpable presence as he walked beneath their towering peaks looking for a way through them. Elijah learned slowly how to court them and was rewarded with their secrets: the canyons and caves and valleys that sheltered him and led him onward toward the north and the west. He had been taught how to proceed with care and oftentimes with prayers to a myriad of Gods. Each time he prayed to these Indian Gods, he prayed as well to his own asking forgiveness, for he felt as pressed by this strange and magnificent wilderness to pray to foreign Gods as he had felt pressed by the Inquisition to pray to the Christian God. Surrounded by mysteries and dangers, he hedged his bets and prayed to all the Gods he'd heard tell of as well as nameless ones that might exist without man's knowledge.

But Elijah had lost track of God over time, just as he had lost track of the years. In the beginning he tried to order sunsets and sunrises into days and the cycles of the moon into months and name them, as he always had, but the years themselves he lost track of. He only knew that he had been but eighteen years old when he left with Coronado in 1540 to find the seven cities of gold. How he laughed at that now, having indeed once found gold, not very much, in fact a very little, in a stream reflecting sunlight, when and where he least expected it, and certainly not where Coronado had looked for it. Perhaps he could have been a rich man had he followed that bit of glitter to its source, but by then he was more interested in finding sustenance than wealth. When he was eighteen years old his beard grew in soft and golden, and now it was gray: his beard and the hair on his head and body, all gray. His eighteenth year was the last year he counted. After that he simply lived. He knew he was an old man by that gray hair and the pains that plagued his lean, hard body: pains everywhere a bone could bend.

When had he lost track of God? Jesus or Adonay or, as he sometimes shouted out to the heavens, "whoever you are, oh powerful one or many, as the case may be"? It did not matter for he had come to believe that he didn't matter to any of them. He only knew that once it had mattered to Christians that he was a Jew. He didn't feel like a Jew. He felt like a man alone to whom the rituals and traditions of both Catholicism and Judaism had no meaning. He felt defined by dreams he could not share with anyone, Jew or Christian, and compelled by the beauty and enticement of a land he had learned to explore alone, carrying little in the way of provisions, traveling light and traveling farther because of it. So why had he believed that God, or chance, would favor him? Elijah Benveniste, an exile wherever he turned, laughed at the irony of his name and his destiny. Having no one else, and no longer hedging bets he knew he couldn't win, Elijah began to talk to himself, to tell his tale of the years, honing it, savoring it and it was his own voice that got him through the days, when every step caused pain, and the nights, when lying still caused pain as well.

His life, as himself, had really started after Coronado's expedition when he had returned to Vera Cruz and realized he was tired of human talk, human vanity, and human arrogance. He preferred the sound of the wind in vast places. He decided, then, to go back into the wilderness alone, to seek alone, not golden cities, but whatever he might find. Elijah was curious and yearning to see sights he could not even imagine: young then and needing a miracle to connect him to life, some other kind of life, for he couldn't bear the life he'd been born to, a life in a society that called itself "civilized" but was really unspeakably foolish. He was equally disgusted with the insanity of the Inquisition, and the inexplicable and dangerous religious fervor of his own people. These were so desperate for the attention of a God who had abandoned them that they risked, not merely death, but terrible suffering and pain, to practice their rituals, not even knowing if the rituals were the right ones or rightly done. So Elijah reasoned and despaired of finding reason in this world that called itself civilized.

The mountains were no harsher than these Gods and in the mountains he had found not only beauty but logic as well. Elijah could not wait to rid himself of the soldiers who had been his companions in the inevitable intimacy of a life of traveling through the unknown and the threatening. He longed to go back alone to a land that became his companion, his mother, his father, his lover and child.

He had begun on horseback with entirely too much baggage but he still had much to learn about letting the land sustain him. He had ridden slightly ahead of a hurricane that he survived only by burying himself as deeply as he could in the ground and watched as the terrible wind blew ships inland from the sea, uprooted trees that reached too far into the sky and blew his horse over his head and beyond his vision. Later in his half-conscious dreams under the stars he believed he remembered that the wind had blown him too, half way back to Santa Fe.

He remembered it that way because in fact the wind blew away his memory and he wandered into Santa Fe without it many months later. Some Pueblo Indians there found him and thought he must be holy because he was so clearly mad. They took him in but he yearned to be out and to lie alone in the mountains, under the stars. He learned to stalk and trap animals for their meat and fur and began to wander farther and farther north and west, coming back in the winters to sit by fires, eating until he put on fat, and tell tales. He would trade his furs for finished products: clothing and tools, and, once again, a horse.

One year he lived with the Utes and fought with them against the Comanche and was taken into slavery by the Comanche. So he worked and lived with the Comanche for seven years. While he was with them he met a woman who told him about her own people far to the northwest and how she had been taken by another tribe and traveled with them through bleak and barren lands before they fought the Comanche and lost and she was taken as a slave. This woman told Elijah how she missed the great forest land of her home and the vast ocean that supplied them with food. She described the thousands of colors that appeared in the forest after a rain and sang the songs of her people and inspired him with a desire to escape with her and travel back there.

They walked a long way through land so dry and barren he thought they would die of thirst before they would starve but she always found water and something to nourish them. Sometimes it was just a thin watery soup more like tea than food, sometimes animals so small they sucked the bones dry and still felt hungry.

Being only two, and without bows or arrows, they could not think of hunting the bison that roamed there. The woman was afraid of the Buffalo hunters they spied from a cave. She feared being taken again into slavery. By himself, Elijah would have taken his chances and joined them, and later he did. But first he traveled with the woman.

By the time the snow began to fall, they had traveled up into the foothills beneath the ridge of mountains that formed the strong arched spine of the land. He would look up at the peaks, each with its own halo of wind-driven clouds, and knew that he could die in those mountains but still they delighted his heart with their harsh beauty. When the snow deepened, the woman showed him how to make a shoe of rawhide and tree boughs shaped into a large triangle with straps to attach these under their leather boots so they would float atop the snow instead of sinking into it. She showed him also how to cut a cave into the largest drifts to keep them warm. They weathered a winter living on the meat of squirrels, deer and once, a mountain lion. They had not intended to hunt the lioness but had somehow found themselves between the mother and her cub and had no choice but to fight and kill her and once she was dead, of course they ate her. They found the cub and cared for it, sharing their food with him, but when the weather warmed and the snow thawed, the cub ran off and they never found its body so hoped that it survived somehow.

Finally they reached the land he called the land of the beginning for it spewed forth boiling water from the innards of the earth and the sudden, graceful, arching spray seemed to reach the highest stars. This strange and noisy land tempted him to believe in the Catholic story of hell. For this land was covered with holes in which boiling water seethed and bubbled. It was beautiful to see but dangerous and they watched while a buffalo sank suddenly into a hole that opened up beneath his weight and sucked him down and then only bare boiled bones rose to the top.

The pools in these holes were of the most beautiful colors: as blue as lapis, as green as malachite, and enticing. These colors were hypnotic and the woman had an irresistible desire to look into their depths. She walked slowly and prayerfully, making no sound, light on her feet and careful not to disturb the gods that could rise up in anger and tear the ground from beneath her feet. It was not the Gods she needed to fear and appease, but the earth itself, which cares nothing for appeasement. Her weight, so little compared to the Buffalo, was still too much for the earth that had grown thin and crusty with so much boiling. Elijah called out to her to step back for he could hear it coming, the breakage, the rumbling, and his call harmonized with her scream as she fell into the sapphire cauldron. Then he could hear only the rumbling. Perhaps that was when he lost track of God.

He turned back to find the Buffalo hunters and hunted with them and lived with them for many months or was it years? He lost track of the time. He learned much from them and when he left them he had many tales to tell when he returned to winter with the Pueblos. Then he became ill and was taken to the woman who could cure him, the proud *coyota* who deigned to love him. He remembered her in dreams and, more and more, against his will, when he was awake, hypnotized with walking.

Elijah had been taken with a fever that turned the world upside down and confused the days and nights in his mind. He remembered cramps like something alive inside of him that pinched and twisted his guts until he threw up whatever he had tried to eat. He remembered his skin burning hot and then being so chilled that he shivered, aching all over, until he was soaked in sweat and awoke to a world of spring warmth and color. He remembered that when he came to her everything was still covered with snow so he knew he'd been with her for many weeks. The woman took Elijah out walking then and showed him the buds on the trees and the spurts of green in the garden. She told him the little she knew about her own father, one of those Spaniards who had come from across the sea with Pánfilo de Narvaez to explore the lands between the Rio de Las Palmas and Florida.

"Six hundred men started out" she told him with awe in her voice, for most of them had died or disappeared, her father being one of those who had survived and eventually disappeared. Some nights she told him the stories she remembered her father telling her before he died, not such an old man even then, but it was not the years he told his grieving daughter, it was the distance that made him ready. This she told Elijah and Elijah understood. A life of exploration was hard on the body and the soul, but it was still harder to resist the pull of the wild.

She told him how shipwrecked sailors had killed their horses for food and tanned the whole skins of the forelegs to be used as containers for water, how they wove the hair from the tails and manes into ropes for rigging the sails they made from their own shirts, how they used the horses' lungs to make bellows to fan the flames they needed to melt down their stirrups, spurs and crossbows to make nails, saws and axes. With those tools they built five boats from the materials they found growing in the swampy land where their ships had floundered and wrecked. It was clear the woman was proud of her father's resourcefulness and the fact that he had survived where so many had died of drowning, disease, starvation or the desperate drinking of salt water. Living sometimes only on daily handfuls of raw maize, sometimes for weeks on only blackberries or some root that had come into its season, or on oysters as the Indians they encountered showed them, and once to her father's knowledge, their own dead, hundreds of men scattered and became tens and tens became a handful. She was proud too that her father had refused to partake of human flesh and had yet survived to come so far inland to the land of the Pueblos from that place where they had been blown ashore from the eastern sea.

Then Elijah would tell her the stories he had heard about that same expedition for there were four of the survivors, a friar named Marcos, a black freedman named Estevan and two others, who returned to Spain to garner fame all over Spain and New Spain for the tales they told, those tales being their fortune. Their names were included in written histories for the parts they had played in these stories and the stories to come for these men convinced Francisco Vasquez Coronado that there existed cities of fabulous wealth so that Coronado was inspired to organize his own expedition. Elijah told her he had joined Coronado's expedition when he was but a young man of eighteen. He didn't explain that so many of them had left to face the unknown but glamorous dangers of this new land to escape the well-known and ignominious dangers of the Inquisition. He suspected her father might have had similar reasons for joining the earlier expedition but he didn't know if this was something a man would tell his half breed child.

Elijah had been so weakened by his mysterious illness that even drawing a deep breath tired him and he stayed with her until mid-summer. When he saw that she was big with his child he began to think of staying there with her forever and he knew that he should. He thought of the joy of raising a child but no sooner had he begun to think of staying anywhere forever, than he began to have visions of deep forests laced with streams and waterfalls and high mountain tops where only the tiniest flowers grew: "forgotten by the wind" these flowers were called by Indian people he knew. The reds and purples and greens of the forests and flowers invaded the darkness of his dreams. He dreamed also of walking up a steep and rocky path, a path made by Elk, and knowing when he emerged from the deep woods at a place high above a river he would see the world around him and be glad as if he had finally understood God. But before he could reach this high place he would hear the woman's voice, a whisper but compelling, calling him the way she called her horses and he would wake with a tightness around his chest as if she had roped him and was tightening the rope. He believed that he loved her but he just couldn't let her tether him to one spot when he longed to walk as far as his eyes could see, always curious what he would find around the next bend, over the next mountain, at the end of the trail he blazed for himself.

Finally he realized he was closer to the mountains than to any human being and he went out again to find whatever he might find. He felt guilty for leaving the woman and the unborn child and even guiltier that last day promising to return when he knew his promise was not only a lie but unnecessary. She had never asked him to stay forever, never asked anything of him, had included caring for him during his sickness in her life but had only reluctantly allowed him to help her with chores when he began to recover his strength. He remembered that she didn't say a word when he left but offered him a talisman. When he saw that it was a small silver six pointed star on a chain, similar to one his sister had given him when he left his home back in Spain, he understood that this half breed woman knew all about him. When he tried to speak more words to her, she touched his lips with her finger as if to admonish him not to make a promise he might not be able to keep and she herself said nothing, nor did she shed a single tear. She motioned him to bend so she could put the chain around his neck and then smiled at him and kissed him gently on the mouth. She had everything she wanted from him growing inside her.

When he left, Elijah expected to continue traveling all the way to the end of his quest, crossing that terrible land he called the land of the beginning and the end, determined to pass through it to the northwestern sea. But his sickness had left him weaker than he remembered ever being and he realized he might be forever weak for he was older now and he could never travel as fast or as far as before his time with the horse woman who lived her hermit life on the outskirts of the Pueblo. He thought he could make this last trip by sheer doggedness, going slowly but surely, resting when he needed to, talking constantly to keep himself company and just refusing to give up.

He reckoned without the desert heat at high noon, hotter now he was older and without the raw harsh cold of the desert nights that lay between him and the warmth of mountain caves and thermal springs. He began to circle about looking for easier routes until no matter which way he turned he would run into that sheer physical exhaustion and pain that drove him back and knocked him down, and he never saw that terrible beautiful land of death and ecstasy again. Nor did he find the place he had so fervently sought. Year after year he stopped in places he was accustomed to during the seasons he was comfortable and came back always to some inhabited place to trade his furs and talk. Occasionally he came close to the place where the woman lived and would spy on the child he was ashamed to claim. He felt certain that if the woman ever saw him she would not recognize him because all that had remained of his youthful good looks and strength had gone into that one child he had conceived with her.

The first time he watched her he didn't really see her at all, as she was tucked into a woven blanket in the crook of her mother's arm. He knew the baby was healthy and strong by the smile on the mother's face as she nursed her infant. He did not know then if his child was a girl or a boy but he felt happy that the mother was so clearly delighted, singing to her baby and lifting the tiny bundle up high to survey their sunny world. He wanted to leave a gift but he was ashamed to show himself. He remained hidden in the shadows until the sun went down and the mother returned with her baby to the warmth of the hearth. Then he hung some beaver pelts on the branches of a *piñón* tree knowing she would find them there when she went to gather the precious *piñón* nuts that would soon be ready to harvest. He remembered she was a woman who used all the bounty of the land.

When he next saw his child two autumns later, she was running and her mother was calling her, so he knew that his child was a girl named María and that she was brave, perhaps a bit headstrong and very beautiful for she came close to where he hid among the trees until her mother made her come away. Elijah had learned to move quietly and to make himself invisible but he thought perhaps the child had seen him for she had stopped just long enough to draw a deep breath and looked straight at where he crouched. Perhaps she thought he was a bear hiding in the woods. She was not afraid but she did run back to her mother who was calling her most insistently. After that he longed to see her grow up and he made a point of coming every year to watch her progress and always left some precious thing where she herself could find it, an elk horn, a perfect bird's egg abandoned in its nest, a bit of rock with strange markings like fairy footprints, a piece of malachite, an eagle feather. He always left these gifts in the same spot and so each year she looked for some treasure there. The last time she called out "Where are you? Who are you?" She was old enough to know someone was there and young enough to be unafraid. But he did not answer and the next year, there would be no treasure in her special magic spot by the grove of *piñón* trees.

Now he rotted, losing muscle, losing breath, losing teeth, hair gone to gray, and eyes misted over with some troublesome fluid, so he saw with his ears and his nose these days, and with his memories, for the valleys and paths of his past wanderings remained familiar to him. But he knew that all things good and bad, happy and sad, come to an end and he understood that he would soon embark upon a new exploration that no one had returned to tell about. At first this frightened him but then he realized that this was why men created gods, someone to guide them into the most daunting of unknown destinations. He began to hope that God had found him or that he had found God, he wasn't sure which, but at the end he was no longer bitter that he had not found the destination he had set for himself or that no one would glorify his name with a chronicle of his travels. He was happy to lay there and listen to the silence of the snow and he smiled because he felt warmer than he had in years.

Chapter Four
El Valle
San Luis 1989

From the Denver Post, April 28, 1989
POACHING RAID RULED EXCESSIVE BUT NOT
RACIST

The massive poaching raid through the San Luis Valley last month intimidated residents with an unnecessary show of force, but there was no evidence of racism or brutality, a commission appointed by Gov. Roy Romer reported Thursday.

The four-member panel had sharp words about deployment of a helicopter and large numbers of federal and state officers who swept into mostly Hispanic rural communities at dawn to arrest suspects. The arrests culminated a two and a half year sting operation aimed at poaching for profit.

Fifty seven people were arrested by 275 (two hundred and seventy five) state and federal officers across the southern Colorado valley and in northern New Mexico. Romer appointed the commission after residents complained of entrapment and excessive force.

Lois had to be at the Church meeting hall in San Luis by eight in the morning so she was up and out like a shot by four. There were no other cars on Colorado Blvd. which was famous for all day gridlock and it was an eerie feeling having that thoroughfare all to herself, as if the world had finally come to an end and she had somehow missed it on the ten o'clock news. A full moon was heading west in that royal blue early morning sky and lit up the parking lots, the warehouses, the used appliances stores (completely financed at 21%), the KFCs, the discount shoe-stores and bowling allies built on the ancient land of shale and bones. Neon signs from liquor stores threw striped shadows through plastic blinds on beds of poverty and despair endured alone, the pay-by- the-week kitchenettes, the one-night-stand, just-passing-through motels, advertising clean, safe rooms forget the amenities, clean and safe will do just fine thank you. She passed the hospital complex, quiet now, no ambulance sirens, no emergencies in that hour suspended between night and dawn, a surreal time. She passed Glendale, the clubs finally closed, even the nude dancers gone home wherever home might be.

In two more hours the street would be filled with trucks, buses and cars from gritty Commerce City to affluent Cherry Hills, filled with the smell of hot tires, hot brakes and fast food, filled with music, rock and rap, classic and country, filled with folks speeding and cussing, looking at each other nasty or just curious or maybe incredulous, looking for trouble perhaps, reading bumper stickers at the lights, starting fights, cutting in, cussing, crying, damn!

Lois would be long gone by then, out of the city and out of the twentieth century. Lois remembered when Glendale and points south (one shopping center after another) was all open fields. She imagined cattle grazing there. She'd heard there was once a blacksmith shop at the corner of Alameda and Colorado. She passed a refrigerated grocery truck, so lost in thought she almost missed her exit for I-25 South.

The sun made a glorious appearance on the horizon as she drove through Colorado Springs and Lois was tempted to take a detour through Garden of the Gods but thought better of it and focused on making good time to Walsenburg. At Walsenburg she would turn off the interstate onto highway 160, a curving, two-lane road with no place to pass the frequent slow moving trucks carrying loads of hay or potatoes.

Her own dream of living on the land was something Lois had tried briefly and not all that valiantly, giving up after three harsh winters because she believed or was convinced that she, in those days they, should explore other options. Her ex-husband settled back into what he called "civilization" so easily because her dream had been his nightmare, but she never stopped mourning the sound and the smell of the mountain spring and the magic five o ' clock light through the trees.

When Lois arrived in the town for the first time she saw the bell tower of the church but not the dirt road that led around to the back of it and the meeting hall, a low non-descript building hidden by cottonwoods, so she kept going on the main road through town and stopped at a Conoco station to ask directions to the Church meeting hall. She pulled up intending to go inside but the proprietor came out to her car instead and she leaned out the window to ask him where to turn off to get behind the church and he answered without missing a beat:

"I'm surprised you don't ask me for the synagogue."

Lois had no time to get over her considerable surprise before the man began to recite Hebrew prayers to her. She wondered where he had learned Hebrew but she asked him how he knew she was Jewish.

"Takes one to know one." He said with a large grin. He reminded her of her own father with his round face, wide smile and sparkling eyes.

"My grandmother was Jewish." he told her as he pulled from inside his shirt a chain from which hung a Star of David as well as a Christian Cross and a Native American Circle. He smiled and went on "I speak several languages: Spanish and English, Hebrew and Arabic, a little French, less German."

Lois was first amazed and then excited. She loved chance encounters, the kind that could change a person's direction in life. She loved the sense of exploring unknown territory and optimistically expected the wonderful and fantastic. His name was Orlando Salamanca, the last name being for a town in Spain from which his ancestors had originally come. Lois was so excited that she could easily have spent the rest of the morning questioning him but she knew she was running late and told him she would be "right back" . . . then realizing she could be several hours at the meeting house she amended her promise and told him she'd be back as soon as she got done at the meeting. He of course knew all about the poaching raid and about the group of radical lawyers coming into the town to meet with the Coalition that was formed to fight this latest invasion of the Valley. In fact he had a favor to ask of her.

"Do you know who you are going to represent yet?"

"No, we'll be assigned to clients after the meeting."

"Can you ask to represent someone in particular?"

"Sure, who did you have in mind?"

"His name is Rocky Hernandez and he won't be at the meeting. He is still hiding in the mountains, didn't want to spend even a single night in jail. I know his mother, María. Ask for him, they'll have his paperwork."

"You got it."

"See, it was meant you should get lost and stop here. Come back after the meeting and I'll give you directions to María's place. She'll feed you when you get there. And then we can visit later." His smile warmed the cold morning air.

Lois turned and circled back to the meeting house which was filled with defendants, their families, political activists making speeches and lawyers from Denver, Alamosa and Colorado Springs all milling around like summer campers waiting to register for activities. She found the right person to ask for her assignment and was granted her request to be assigned to Rocky Hernandez and given a copy of the charges against him. Several people seemed to know that, if she could arrange immediately with the local prosecutor that Rocky would not be locked up but set free on a PR bond, he wanted to turn himself in and get the whole thing over with. Most of the other attorneys were already interviewing clients that were out on bond or going over to the jail to visit clients there. It seemed that Rocky was the only one among them who was a true wild child, having lived for so many years in the mountains, in the open, that he was phobic about spending a night or two in the jail, even with police officers who were friends, sympathetic because they had grown up with him and sympathetic too because some of them had been charged with poaching as well. For the first time in her legal career Lois would find herself on the same side as the local policemen.

DROP ALL CHARGES!! IMMEDIATE REPARATIONS!! . . . one activist had written in bold letters on the flier and another had spoken at length about the necessity of showing a united front, avoid plea bargains, stick it out to the bitter end. It was like asking union members to hold out during a long strike while their families went hungry. "Fat chance" she thought to herself. Lois listened to a couple more impassioned speeches, got lists of phone numbers of people who wanted to help as well as a copy of the latest newsletter *La Comisión Independiente 6 de Marzo* knowing as she read it that very few individuals would have the energy and resources to hold fast to its principles long enough to take their cases to trial. It was so much more effective to pick on poor folks with families because poor folks with families were inevitably too overwhelmed with the exigencies of daily life to devote much time to causes. There were a few, always a few, heroes but heroes were heroes because they were few and stood out from the rest.

Lois returned to the Conoco station where she found Orlando reading. He called his wife from the back of the shop where they ran a Laundromat and she came out front to meet Lois, with a smile as wide and warm as Orlando's. Then he wanted to show Lois his library. Behind the counter stocked with jumper cables and batteries, candy bars and cigarettes, he had his collection of books on history, philosophy, psychology, mysticism, many by Jewish authors. Most of the books had been given to him by people he met who had passed through on their way to Taos or Santa Fe and came back to visit. But she needed to be on her way and so they planned another visit just to talk about the books. Orlando told Lois that Rocky's mother was Shoshone and very wise, a *curandera*. He had some books he wanted to send to her and gave them to Lois to take with her.

"Expect to stay the night" he told her, "perhaps she will take you into the mountains on horseback to find your client."

Lois was glad to have Orlando's directions which she followed carefully. She never would have found the ranch without them. The road she took out of town was a dirt track behind a run-down store that sold cigarettes, junk food and liquor. She followed it as it curved here and there for no apparent reason, avoiding the temptation to turn onto other wider roads that would have taken her to New Mexico or dead ended at a reservoir. She saw the Church he told her about and stayed the course waiting to turn onto another county road just behind the San Francisco Post Office and sure enough at exactly .4 of a mile after the church she found her turn. She followed that another .3 of a mile and saw a long low adobe house all alone on the horizon.

Orlando must have called ahead because María was outside waiting for her. Lois introduced herself and followed María into the kitchen. María fed Lois with her grandchildren while various men walked in and out of the kitchen on their way to or from their own homes. Each time she was introduced, Lois felt awkward being treated like an honored guest but she was indeed honored as any guest would have been, it was the way it was done in the Valley.

After a dinner of rabbit stew and *pozole*, María cleared the dishes and instructed her granddaughters to wash and dry them while she and Lois talked outside on the porch. With the sun down, it had gotten quite cold and María offered Lois a down jacket that smelled of wood smoke and herbs. They sat outside watching the moon rise and talked about the young man in the mountains. María knew he wouldn't want to go through the kind of long political, legal process that was being discussed. They went back inside to read the newsletter and María put on her half glasses and looked carefully at the document held at arm's length in order to see it.

PON'TE TRUCHA!

> Three weeks have passed since the invasion and terrorizing of the Sangre de Cristo Land Grant communities. We faced challenges, fear and confusion. Now we must organize for a long fight as we face the aftermath: publicity, legal proceedings, investigations, psychological trauma, provocations, expenses, etc. . . . To turn this entrapment and raid around so that we can define our future we must put aside petty rivalries, old jealousies and personal differences. Hunters must resist early plea bargaining so we can see what the prosecutor really wants. Hunters should not waive any of their rights without considering what impact this will have such as weakening the overall strength of a united defense effort . . .

María chuckled when she read the exhortation to put aside petty rivalries.

"It's part of the culture" she explained with a sardonic smile to Lois.

"You know I sometimes think that all these petty rivalries are a really necessary part of the culture, for the men anyway, necessary for them to feel like men. How to explain this? Before the Americans invaded and this land was part of Mexico, the different Indian tribes rode around raiding each other, Navajo, Comanche, Utes, Apaches all stealing horses from each other but also women and children they'd take as slaves and then the Spanish, they would buy them. The Spaniards, really mixed people for generations now, although they don't always want to acknowledge their Indian grandmothers, they called it "ransom" but it was really slave trade because the people they ransomed had to stay with them to work off their ransom. So the Spanish had households full of slave servants. Sometimes they adopted the people into their families, sometimes they worked them too hard, but that is another story. My point in telling you this is that the men made their place in society, their honor and their wealth by raiding and stealing from each other. It was a tradition you understand? Now they can't do that anymore so they maintain their honor with these petty rivalries. A man can no longer steal horses from his neighbor's herd so he takes his prize cattle dog instead and they fight over that. Lots of fights over dogs these days. Go sit in the courtroom when the judge comes to town and just listen, lotsa dog cases."

"So all this raiding and slave trading, your grandparents told you these stories?"

"Hell no, my parents were both pure blooded Shoshone from the Wind River region. No slaves in our family history. No I read all that in a book."

Lois laughed then and María laughed with her. Then she got quiet thinking about Rocky, the youngest of her thirteen children.

"My son is a loner" she said sadly. "It sounds good, the idea of a united defense effort and then taking the offensive and making the government accountable. But that is the nature of government, to oppress. Do they really think the Mexican government is any better? Land grants? Where do they think those came from? God? They came from a corrupt Spanish king who had no right to grant these lands to anyone. Then the Mexicans won their independence from Spain and from France but the Indians of Mexico are no better off down there than the Indians up here.

Well, enough history! I will be very happy if you just keep my son out of jail. He stays out of these politics. We don't care about the treaty of Guadalupe Hidalgo. That is between two governments that had nothing to do with us. We don't want this fight. Every day we fight to survive; we do this quietly so we will be able to pass on a spiritual home to our children and grandchildren. My son will always hunt. He knows the mountains so well that he could hide forever and they would never find him, not even with all their helicopters and dogs. But he wants to come out and see his family and sit by my fire in the cold winters. Will your friends be angry at you if you arrange a plea bargain for Rocky?"

"Your son is my client and I will do what he directs me to do. I can't even let you decide, only him. That is my ethical responsibility."

"My friend Orlando told me I could trust you. He has a sense about folks you know. You have some books for me?"

María looked up at the stars beginning to appear in the west while Lois went to her car and retrieved the books that she had forgotten.

"I notice you like to read philosophy as well as history."

"Does that surprise you? Once this houseful of kids grew up and left, I needed something to fill the time. I'd go to town and stop by Orlando's to listen to him talk. My husband doesn't talk much, just grunts when he wants something, "get my *lonche*" he barks at me "Eat" I yell at him and slam the plate down. I barely remember when we were young and romantic. Those kids came fast, not much love in between . . . but enough about that. I just became friendly with Orlando's wife Viola and we would both listen to him talk, about this Jewish thing. He thinks he's Jewish and gets very excited about it. Most folks in the village make fun of him, maybe they are afraid he will find out they are Jewish too, but you know what I think? I think he has more brains than the whole lot of them put together. He told me you are Jewish?"

María laughed and confided that Orlando told her the Jewish lawyers were the best. Lois laughed with her. She realized that they laughed a lot together and she felt comfortable with this woman as she had with Orlando.

"Well hopefully a half Jewish lawyer is good too. My father is Jewish, my mother is Mexican. She is from a town about this size, Cimarron, near Raton. Her parents moved to Denver when she was very young."

"Oh, who was your grandfather?"

"His name was Isaac Mendoza. I never got to know him. He died when my mother was thirteen."

"I'm sorry. The name doesn't ring a bell but most of the folks I know from New Mexico live in Questa or near Taos. But I do know where Cimarron is. They have that old hotel there?"

"The St. James, It was on national television one Halloween, some show about haunted places. They say some famous gunfighters stayed there."

"Yes I think I remember that. Well, let me show you the guest room. It's not haunted but it used to be my girls' room and there are still a lot of their dolls in there. I hope they don't scare you in the night." She made a pretend scary face and smiled in her motherly way.

María led Lois down the narrow hallway to a large add-on room at the end. There were bunk beds along one wall and a double bed in a corner. There was a crowd of beautiful dolls on the bunk-beds, many handmade in costumes that identified them as Indian or Spanish. There were also various religious pictures on the walls, lace curtains on the one window and some colorful hand-woven shawls draped over the one armchair. On the pillow of the bed lay a cotton nightgown with embroidery around the hem, sleeves and square neckline. Lois had seen such embroidery on expensive dresses in import shops. She hesitated to wear it to sleep.

"No, please, wear it and there is a warm robe in the closet there at the foot of the bunk beds. Please, be comfortable. You know we really appreciate that you are going to help Rocky. He could not stand even a single night in jail."

In the night, Lois heard whispering and dreamt that she was meeting Rocky but even in her dreams she could not have imagined the next morning.

Lois lay in bed a bit longer than usual listening to hear when the one bathroom would be clear. After María's grim husband ate and left the house, Lois got up, used the bathroom, put on the warm fleece robe and went to the kitchen to look for María. María was out feeding the chickens but there was a plate on the table with a note telling her to help herself. She found tortillas still warm wrapped in a napkin in a basket, like her grandmother used to serve them. Various pans on the stove top held scrambled eggs, sausage and potatoes. There was a small bowl of green chili on the table. It was more than Lois was used to eating first thing in the morning but she realized the country air made her hungrier than she would be in town. When María came back and caught her finishing a fat burrito, she grinned and said

"We have a saying: *panza llena , corazón contento*, that means . . .

"Yes I know, a full stomach, a happy heart."

Then they went out back where María had already saddled two mares and told Lois they would ride up into the hills and meet with Rocky. Lois was glad that she had packed some hiking clothes for the trip. A couple of the lawyers had come in from Pueblo or Colorado Springs and had afternoon court dates after the meeting, but most of them had driven in from Denver 4 hours away and had made plans to stay over at least one night and some were making a mini vacation out of it, going down to Taos in The Land of Enchantment. Lois was dressed and ready to ride in a few minutes. She was glad the horse was not very tall and she could make a good show of swinging up into the saddle. The air had warmed up considerably as the sun rose higher in the sky so she took off her jacket and tied the arms around her waist, put on the leather gloves that María offered her and took a deep breath of the fresh morning air before giving her horse a light tap and taking off after María into the hills.

It had been years since Lois had ridden a horse and at first she was afraid to prod her horse to the speed that María was going but she had no choice and discovered that a full gallop was easier on her than the initial trot. Within minutes she was enjoying herself and not the least bit afraid. It took them twenty minutes by her watch to begin the climb into some hills and gain the cover of trees. They slowed their horses to a walk and wound about through the woods, María following a trail of sunlight through the trees rather than anything discernible on the ground. Lois understood that Rocky would be indeed hard to find, unless the Feds knew the exact angle of light to follow at the exact hour and minute of the morning.

María stopped her horse near a creek and tied the mare to an old fence post that no longer had any fence to hold up. She whistled and by the time Lois caught up to her and dismounted, a small, thin, childlike man appeared from out of nowhere on the other side of the creek which Lois now saw was frozen like glass and too wide to simply step across. She was wondering how best to negotiate the ice when Rocky began to throw handfuls of gritty dirt and some pine branches onto it to make their crossing easier. As they approached his side he held out a longer thicker pine branch to hold onto as they jumped up the slight embankment. Close up he looked barely half his thirty years. He was shy and not comfortable speaking English, maybe not comfortable speaking at all.

María spoke to him in Spanish and Lois, understanding only the occasional word waited to be introduced and softly touch her client's hand. María then continued speaking in rapid Spanish to her son and Lois saw him nod and smile with relief. María was ready to put up her home to make his bond but under no circumstances was Rocky to have to spend any time behind bars. She understood that once she had worked out a bond agreement with the DA, María would make Rocky available to come in for an arraignment and to set a date to enter a plea. Lois did her best to look confident. As suddenly as Rocky had appeared out of the bushes and trees, he disappeared and Lois and María rode back to the ranch.

Lois changed and left for the courthouse, not knowing what to expect and glad that it was still only Thursday because she was determined not to leave San Luis until she had made the world safe for Rocky Hernandez. This of course she could not do. But for now she would content herself with just keeping him out of jail. Predictably, the deputy prosecutor in San Luis claimed to have no authority to enter into any kind of binding agreement but he would recommend . . . . she wasn't buying it, and wanted to know who did have authority to enter into a binding agreement and was told with a touch of smugness that the regional prosecutor, the boss, had his office in Alamosa. Did he really think that would stop her? She'd driven all the way from Denver, another 60 miles wouldn't matter. Naively she called ahead to announce her intention to meet with District Attorney Derrick Gardner.

So off she went while everyone else went to lunch. When she marched up to the office and one of the secretaries practically spread-eagled herself across his door as she announced that Mr. Gardner wasn't in, Lois figured something funny was up. Just why were they going to so much trouble over Rocky anyway? He was small potatoes. But so were they and being a big fish in a small pond could go to some heads. OK, OK she was leaving.

She went over to the courthouse thinking to find the prosecutor there since she assumed he would have to show up for the afternoon docket. She was headed toward a telephone to make a call back to San Luis when she heard a large blustery man behind her call out in a hale and hearty way: "Well if it isn't Derrick Gardner" and thrust his large hairy hand out toward a gentleman who was approaching from the side entrance. She simply inserted herself between the two men and held her own hand out to shake that of her opponent. Of course he squeezed it hard showing off his masculine strength, she'd gotten used to this from a certain sort of professional man.

"Hello Mr. Gardner. I'm Lois Gold and we just talked on the phone about an hour ago. I guess you forgot to tell your secretary that I was coming because she didn't seem to know where you were."

"Well, hello Ms. Gold. I'm glad you found me." ("Bullshit" she was thinking.) "Is your client with you?"

"No Mr. Gardner. Not that I didn't trust you or your deputy or anything but I thought we should get something on the record before he came all the way to Alamosa."

"Well, let us go see if we can catch the Judge in chambers before he goes back to court after recess. We've been involved in a rape trial today."

In chambers, Lois made her arguments to the judge that Rocky should be allowed to go free on a PR bond and talked about family ties being what kept him in the community and in fact if he didn't turn himself in which he was quite willing to do with the proper assurances, the Feds wouldn't be able to find him anyway and here he was *wanting* to come in out of the cold and get this whole mess straightened out.

The Judge said he didn't have a problem with that and gave the prosecutor a look like he didn't much approve of the entire raid in the first place and the prosecutor smirked and said he didn't have a problem with it either except that Rocky wasn't around and he didn't think he could call up the cops in San Luis and just ask them to bring Rocky in to the District Courthouse because he knew he wasn't real popular with those cops down there. He gave Lois a phony baloney collegial smile thinking that, being a defense attorney, she would waste no love on cops generally and that was something that they, as two professional folks, could have in common whatever their political differences. But Lois surprised him a second time that day and said that the cops liked *her* pretty well and she would just call up ole Abe Medina like she knew him all her life and ask him to bring Rocky to town when he came in this afternoon to get his wisdom teeth pulled. She'd managed to glean that much information back at the jail before setting out for Alamosa.

"He'll need a ride home anyway after that procedure, don't you think?" giving Mr. Gardner a phony baloney honey sweet, "ain't-I-the-friendly-one-though" kind of smile right back. Lois was beginning to enjoy this.

María must have brought Rocky into town while Lois was driving to Alamosa because, when she called, Abe had Rocky with him and they were just awaiting her call to get started. By the time they arrived the rape trial had resumed so Lois and Rocky had to wait in the law library for several hours and didn't get in front of the sympathetic judge until nearly five o'clock. While Rocky hid behind the stacks, pretending to be looking at the books, Abe Medina explained to her why they had been so reluctant to let Rocky out on bond, and why Rocky had been so reluctant to come down out of the mountains. The friendly prosecutor had hoped to intimidate Rocky into leading the cops to his older brother who was the suspect in a murder case.

The murder was only local news and was overshadowed by the big Federal operation but the local prosecutor and the police in Alamosa had been looking for Tony Hernandez for months. When Rocky sold an antelope to the federal undercover agent, the guys in Alamosa were already licking their chops thinking the feds would catch Rocky in their net. They knew they couldn't expect much help from the cops in Costilla County, some of whom had also been arrested on poaching charges. They hadn't counted on the public outcry that would be raised over the poaching raid and maybe now they figured they may as well put that murder investigation on hold while the entire area was in the media limelight.

Then, one thing leading to another and with time on their hands, Abe told Lois about a guy who was shot in the head while allegedly trying to escape the police, white officers near Creede.

"The thing was, the bullet went through the front, not the back, of his skull and there was a hole in each of his hands right through the palms, sort of like he'd had his hands held in back of his head, sort of like he was doing what those Anglo cops told him to do, but that evidence got suppressed somehow and that cop was never even warned let alone indicted for murder. Hell, killing Mexicans, killing Indians, killing Blacks, it don't make no matter." He shook his head sadly and then got up with that show-must-go-on attitude that people got when they didn't know what else to do or say . . . "Gotta go, get these damn teeth pulled."

The judge couldn't have been friendlier to Lois and that seemed a good portent of things to come. He also managed to throw several irritated looks Mr. Gardner's way. A date was set for Rocky to appear in court in San Luis and Lois nailed Mr. Gardner to a plea agreement that his deputy there would have authority to recommend to the court.

"I don't want to have come running back up here to make sure we can enter into a binding agreement"

"I wouldn't want you to have to do that either." And Mr. Gardner smiled a "no hard feelings?" smile and Lois allowed her hand to be squeezed too hard one last time.

Abe was waiting for them, his mouth all numb from Novocain and Rocky got into the driver's seat of Abe's cop car while Lois followed in her car. She'd already been invited to spend a second night at the ranch and she thought she might also stop along the way for that promised visit with Orlando. She'd been told coming to the Valley would feel like coming home and so far that promise was proving true.

Chapter Five
Jacob
Flanders 1579

"Why did creation begin with a single human being? For the sake of the righteous and the wicked, that none might ascribe their differing characters to hereditary differences. And lest families boast of their high lineage. This they do nonetheless —how much worse would it be if all were not descended from a single source!" Talmud

Jacob was a strong and healthy child who spent as much time outdoors as he was permitted but during his twelfth year he and his father both became ill with a lung ailment, which left them feverish and weak and coughing constantly. It happened during a time when Miriam was on a journey to visit some friends. Where she had gone and who she was visiting was not something she divulged, although she warned that she would be gone for several weeks if not months and not to worry about her until winter. There was at that time a constant movement of people across the seas and the landscape, which Miriam frequently guided so Pieter suspected she was going to lead some Jews from the south to a city in the north and toward the east that he heard had offered asylum to persecuted Jews from Iberia. Whatever his speculations, neither Pieter nor Mayken asked questions they knew Miriam would not want to answer. They knew they would miss her presence, and even worry about her safety although she had about her an air of the invincible, as though she was a force of nature rather than a mere human being, but they could not know how badly they would miss her healing skill. Had Pieter and Jacob taken ill before she left, she would of course have stayed to tend to them but everyone in the household had been in good health when she left with instructions to Pieter about Mayken's sleeping medication should that be required.

Thus when the two men of the house fell ill with the fits of coughing, fever and insurmountable weakness, they called a Doctor from the town. This Doctor applied leeches to Jacob and Pieter to suck out the bad blood. It seemed to Jacob that his father lost enough blood every time he coughed. Jacob himself did not cough up blood but sometimes felt like he was coughing up his innards and once experienced such an excruciating pain in one side that the Doctor was certain he had cracked a rib.

Miriam was gone longer than she had expected to be and when she arrived back home, two months later she was dismayed to see the two so debilitated by the lingering illness. She went out into the countryside to gather herbs and made steaming concoctions, some to inhale, some to drink and some to bath in. Whereas the town Doctor had sought to heal them by having their blood sucked out of them by the disgusting leeches, Miriam seemed determined to make them sweat and piss out the source of their sickness. Under her care Jacob recovered completely but was so weak that he spent two more months in the house, and followed Miriam around everywhere, offering to help with household chores and asking why she did what she did the way that she did it until even placid Miriam began to get impatient for him to return to his boy's pursuits outside.

He observed that every Friday at dusk, Miriam disappeared into a closet- like room behind a tapestry in a large hall of the house. She would carry with her a basket covered with a cloth and was very secretive. If she caught him following after, she would send him on some errand and be gone when he returned to find her. Her reluctance to let him follow her into the hidden room when he was used to following her everywhere else of course made him curious and one Friday he found the key she used to unlock the room and went early to unlock it himself. After he replaced the key in its hiding place in a box that looked like a book, he went back to the room, opened the heavy door slowly and as quietly as he could, wincing when it creaked, closed it as carefully and took a quick look around. The room was nearly filled to three edges with a heavy wood table covered from top to floor with an exquisitely embroidered, lace trimmed cloth. On the fourth side sat a magnificently carved wooden chest. Before he could open the chest to investigate its contents, he heard Miriam footsteps, and quickly slipped under the cloth to hide under the table. He could see the rest of the room from the border of lace that fell just at eye level when he sat on the floor.

Miriam was surprised that she had to fumble with the key to get the door to her secret room unlocked. She didn't realize that she had in fact locked it with her first turn. Jacob watched her as she opened and walked through the door and approached the chest the intriguing chest. She opened it and brought forth two candle holders, two candles and a flint. She had bread in the basket and lifted a bottle of wine and a glass from the chest. She then came to the table to set these things out. Afraid she might touch him with her toes, Jacob attempted to move slightly away from her direction without realizing that he had seated himself on one edge of the long tablecloth. The cloth moved slightly with him but Miriam still didn't notice. Then as she attempted to center the candles in the circular design in the middle of the cloth, she saw that the cloth was awry and tried to straighten it. She had to tug and the candlesticks fell over and Jacob cried out the same moment that Miriam did.

Jacob crawled out from under the table very embarrassed and afraid he would be punished, but when Miriam saw it was only him, she was too relieved to be angry at him and could only laugh. She decided the encounter was a sign from God that she had waited too long to tell Jacob the secret of his heritage, his legacy of terror and secret joy.

So it was that Jacob had his initiation into manhood and the society of his brethren. It wasn't really legal according to Judaic law because there was not the requisite number of men but in Miriam's opinion one wise woman was worth ten men anyway. First she swore Jacob to secrecy and then told him about the dangers of being a Jew in those times. He realized then what she was getting ready to tell him and, not waiting to hear the bad news, just asked her if he was being sought by the Inquisition for the presence of that institution in the lowlands was part of the daily background to their lives. He'd have to have been blind and deaf not to know about it. He began to contemplate whether he could withstand the terrible pain of his entire body burning, (as a toddler he'd once touched his finger to a flame and was thereafter very careful around fire) or the excruciating humiliation of being whipped and driven stark naked down the streets carrying a huge cross. Miriam knew this would not be welcome news to the boy and wanted so much to be able to get past the initial shock and move on to what was wonderful and worth preserving in his heritage. But first she had to get his mind off the horrific images that were the inevitable consequence of her announcement. Although he was clearly made anxious by the news, he did not seem entirely surprised. He'd long known he was adopted and often wondered about his real parents but didn't want to hurt Mayken's and Pieter's feelings by asking about them.

Miriam told Jacob a story to cheer him up and put him in the mood to hear the better part of what she had to tell him. Her story was a story about a boy Jacob's age who could understand the language of ravens and other birds. This boy, like Jacob himself, was taken from his parents at an early age not by any other human being but by a strong wind because, in stories, the forces of nature become characters just like the people and act and think and sometimes talk just like people and of course Jacob was used to such stories from Miriam.

"So . . . let me tell you about another boy just about your age, and I'll call him Jacob . . ."

"Why give him my name?" asked Jacob

"OK, we'll call him Joseph then."

"No, you can give him my name; I just wondered does his name change every time you tell the story?"

"Of course, it's a story and I can change it however I like. So, then, Jacob, Joseph, let's call him Adam, how is that? Adam was taken by the wind and carried into the water which carried him to a large fish which swallowed him and then spit him out in a faraway place where he lived with shepherds for many years. Adam had learned during some earlier adventures (for in these stories there is no end to what has happened before or what will happen later) to understand the language of the ravens and other birds and he overheard two sparrows discussing the plight of a king who was kept hostage in his palace by a plague of ravens, so many of them blocking the doors and windows of his palace that no one could enter or leave it. The King himself was starving inside."

Jacob began to laugh at the idea of a wealthy, powerful ruler trapped and starving.

"You mustn't laugh at another's suffering Jacob, even if you think he deserved it."

"OK, I'm sorry. Please continue the story."

"You promise not to interrupt?"

"I promise."

"Alright then. Adam decided to go to the King's palace and see what he could do to find out why the ravens were keeping him prisoner. Of course the boy was able to speak to the birds and was allowed to pass and once inside he offered his assistance to the king as a translator."

Miriam drew the story out mimicking the voices of the boy and the King and even the Ravens making up some gibberish to make Jacob laugh again, but he remained somber and attentive as promised.

"What the ravens told Adam was that two of them carried the souls of two Jews who had been murdered by robbers and they recognized some of the king's servants as those selfsame robbers. They were there to seek justice and to find messengers to tell the murdered men's' wives of their deaths so the wives could remarry, for no woman could remarry not knowing whether her husband was alive or dead. In order to appease the ravens, the King had his guards arrest the three servants who the ravens pointed out to him as the murderers and they were hung the very next day. The King also dispatched messengers to the widows to let them know their husbands had been killed so they could mourn and later remarry. Then the ravens flew away and the King, in gratitude to Adam, made the boy his advisor and then son-in-law. You know that the boys in these stories always end up marrying the King's daughter don't you?"

Jacob nodded yes and smiled but did not interrupt with any comment or laughter.

"At the wedding there were folks from all over the land including Adam's parents who had become wanderers after they lost their son. At first they didn't recognize him but he recognized them and brought them to the palace to live with him. So what do you think of that? You can speak now, I'm done."

"Why did you tell me this story? Are my parents wanderers? I would never recognize them. I was just a baby when I came here. I don't remember anything. Were they Jews? Were they burned? What about mother? She talks to birds and I heard the servants here talk about her. They wondered if she was a witch talking to animals and birds and they whispered but I was very quiet, hiding behind the chimney and I heard them and I know they were wondering if she might be burned someday too. They burn witches and they burn the Judaizers. Are you a Judaizer? Is that what this is? Judaizing?" and Jacob ran away crying and afraid so that Miriam had to leave her candles and bread and wine and ritual and Sabbath joy to run after him and apologize and try to comfort him and allay his fears. Although he was trying to hide again, Miriam found him easily and put her arms around him while he cried and when he stopped she told him that part of growing up to be a man meant realizing that the world was full of pain as well as pleasure, evil as well as good.

"Jacob, all grown people wake up with fear every morning and we all learn to put it aside and go about the business of the day and that includes taking pleasure in the goodness and beauty around us, just for today. Then tomorrow we can start all over again, one day at a time. You can do that."

Miriam also told Jacob that the Jews were an ancient and chosen people. "Chosen by whom?" he wanted to know. "Chosen by god" Miriam told him and told him as well that Jesus himself was a Jew and this raised a question in his mind. "If Jesus was a Jew why did the Christians hate the Jews enough to want to kill them?" She said she did not understand this herself and that it was time to light the candles and say the prayers over the bread and wine. He listened and tried to repeat to himself the strange sounding words: Baruch Ata Adonay, Eloheinu melech O'olam . . . King of the universe . . . King of the universe, he was left with another more urgent question: Why did the King of the universe allow his chosen people to be persecuted? Again Miriam could not answer. Why indeed would a powerful father allow his children to be so mistreated all these centuries? She had no answers but for her to defect, to convert, and to repudiate a god she carried within her soul as the very life breath that had kept her going throughout the ages was simply not a choice. She struggled to convey to Jacob the joy of worshipping the one only God of the universe but she was without the words that would fly in the face of the realities he had already witnessed all around him and win him over. She prayed instead that one Sabbath evening he would feel it within himself.

Miriam did not tell Mayken about the initiation any more than she had ever given her any hint about the circumstances of Jacob's birth, but Mayken dreamed things and pondered her dreams, lonely as she was in her different and difficult reality. One day as they prepared breakfast together for the still sleeping boy, Mayken told Miriam a dream she had had of a baby, already dead, being burned at one of the Spanish rituals that were still carried on at the behest of Charles' son and heir, the emperor Philip. Somehow in her dream, the baby, the child of a Jewess she told Miriam, was mixed up with Philip himself, the two of them wrestling as the flames carried their images heavenward. Miriam told Mayken it sounded like a good inspiration for a painting and tried to encourage her to return to her art but Miriam worried that Mayken had guessed the truth. It was a mystery to Miriam just exactly what Mayken did know; perhaps her wild imaginings were in fact real in another place and time. Certainly this dream had a basis in a reality that had occurred in Mayken's own town and touched her life for over thirteen years. It made

Miriam wonder about all the other dreams Mayken had described to her that she had not recognized. These dreams of Mayken's made Miriam afraid, but in this case afforded her some measure of relief for she had always felt guilty for not telling Mayken about her son and now she realized that god would tell Mayken what she needed to know and that this was out of Miriam's hands.

Afraid to incur their resentment, Miriam did not recommend to Mayken that she dismiss the gossiping servants but she did advise giving both women more time off for their own families so they would be less inclined to study Mayken's moods and behaviors. Together, Mayken and Miriam purchased food from the local vendors, some of whom came to the house. They also maintained a kitchen garden and Jacob helped them in this outdoor chore. Miriam prepared wonderful meals while Mayken often calmed her racing brain with the hard but soothing work of laundering the household linens and their clothing. And together they cared for Pieter who had never fully recovered from his illness and later that year would die of its lingering effects. It was as though his life breath just drained invisibly but inexorably from his body and Miriam's inability to heal him became the inspiration for a long list of unanswered prayers and questions.

"Who are you?" she often asked under her breath, "Who are you and where are you hiding and for how much longer?"

Pieter's funeral was well attended by the elite persons of the town who had commissioned portraits from him over the years and servants were sent to Mayken's home with baskets of food to help sustain the small household. The master's death made a good excuse to then finally dismiss the servants who had wondered whether Mayken might not be a witch but Miriam who took over while Mayken grieved sweetened the dismissal with generous gifts to allay their future resentment. The painter's guild made gifts to the widow and orphan of their brother but it was Miriam who traveled afar and in secret to find buyers for Mayken's own strange but wonderful paintings and this was what ultimately sustained them for many years even after paying for Jacob's crossing to the new world.

Each Friday night before and after his father's death, Jacob was drawn to join Miriam in her Sabbath worship. He learned to repeat the strange words and what they meant, and of course he questioned why he or anyone should offer prayers of gratitude when there was so much yet to be requested and granted. But over time he internalized a certain pride in being included in this ancient and secret society. It made him feel special and even hopeful. Not unlike Christianity, Judaism offered the promise of some future joy if only one could sustain his faith through the valley of death that life turned out to be. When he thought about it too carefully with his mind, it didn't make sense, but he wanted to believe it so, in the course of time, he did.

As the weather warmed, Mayken and Miriam often took long walks through the countryside, gathering herbs, enjoying the sunshine, not often talking, each lost in her thoughts and comfortable with the other. One day Miriam stood and stared long and sadly at a cave that once sheltered Jacob's parents and Mayken recognized the spot from one of many dreams she had about other people's realities. When Miriam finally admitted to Mayken that she had long been harboring a secret about Jacob's birth, Mayken did not seem surprised and barely broke stride. But both women began to plan for their beloved Jacob's departure. They knew they couldn't protect him forever.

One morning, shortly after his fourteenth birthday, Jacob awoke to the sounds of the morning birds and the sweet musical sounds of kitchen utensils stirring and clinking as the two mothers prepared his breakfast. Jacob felt himself pulled gently back to sleep for just a few more minutes and in that brief time between waking, dozing, and waking again, he dreamed he was carried over an endless expanse of water by a huge bird. He was quite comfortable and not afraid and the bird put him down gently in a boat that rocked back and forth and rode the waves that narrowed into a river and the river ended in a swamp of tall reeds where long-legged birds sang like humans and stood guard over his sleep. He thought perhaps his mother could explain the meaning of this dream to him but he didn't have time to explain it to her over breakfast as he was late for church. At Miriam's suggestion the two women and Jacob had maintained a regular attendance at church ever since Pieter's passing and Jacob was even encouraged to join the choir. At first he wondered about this but Miriam explained it was part of the necessary secrecy about his origins. Jacob was uncomfortable speaking Christian words of worship but his feelings of treachery and dread vanished when he sang the same words. Set to music, language became universal and transcended the petty meanings that set one human being to hate or fear another. It did Jacob's Jewish soul no violence to lend his boyish soprano to the chorus of voices in the Cathedral nor did his

Jewish voice render the hymns of Guillaume Dufay and Balthazar Resinarius any less exquisite. Nonetheless, Miriam and Mayken feared that even Jacob's fervent participation in the Cathedral choir would not long keep him hidden from the interest of Philip's inquisitors. First they talked about sending him to Amsterdam where there was a Jewish community and refugees from the inquisition could find help. But Mayken was apprehensive about this because of her strange chaotic dream set in a city of waterways. Mayken was worried that the time of peace would end and she knew she wouldn't feel that her son was safe until he was out of their world altogether and in the new world across the sea.

"But you know if we do that we will never see him again?" Miriam asked and warned at the same time, but Mayken was adamant that she did not have a good feeling about Amsterdam and that his destiny lay across the sea she was sure of it. Miriam had come to trust Mayken's feelings about these riddles for which there was never a completely trustworthy solution. Life itself was a constant danger. And so it came about that Jacob was sent on a ship that did indeed come from Amsterdam and would take him to Vera Cruz where he would then be met and taken to a community of Jews in a province far to the northwest. He could work off his passage so the women gave him the gold coins they'd saved to hide under his clothing and next to his person for use once he arrived in the new world. Just the phrase "new world" was both frightening and exhilarating. The plans were made by another of Miriam's many mysterious acquaintances, a man who went sometimes by a Spanish name, sometimes by a Dutch name, but to Jacob, his name was Moses.

They were at sea not quite forty days and forty nights, and for Jacob it felt indeed like the end of the world losing both his mothers and leaving the familiar town for an empty, gray vastness. Day or night Jacob could not often distinguish where the sea ended and the sky began. He maintained a sense of equilibrium by singing the familiar hymns. Sailors, merchants and a few missionaries clung to him with their eyes when he ordered the timeless vacuum of their voyage into cadence and melody. For Jacob the singing vibrated through his body obliterating pain, hunger, fear and loneliness. He would sing the first couple of hours deliberately, conscious of each note rising through his body and then he would fall into a trance, working at tasks mechanically while he sang several more hours before he fell into a long sleep, often longer than the whole of the pale gray hours of the day or the fathomless dark hours of the night. He would work without noticing what he did and was surprised when his muscles ached later.

When the cries of the first gulls pierced his deathly slumber his memory of the voyage was a dirge of unbearable beauty broken by death and rebirth as regular and inevitable as the roiling of the waves. Although he would never see the ocean after he left Vera Cruz to travel hundreds of miles on foot and horseback to the north and the west, he would never stop longing for it.

Miriam did not know how long she had lived when she said good-bye to Jacob and her memories seemed to grow more and more remote each day he was gone. She prayed over the candles to have her memories restored to her in all their former vividness. Her life was receding from her even as the shore had receded from Jacob's vision and she shared with him a sense of drowning in a lost history. Even her sleep was dreamless and she lost track of the day and of the hour. Miriam envied Mayken who could paint the faces of peasants she'd only briefly glimpsed as they crowded the streets on festival and market days. Not just their features but their souls as well as though she'd known their joys and sorrows intimately. Often it seemed to Miriam that Mayken accepted the joys and sorrows of strangers as her own, herself a bottomless vessel open to yet one more smile, one more tear and one more and one more without end. She had always worried over Mayken but now, as her memories were leaving her, she longed for that fullness.

One night when the moon was as full as it was the night she said good-bye to Jacob, Miriam finally dreamed. It was a funny dream and she woke up laughing even as Jacob himself laughed that very morning to see the sun rise on a vision of land. Miriam dreamed that a peasant, come to town on market day, had lost his kids brought for slaughter and he ran through the streets chasing and shouting at the bleating goats, making such a comical ruckus that it was her own laughter that woke her. Miriam felt better throughout the day. Sometimes she would laugh out loud at nothing at all and then ask Mayken "What do you think? Jacob is fine, maybe already there and safe at last. What do you think?" And Mayken would think for a while before answering always the same thing that yes she thought Jacob was happy that day and safer there than here but still had a long journey to go. Miriam didn't know if she meant more traveling or simply life itself so she let it go until she had to ask again, Jacob so constantly on her mind that day as always.

And that very morning, the gulls screeched into Jacob's ears so he thought they spoke to him like birds spoke to his mother Mayken. He was laughing at himself when the cook came running out on deck after a small goat that had run from his sharp knife. This was the last of the goats they had brought along for food and they had hoped that he would grow some during the voyage but he was still so small. Jacob joined in the chase and caught the animal. "He's too small to feed anyone sufficiently. Let me keep him for a companion in the new land. We are both young." And the cook agreed as long as none of the sailors or other passengers objected. Of course no one objected to granting the wish of the young man who sang like an angel so they all made do with onions for the last couple days. There would be days ahead when, having no one else to sing to, Jacob would sing to his goat that he had saved from death.

Mayken heard Jacob's voice in the cry of the morning crow. Every morning she heard his voice until the day she died.

Chapter Six
A Story
San Luis 1989

In the Talmud it is said that God created human beings because God loves a good story

One short month after Rocky's arraignment, Lois returned to San Luis for his sentencing. He had been offered a very good plea bargain and even though she thought she could get an acquittal, she took one look at her client shaking like a leaf in the courthouse, intimidated by the suits, and realized he wanted to take it and get out of there. No amount of advice would cause him to change his mind, and she remembered what his mother had told her and respected it.

The sentence was to be a fine and no jail time as they had agreed upon and there was no reason to believe that the Costilla County Judge would not accept the DA's recommendation. It was just damn funny to Lois that the deputy DA tried the same damn thing that hadn't worked the last time they'd been through this. He claimed in the courtroom that he had no authority to recommend no jail time whereupon Lois made clear to the judge that that was part of the plea agreement and that, if jail time was to be contemplated, her client would not enter his plea upon the record and they could go forth with the trial, she was ready (this was not a lie, rather a bluff, a necessary part of any underdog's repertoire of behaviors). The Judge dropped a heavy hint that she wasn't considering jail in any case and they went forward while a courtroom full of other accused poachers glared at that lying *pendejo*, the Anglo DA. The Judge suggested that the minimum fine, mandatory and not within her discretion as to the amount, could be paid over a year and half and those months that the defendant wasn't able to make a payment he should contact the clerk of the court and let her know. The deputy DA, come out to the Valley from Connecticut and maybe not planning to stay as long as he originally thought, gave a grunt of disgust. He obviously considered the native population to be irresponsible criminal elements.

When it was all over and they were walking out into the bright glare of the plaza, Lois spit on the DA's shadow. He didn't see it but a couple police officers did and smiled at her. She felt proud; she'd managed a good straight long shot at his retreating and despicable figure. Her anger purged by a harmless old tradition, she could focus on more positive and interesting thoughts. María's daughter Therese from Amarillo was visiting with her children and she and her husband were going into Taos to go dancing that night and had insisted that Lois go with them. First she was headed to the Conoco station to visit with Orlando. He said he had a special book for her.

Orlando held the book in his hand while he told Lois a story about his old friend Philemon Sánchez.

"Philemon. That is a beautiful name, what does it mean?"

"It means his mother loved him and decided to give him a beautiful name. I don't really know what it means. Perhaps we can look it up later in one of those baby name books. Let me tell you Philemon's beautiful story."

It didn't start out so beautifully. Philemon and his wife were very poor during the depression when they first married and very much in love. But a local Anglo rancher who was rich and owned many thousands of acres of land was in love with her too and Philemon began to feel bad that his beautiful wife had to live in poverty with him when she could have lived in luxury with the Anglo rancher for he was sure that the rancher had asked her to marry him and she had refused because she was in love with Philemon. He had heard this story from his wife's sister who had intended to reassure him about his wife's great love for him but only succeeded in making him feel worse about what he couldn't offer his beloved. Then in 1929 when they had been married less than a year, Philemon left, abandoned his wife who was pregnant although he didn't know it when he left, maybe she hadn't known it yet herself.

"Are you making this up? It sounds like a soap opera."

"Well where do you think they get those ideas for the soaps if not from real life? I am not making this up and it gets better I promise you."

"Please don't tell me she marries the Anglo rancher and he thinks the kid is his and then one day Philemon comes back and falls in love with his own daughter or something like that."

"That sounds more like Greek tragedy but no that is not what happened."

"OK I'll keep quiet and let you tell it."

"Thank you very much." and Orlando smiled at her and continued to wave the book in his hand as if the book had some part to play in the story.

"Of course the rancher did come to visit Angela, such a perfect name for this woman in this story, and he did offer to help her out and pretended to be sympathetic about her husband, pretended to worry about what might have happened to him for surely Philemon would not have deliberately abandoned such a fine wife, saying such things to rub it in that her husband had left her and that he was there, a loyal and kind friend."

"Maybe he was a loyal and kind friend. Not all wealthy Anglo ranchers are bad people."

"I sometimes think to be wealthy, one must be bad."

"Well I do understand *that* but go on with the story. I promised not to interrupt."

According to Orlando, Angela refused to take anything from the rancher in order not to be beholden to him and she went to work in the homes of all the other wealthy Anglos, cleaning their houses and washing and ironing their linens and it was a hard life for a pregnant woman. Then when her daughter was born she had to take the baby with her while she worked but she provided for her needs and that of her child and never complained being not only proud but optimistic and it seems that she believed what the rancher had said hypocritically, that her husband had met with some misfortune and would never have left her for she had faith in his love and so she prayed for him, that he was alive and would get well if he was sick or hurt somewhere and come home to her and then her prayers were answered. Philemon came home, fully expecting Angela to be living in luxury with the Anglo rancher, and was both glad that she had waited for him and sorry that she was working so hard.

Philemon resolved he could work as hard as his wife and love her as deeply as she loved him, and have as strong a faith and if he could do all that what more could God ask? He had brought with him several books. He told his wife and later Orlando that it was the owner of the books who had convinced him to come home.

"Why what did the person say to him?"

"Not a thing. The man who owned the book died. He was struck by lightning and Philemon saw it happen, saw his friend, for the man was his friend, fall from the sky like an angel and he resolved then and there to go home and face whatever consequences might await him, for he was alive and glad to be alive.

He took the books because he wanted some remembrance of his friend but he never read the book he brought to me, couldn't understand it because it was written in a foreign language, even the letters were foreign. He brought it to me to find out what letters they were because he had heard that I knew several languages. I told him that the letters were Hebrew and he gave me the book because he thought I could read it and perhaps because he was afraid to keep a Hebrew book in a Catholic home. Anyway I have had this book many years now waiting to give it to the right person. "

"Why me? I don't read Hebrew. I was brought up reform. All I know is the Shema and the Friday night prayers, you know, over the bread and the wine even though my mother didn't do Friday nights. I must have learned those for Passover with my father's family."

"But I see that you live your life by the commands to do good deeds, to share and seek justice. Isn't that why you are here? But if you look inside the front cover of this book you will understand why I am giving it to you."

Lois looked inside the front cover of the book and was startled and amazed to see her grandfather's name written in heavy calligraphic letters and then the address in Denver on the west side, the last place he had lived. And then on the second page, and all this from back to front and right to left, was an inscription from a rabbi who had been a well-known and highly regarded teacher. Apparently her grandfather had sought out this rabbi to study with for the inscription was to his beloved student Isaac Mendoza, and it bade him have faith. The inscription was in English but the way the words were ordered, it was clear it was written by someone for whom English was a second language. The name of the rabbi was Polish. It was dated: September 28, 1930. Her grandfather had disappeared the following spring. Lois was in shock to see her grandfather's name written so elegantly and so solidly, proof that he existed outside the whispered myths of family.

"How on earth did you know this man was my grandfather?"

"You told me when we met that your real name was Luisa Mendoza Goldberg and I remembered Mendoza of the Hebrew book. Everything happens for a reason."

"That's what my mother has become fond of saying. I'm not sure she ever believed it before but she's becoming downright mystic. She took a class in Tarot reading at the Adult Ed Center. Did Philemon tell you much about my grandfather? Don't tell me now. I can't listen to anything more about him now. But please for sure next time. I'll think about this a while and then next time you will tell me more. OK?"

"You never met him of course."

"No."

"But you missed him just the same. I understand."

Luisa didn't answer and Orlando waited but a moment and then brought out some photo albums to show her of his family. Then he tried to explain the Byzantine politics of the Valley and Lois explained her theory that the U.S was following a pattern already blueprinted in Gibbon's *Decline and Fall of the Roman Empire* and together they speculated on a future of nationalistic divisions on the North American continent during which the various groups that looked to historic traditions to maintain cultural identities would ultimately be undone by history itself, becoming as homogenous as the twentieth century European nations. Where once there had been Celts and Franks and Goths and Druids and Scots and (aha) Anglos and Saxons and Normans and Vikings now there were Europeans. History had a way of devouring and digesting cultural traditions leaving universal mythology and the same inexplicable mystery in its wake. It all boiled down to the same struggles between humanity and nature, humanity and god, humanity and fate, humanity against itself and left only the same unanswered questions.

Orlando observed that the Jews had managed to maintain a distinct cultural identity for thousands of years most probably because they did not have a homeland and had no choice but to make their home in an idea. That idea had expanded and developed and been the subject of the focus of the Jewish people all over the world wherever they existed as visitors. Now that Israel offered the promise of a physical refuge for the Jews of the world that focus could easily dissipate.

"You can't have it both ways," he said with an air of wisdom, but also inviting argument for he loved a good debate.

"So you are saying that a dream can keep people together but reality is the death of the dream?"

This was not the response Orlando had expected and he did not know what to say. Lois seemed so sad and they were both silent a moment, until Lois remembered with a resurgence of energy that she was late.

"But I must go now. I promised María's daughter I would go dancing with them tonight in Taos and I am already late. Would you call over there for me and let María know that I am on my way?"

"OK for now. But you must promise me we'll continue this discussion next visit. No one in this town is interested in these matters."

"Why don't you and Viola come visit me in Denver sometime?"

"No I never close the shop except on Saturday."

"Why not?"

"Who knows who might come through? If I'd been closed last month I would have missed you."

So Lois left Orlando waiting to make fated connections, a steadfast hub in a wheel of history, and drove to the village of San Francisco where María waited patiently to serve her green chili and pozole, with some elk steaks (out of season?). Lois met three more of María's many children and well after dark Lois, Therese and Therese's husband Dennis drove off to Taos to go dancing at the Sagebrush. Dennis could dance with both of them unless of course some handsome vaquero was to ask Lois to dance and Therese grinned and winked at her mother.

In fact a handsome vaquero did ask Lois to dance even before they had a chance to take off their jackets or find a table. His eyes were so joyful she felt happy just looking at him and she gave her jacket to Therese. Lois had never danced to country western music before but Juan Carlos led her gracefully around the floor with a sure hand and she found it easy to follow as long as she just looked into his eyes and didn't try to pay attention to the couples swirling around them. He danced fast with flair, literally kicking up his heels and gallantly shielding her from collisions on the small crowded dance floor. When the band played a slow waltz, he held her a respectful distance away from him and asked where she was from and what kind of work she did. He was so courteous they barely touched but the waltz felt like a long sweet kiss. The Texas two-step had become fashionable but, for Lois, the essence of "the cowboy way" would always be the waltz.

Juan Carlos had been raised on a ranch in New Mexico where his mother was the nanny to the owners' children. He once had dreams of being a pro-rodeo cowboy but now, in his mid-thirties (she barely believed it, he looked so young) he lived in Denver where he worked all week as a welder and came down to New Mexico on weekends to visit his parents and talk about moving back someday. Lois gave him her name and telephone number on a napkin when he asked her but she didn't seriously expect to hear from him again. Therese knew better of course. "You'll be married within the year. I can see it in his eyes."

"What about *my* eyes?"

"Well you like to pretend you are really cynical but he'll persuade you. You may be a lawyer but that's still no match for a New Mexico vaquero. Besides you two danced like you'd been together for years."

§§§§§

In her dream, Lois was driving into a dark forest on a narrow dirt road with huge old trees forming a canopy overhead. Animals ran out and stared into the headlights of the car before running back into the woods. She could see their eyes reflecting the beams, nothing more than their eyes and the white under tails of the deer. She felt at home driving deeper and deeper into the darkness. She could hear the creek as it rushed under the road through a culvert. An owl rose up in the sky, opening wide wings in the moonlight, swooping down on a mouse or a rabbit. In her dream, Lois remembered riding horseback in the dark, barely making out the road in the half moon lit night, letting the horse take her home, slowly, tired and peaceful, content to be near the barn, at home with the owl and the deer and the scampering little animals that crossed the road lightened by the moon, darkened again as clouds drifted across the sky, at home with the sweet clean rain that fell gently in the night, a summer night.

In her dream, it was always a summer night. A late summer night with the barest hint of autumn chill in the air, but Lois, in her dream, dreamed again of autumn leaves and fires and the scents of pine smoke and apple wine fermenting behind the wood stove. In her dream, Lois remembered beyond memory to leaving a forest in West Virginia, leaving a forest in Europe, leaving a forest in Palestine. Lois dreamed of leaving a forest in Palestine. And each time she left, Lois was part of a group of people that grew more numerous with the years and it felt like a dance they were doing in her dream, over the earth, here and there, back and forth, sometimes fast and furious, sometimes slow and sleepy, turning grief and loss into music and then dancing to it.

Chapter Seven
Jacob in the New World
1579-1589

"You shall love your Eternal God with all your mind,
with all your strength, with all your being.
Set these words, which I command you this day,
upon your heart.
 Teach them faithfully to your children,
Speak of them in your home and on your way,
When you lied down and when you rise up.
Bind them as a sign upon your hand; let them be
symbols before your eyes;
Inscribe them on the doorposts of your house and on
your gates."
Translation of Hebrew Prayer

When Jacob landed in Vera Cruz he was met by a man who introduced himself as Juan di Vittorio and asked if Jacob had a book for him. As he spoke he flashed ever so quickly a small six pointed star engraved at the intersection of the elaborately decorated silver cross he wore hanging from a chain around his neck. Jacob would then and there have unpacked the book, but Juan smiled and said that first he would take Jacob home to wash and eat and then he could unpack his belongings in peace and privacy. He was not concerned about the goat, there would be plenty of room for him in his courtyard, so the man and the boy and the goat set off to negotiate their winding way through the noisy and colorful town. "Wait 'til you see Mexico City" Juan told the wide eyed boy who was craning and twisting every which way to take in all the sights. Antwerp had been somber and dull compared to this port filled with colors.

The man walked very fast, hurrying Jacob along with him, saying he could tour the town another day but today he wanted to get him to his new home to meet the man's wife and daughter who were anxiously awaiting their visitor. When they turned into the man's street it appeared that the entire street was fronted by a long adobe wall with wrought iron gates every few yards. Above the gates were tiles with the painted crests of the families who lived behind each gate. Jacob was fascinated by the tiles painted in vivid reds and blues, yellows, greens, as beautiful as the stained glass windows in the Cathedral at home. Here two fabulous creatures reared up and raised their leonine heads to face one another, there a unicorn also reared up on its back legs, another showed a saint in simple peasant clothing standing in the foreground with a wonderful mountainous landscape behind him, another depicted the Madonna surrounded by roses, each tile picture more beautiful than the last and Jacob spoke to his companion in admiration, saying he would like to learn to create such beauty himself. Juan said nothing until they stopped at his home. The tiles above his gate depicted no fabulous creatures but only a complex geometric design in reds and yellows. Looked at in a certain way it was possible to discern a six pointed star but you had to know what you were looking for. Juan noticed Jacob's disappointment and explained "we do not worship idols nor do we paint them above our homes. Instead we have this . . . " he opened the gate and when they were safely inside he showed Jacob a long narrow silver filigree box affixed in the doorway to the home. "In this box is a scroll containing a prayer and we attach it to the doorposts or our home as it was commanded by our god to do." Jacob admired the intricate craftsmanship of the silver and thought perhaps he had found an art that would be acceptable to learn.

Juan's wife and young daughter came outside in the warm evening sunshine to greet him and while the woman took his things up to the room that would be his, the little girl took the goat around through a garden to a shed behind the house. Jacob could hear chickens cackling, a pair of doves cooing and a parrot shrieking *HOLA* over and over until finally he responded with an *Hola* of his own and the parrot was quiet. He'd never seen a talking bird before although he'd heard of them. Juan led Jacob after his wife to his room in a small corner turret. The small room was almost crowded by a narrow wrought iron bed and a large beautifully carved walnut wardrobe for his belongings. There was also a curved iron staircase that disappeared into a hole in the ceiling and when he climbed up he found himself standing at the top of the turret, covered overhead but walled around only to waist level with a bench built around the inside of the low wall so he could sit up there and look all around at the city below. He also noticed a deep green vine with large waxy yellow and red flowers that had grown up the entire side of the turret and all he had to do was lean over a bit to sniff the exotic flowers scent. He was so taken with the charm of his new accommodations he almost forgot that Juan and his wife Beatrice had followed him up the stairs and were smiling at his reaction. When he finally brought his eyes down from the skies and up from the flowers to thank them he could see that they wanted to make his life in his new home as pleasant as they could. They would be his new parents, his new family. After enjoying a meal of fish and fruit in a beautiful wood paneled room, Jacob presented the precious book that had been given to him by the man named Moses in Amsterdam to his host and Juan explained that they would study its contents together. Juan passed it to Beatrice who admired it with tears in her eyes, then put it in a special hidden space built into one of the carved wood panels on the wall.

Later that night when everyone slept, Jacob gathered his bed covers around him and climbed the stairs to the open space above his room to stare at the full moon. It had risen larger than he'd ever seen it, low on the horizon, and then slowly climbed the arc of the sky, growing smaller but remaining bright as daylight and brilliantly silver. He struggled to keep his eyes open for he did not wish to miss a single moment of the moon's glorious journey through the sky although in fact he did doze sometimes and dreamed marvelous stories that he would remember later as if they were memories of his real life. On that night he dreamed himself a grown man creating works of art made of liquid silver and solid moonlight. And he dreamed as well that he followed a path of light to its end on earth.

Over the next two years, Jacob studied with his mentor, learning to read both Spanish and Hebrew and to keep his knowledge of the latter secret. Together they pondered the mysteries of the Cabala and when their minds wearied, they enjoyed the accounts of expeditions to the north led by famous and illustrious men. Although Jacob was a good student his greatest love was to wander the roads of the town and out into the countryside. He always wanted to see what was around the next bend in the road, wanting to explore each connecting road, needing to know where the road ended. He would imagine himself exploring the vastness of the north. He could wear out any companion who dared to walk with him and was not afraid to walk all night on those nights the moon was full. As much as he loved his new family and home, he knew that this port town was just the gateway to a whole new world that he felt a compulsion to explore.

When he was fifteen years old and had grown quite tall with large, strong and graceful hands, arrangements were made for Jacob to apprentice himself to a famous silversmith in another town where silver was mined. He approached the craft with a reverence and maturity that impressed his teacher and it was not long before important commissions were passed along to him. While he worked he imagined that he handled moonlight and for this magical work he needed a perfect balance of strength and delicacy. He built his worktable up high so that instead of sitting down to work, he stood. His tools were an extension of his hands which were an extension of his arms which were an extension of his entire body. He balanced himself like a dancer or an acrobat while he turned and twisted ribbons of silver around the stem of a candle or wineglass or the imaginary neck of a beautiful woman. When he created a candelabrum he imagined the room it would illuminate, when he created a piece of jewelry he imagined the woman who would wear it. He created a story for each piece and became famous for this.

"And what is the story behind this piece?" his buyers would ask so they could repeat the story to their friends when they showed off their exquisite new acquisition. His silver pieces, which now included small sculptures of fantastic animals, were sold in the capital city of New Spain as well as being exported back to Spain. He was invited to the estates of wealthy patrons who wanted to watch the progress of the pieces they commissioned but Jacob declined to travel back to Saragossa or Seville. Several times each year he would travel back to Vera Cruz with a gift he would make especially for Juan, his wife or his daughter who also enjoyed the stories that went with the objects.

And he began going often to Mexico City where he met many men, some poor and obscure others already prominent and successful, all with dreams of finding lasting fame and greater fortune exploring the lands to the north. If one believed the rumors, there were cities built completely of gold, magical waters that conferred endless youth, not to mention women whose beauty was beyond compare, but Jacob was a realist and did not believe these stories. He was curious about the real lands that inspired such rumors and naturally longed to be invited to join an expedition. To this end he decided to learn new skills and apply himself to the manufacture of more practical metal objects, including decorative horse tack, belts and breastplates on which he embossed a variety of family crests. He did not miss working in silver. His imagination had moved on and his moonlit dreams were now filled with the natural sculptures made by water cascading down mountainsides and through deserts toward an endless horizon.

The Lieutenant Governor of the province of Nuevo Leon, Don Gaspar Castaño de Sosa commissioned Jacob to create distinctive tack for his own magnificent mount. Jacob traveled to the northeastern frontier of New Spain to do this work and got to know Don Gaspar well. Jacob confided to Don Gaspar his obsessive desire to know what lay beyond the horizon and to connect known routes with yet to be discovered lands, to create a kind of map of this new world in his head, not for wealth although that was the easiest bait to attract men to join such a quest, but for the sheer need to discover, to see, to know.

There was also the increasingly ominous presence of the Inquisition in New Spain and everyone was talking about how even his powerful position could not protect Luis de Carvajal, the governor of Nuevo Leone. There were some who said he had remained a man of honor and courage until the end although he was executed by strangulation instead of live burning to give the false impression that he had finally confessed and repented. Others said he deserved what he got, not because they cared that he was a secret Jew, but because he had captured Indians to sell as slaves, despite the clear wish of the King of Spain that the Indians were to be treated with compassion so their souls could be saved for the Church. The court had years ago officially banned the use of the word "conquest" and substituted for that the gentler term "pacification" when discussing the continuing expansion of New Spain into the northern regions. Once the governor was arrested, everyone in the Carvajal family fell under suspicion. His nephew Luis the younger divulged his true religion with such fervor he was deemed a martyr and later books would be written about him. Even then there were rumors that his correspondence to and from his sisters had been stolen from the prison and hidden in a safe place for history's judgment. It was well known that the Inquisitors had granted the younger man's wish for writing materials in the hope that he would send useful information to his sisters who were also in prison. But he was careful, writing coded messages, describing his dreams and interpreting them like Joseph in Egypt and never once compromising his sisters or anyone else even as he freely admitted his own faith in his Jewish God.

So once again, men began moving away from the Inquisition, this time north and overland. Carvajal himself, before his arrest, had received permission to organize an expedition northward to colonize the Indians there. When he was arrested on suspicion of being a secret Jew, his friend and colleague, Don Gaspar Castaña de Sosa decided to take on the project himself. In 1590, de Sosa did finally organize nearly two hundred people, including Jacob, to make the expedition but he neglected to first obtain the required authorization from the King. He perhaps thought that once he had successfully pacified the northern Pueblos, the King would be so grateful he would forgive his trespass.

Before leaving, Jacob visited Juan who advised him not to be a part of this unauthorized expedition and to wait for another chance to travel north, but Jacob was impatient and saw no reason to be cautious. He spent one night above his old turret room under the stars so filled with excitement and joy he slept not a wink. The next morning for the second time in his life, Jacob left a beloved family he realized he might never see again and felt briefly sad about the frailty of human connection. "*Vaya con Dios*" whispered Juan, "*Vaya con Dios,*" said his wife through copious tears, "*Vaya con Dios*" said his daughter shyly looking down at the floor, "*Vaya con Dios*" squawked the parrot making them all suddenly laugh, Jacob more easily than the others.

No sooner did he join de Sosa's expedition, than Jacob was disappointed in his dream of a glorious cavalcade of men on horseback galloping into the north to explore unknown vistas. Don Gaspar had gathered together the entire settlement of the town of Almadén, men, women, children, servants, dogs, and goats crawled along in two wheeled ox carts. The mounted soldiers who accompanied them were forced to move along at a maddeningly slow pace except whenever they were sent ahead to meet with the Pueblos along their route. The cumbersome wheeled procession was a curious sight to the Indians they encountered in a country that had not yet seen such contrivances. The oddity on this expedition was the absence of friars and priests to convert the people to the religion of the cross. There were rumors later that the entire group was a community of secret Jews looking to settle in a land far from the Inquisition. But whether Don Gaspar's dream was to colonize and convert the native people, to make a fortune from mining or to simply find a safe haven where secret Jews could practice their religion openly, it was not to be. Juan Morlete, an agent of the King pursued Castaño with twenty soldiers and took him back to New Spain in chains. Jacob himself did not witness the arrest. After one battle with Pueblo Indians along their route, he had been on the lookout for attacks and had seen the Viceroy's soldiers coming. Fearing they came for him, he hid in a small cave inside a deep arroyo impossible to see from even a short distance. After the last of the distant angry voices had long been silenced, and night had fallen and he felt alone in the land, Jacob turned to travel once again northward. He would never know that Don Gaspar would be tried, convicted and exiled to the Philippines, or that the conviction would be eventually reversed but only after Don Gaspar was already dead, killed in a slave insurrection aboard a ship in the South China Sea.

Jacob himself should surely have died, alone and without proper provisions in the desert, but with miraculous stamina he kept moving north, drawn by visions until he could no longer tell what was real and what imagined. When he saw the old woman with a small herd of sheep he no longer believed his own eyes and cursed God for sending him yet another false hope. But the woman was real and no sooner did she come near enough to speak, to touch him with her breath and her eyes, than he collapsed, finally giving in, he briefly thought, to death. Like his mother, come to him in a dream, the woman carried him to a Hogan that withstood the winds from all four directions and gave him a little water, not too much at first, and he awoke and began to believe that God had indeed led him to his home for he was tired of wandering in the Valley of Death.

Jacob stayed with the old woman for a year and helped her carry water from a deep well hidden in an arroyo behind the Hogan and helped her to care for the sheep and goats that she kept penned up in a corral made of mesquite branches. Each day he herded them out in a different direction to graze. He walked with her in silence. Neither of them spoke much, having become accustomed to silence. But sometimes she would stop to listen to the wind or an occasional crow and tell him what was happening far away. He thought of telling her about Mayken but realized he would be telling her nothing new.

One day he went to the well and bent over it to drink directly from the clear pool of water and he saw a woman's face reflected in the water leaning just over his shoulder and he looked to see who had followed him so stealthily but there was no one there. When he brought water back to the corral for the goats and sheep he asked the old Indian woman if the well was haunted by a young female ghost and the old woman laughed and said maybe it was but maybe he had fallen asleep at the well in the coolness beneath the trees and overhanging rocks and had dreamed about her. She told him to pay attention to his dreams for they would tell him his future and she told him about Joseph who was a slave in Egypt but became a powerful man because he could interpret the dreams of the Pharaoh. Jacob was astounded that the old Indian woman knew about Joseph in Egypt and she told about the missionaries who lived to the north and the west.

"You will go there of course" she told him "and you will meet a woman there, the woman you saw in the water probably and you will have a child with her, a daughter."

"How do you know all this?" Jacob asked, but the old woman didn't want to tell him and simply told him that she was only joking with him because he believed everything he was told. Then she told him it was time for her to move on and meet up with her people who had traveled north to Mt. Blanca.

"I will take you part of the way with me, to the settlement of Taos, where you will belong."

She went up into the mesas and came back with two horses, a mare and a gelding and she let him ride the mare and they rode along together pushing the sheep and the goats ahead of them for several days. When it came time to part company, she gave him the mare he had been riding and told him that the mare would take care of him and if he found himself lost or in the dark, to let her carry him where she would because she would take him where he would be safe. She also gave him a new skinning knife which had been given her by a trader who told fantastic tales and Jacob reminded her of him. Jacob was overwhelmed with these gifts and sorry that he could not reciprocate but she assured him that there would be days when he could return such favors to her people and she hoped he would not forget that. Then she told him more about his future, only joking of course.

"If you find yourself taken prisoner by any tribe, made a slave like Joseph in Egypt, remember who you are."

"How do you know who I am?" Jacob asked knowing full well by then that the old woman would not tell him.

Chapter Eight
María
Taos, 1585-1595

"Lo ke la vieja keria, entre suenyos se lo veia"
What the old woman desired she saw in her dreams
Old Ladino proverb

When María was twelve her mother decided to take her to the mission in the new settlement of Taos to work for the priest and there be sheltered and fed and protected for the rest of her life. Thus, María became the housekeeper and cook for the venerable Alonso Salazar who was old enough to be her grandfather but whom she began to love in her heart as if he were a younger man. When she was thirteen she began to pray to the Virgin that Fray Alonso Salazar would look upon her as a woman and want to marry her and give her children. Although the priests were not supposed to marry or have children, they often did and María knew this well.

Every Saturday, Fray Salazar gave her the day off and she went to visit her mother taking a basket of food and some other little gift. Her mother did not live in the Pueblo with her people but half way between the Pueblo and the mission just as she had lived her life halfway between the ways of her people and the ways of the Spaniards because she had been the daughter and then the lover of Spaniards.

Her father had been happy to adopt the ways of the Indians and never spoke of going home or missing the company of Christians. He was happiest teaching his daughter how to catch and tame the wild horses of the mountains. The first horses had come with the Spaniards who came up from the south and the east and run away into the mountains to breed until the mountains were full of the magical wild horses.

The lover had been a mysterious man who came alone after many years of wandering and told her marvelous tales of his travels. She should have known that a man who so loved traveling that he talked of nothing else would not stay long by her side. Perhaps she did. She never even told him that she was expecting his child, although she suspected that he knew, and he was gone long before María was born.

She did not reflect too seriously upon this circumstance but lived her life peacefully with nature, the birds, the rains and the clouds being her companions. Often she made up stories about them. She had a mare which she could ride up into the hills and sometimes when the weather was warm she would disappear for days, sleeping in caves that she found in deep and hidden arroyos and eating the fruits of the cactus. She loved to wander like this when the weather was warm. In the cold winters she was content to stay in her small adobe house and watch the sky in its infinite beauty.

Although she read with difficulty and did not write at all, Fray Alonso called her a wise woman and sent his tribute with María in her basket each week, sometimes a piece of pottery, sometimes a piece of cloth, always something beautiful for her to contemplate by the hearth in the winter while she made up her stories about the animals of the earth and sky and about the earth and sky themselves.

The mother and daughter, growing daily more identical, seemed content but each of the two women had a secret longing. María, of course longed for Fray Alonso to love her but her mother longed for a beautiful horse. When María's father had left her without a backward glance, she never again longed for the company of a man but she began to dream of a large, strong horse, a horse that could fly and would know its own way and leave her to dream as she was carried over the mountain tops and into the mists. She had seen just such a horse on top of the mesa behind her house on nights when the moon was full and large enough to frame its large black silhouette as it surveyed the lands below. Sometimes she told María stories about this horse that went on the top of the mountain to hear god speak for she was convinced that horses could hear the voices of the gods.

María guessed that her mother yearned to capture the horse and when she came one Saturday to find her mother gone, she was not worried but sure that her mother had gone to the mountain to stalk and tame the stallion.

The woman was two weeks wandering in the mountains and then she came back leading the stallion by a bridle she had made of twine. How she had tamed the wild stallion from the mesa was a mystery to everyone and she would tell no one but simply smile when folks hinted at their wonder and curiosity. She promised María that one day, she would tell her the secret words she had whispered to the wild stallion to make him come with her. Only she could ride the stallion and she rode him bareback with just the twine bridle. When she began to get old, too old to ride her beloved and magical horse, she decided she would train the horse to carry María and she told María that the horse would be her dowry.

"But I will never marry" María told her mother with sorrow and her mother knew right then, without being told, that María was in love with Fray Alonso and she went to see him for she knew a secret about him.

María's mother had seen Fray Alonso reciting prayers not part of the Catholic liturgy and had discovered books in his study written in strange characters that did not look like the characters in the other books written in Spanish or Latin. He was so secretive about these things that she guessed he would be in serious trouble if anyone found out about it and she went to him and asked him what secret religion he practiced while disguised as a Catholic priest. She told him she wanted him to teach her daughter his religion and to marry her and he told her it would be dangerous for María to become a Jew as he was, but he was persuaded because the mother told him that her daughter loved him and would never love anyone else and even if the marriage had to be kept a secret like his religion, she wanted her daughter to share that secret with him and have a child with him.

"I know you say it is dangerous to be a Jew in these times and I know that is true, but don't you know that it has always been dangerous to be a woman?" Then María's mother broke her long-ago promise to her own father to keep secret what he had told her.

Fray Alonso agreed but told the mother that her grandchildren would not be from him but from some younger man who would come to María when he was ready to die. He told her he had dreamed this and that he agreed to her requests so easily because of his dream, and that he knew it was inevitable. And then he told her about Joseph in the bible who could interpret dreams and she already knew about Joseph for she had read the story in her halting but dedicated way and had especially liked this biblical character for she also could interpret dreams. Sometimes people came to her secretly, Indians and Spanish both, and asked her to interpret their dreams and gave her gifts but no one would ever admit publicly to seeking her advice, especially the Catholics and it turned out that Fray Alonso Salazar knew this about his future mother in law.

So María got her desire but not in every respect. The passion she was privileged to share with her secret husband was a passion of the intellect. He taught her to read and write in Latin and Greek and he also taught her Hebrew, all the while reminding her of the danger of revealing this ability to anyone else. He told her about the plight of the famous Luis de Carvajal the younger and his sisters and mother all of whom had been arrested by the Inquisition, tortured, and ultimately strangled, because of their beliefs. He told her that even though Mexico City was very far away from the settlement of Taos, Taos was not that far from Mexico City. María thought that the Inquisitors would be far more interested in people with power and wealth, but her husband answered that it depended on how busy they were. "They have to work like everyone else or their jobs will be eliminated."

In the evenings when the practical work of the day was done, Alonso would teach María from a book he kept hidden in different places around the homestead. She never saw where he got it or where he put it, but one time she noticed that a bit of hay stuck to the book, before he hastily picked it off and another time that there was a spot of damp that Alonso could not remove and he caressed the book then and whispered some apology. "I must hide this marvelous book in humble places" he explained to her, "and someday you will do the same."

> "Great is our Lord and mighty in power;
> his understanding is without number. As the
> stars are without number save to him, so is
> his understanding without number. "

Fray Salazar read aloud to her. "Why then" María started to ask, "Why then does not the Lord protect his own?" but Alonso continued as if there had been no interruption, to read from the Kabala about how each thing on earth had its own star to watch over it: each plant, each rock, and how gold was grown in the waters in the bosom of the mountains, this brought about by the flash of a luminous tail trailing after the stars as they moved across the firmament.

Once a year a man, her husband called only Crazy John in the Anglo manner, came to visit and the two men would sit up all night long debating religious questions and drinking wine. Alonso never got drunk but on that one night a year with his mysterious friend who came from far away to the north and the west on his way to

Taos to trade his furs for food and whiskey, bullets for his two long guns and, of course, coffee.

"I believe like the Indians do that we revere the earth and all the natural things on it, after all, we are in their land so shouldn't we treat it as they do? Should we not pray to the gods of this land?"

"Yet you kill animals for their furs."

"I eat the meat and I use the bones to make tools, I was taught this and I offer my prayer of gratitude to the animal that gives its life for my sustenance, I was taught that also. Why do you think I've been so lucky?"

"In my religion we call that 'idol worship' and we believe that one god and one god only, a god beyond our paltry imagination, rules the entire world, including this land."

"So, how do you explain all those wooden statues? You Catholics actually pray to wooden statues, I've seen it in the churches so why criticize someone for praying to an animal that at least is alive or was?"

Alonso in the warmth of the fire and his rare taste of whiskey felt he could trust this freethinking man, a man who, after all, had no respect for the evangelistic fervor of the Catholic priests and would not, therefore, feel compelled to betray him to them and so, Alonso, a little bit drunk, confided in his friend his true religion. María, who always sat listening and never said a word, was visibly shocked but wouldn't think of stopping or reprimanding or explaining her teacher/father/husband so she stifled her breath and waited to see John's reaction. Alonso also waited, shocked himself at his own indiscretion.

"I hear tell a man can get himself killed for that. Am I right or is that another rumor like the cities of gold?'

"You are right." Alonso whispered.

"Well, I'll be damned, you are one hell of a brave bastard aren't you?" and John laughed easily and María and Alonso smiled at one another.

"It's not my business of course but I do admire a man who has the courage of his convictions."

John slept the night and left the next morning, generously provisioned as he always did. "See you next year" he said and then, more thoughtfully, "You take care of yourself old man."

§§§§§

A mist was blowing over the land, hiding the familiar mesas and settling its dampness around María. It was beautiful and mysterious but María was cold and afraid to be lost and carried far away in these unseasonable clouds. They moved so quickly. María walked up the hill and into the dry shelter of a craggy overhang and watched the mist blow past her, darkening the day and she thought she saw a dark man on a dark horse ride with the wind toward her home. She could not be sure for no sooner had she seen him than he was shrouded in the mountainous white clouds and then the sky was gray with rain left in the wake of the magical clouds.

María wrapped her shawl tightly around her shoulders and crouched in the furthest driest corner of the shallow cavern, feeling the rock for vestiges of heat. It rained hard for a while making a wonderful noise around and above her and María could smell the mesquite and *piñón* sweet from the rain. Then it stopped as suddenly as it had started and the thick heavy clouds stretched out into thin wisps of mist that rose and disappeared and the only clouds were those clustered at the tops of distant mountains in the north. The clouds caught and reflected the light of the setting sun and the shimmering wet trees and rocks were burnished gold and copper. María lingered in her walk home, talking to her old and powerful god.

Alonso was walking out to meet her and with him was a strange man. Alonso had been worried about her and was relieved to see her dry and smiling and he appeared excited about the young man who strode along with him.

"María loves to walk the land" she heard him telling the stranger and then he was introducing her to Jacob di Vittorio who's dark aura she recognized immediately and immediately her heart was rent by his beauty. "The man of the mist" she called him and he laughed as though he had seen her too.

Jacob could not have seen María in the cave but as soon as he felt the intensity of her dark eyes he felt as though he had always been held in that gaze and would be held there forevermore. She was prophetic and powerful and her beauty touched his youth, mesmerized him for an eternal moment and he thought he must be in love before he even had time to wonder what love might be.

"María is my wife, but we keep this a secret, you understand and she is a Jew also, the daughter and granddaughter of Jews."

Then, turning to María, Alonso explained that Jacob was a Jew who had come north from New Spain. Facing her, he could not see the look on Jacob's face when he learned that María was the priest's wife but María saw it and looked down at her feet when she felt a smile coming.

"If Senor di Vittorio is of our faith then he must stay with us and let us shelter him and protect him. You have told him of what has been going on here?" then, facing Jacob again, "even in Taos we must be very careful."

"Why didn't you ride Raven this evening?" Alonso asked María on the walk back to the house."

"The lightening spooks him and sometimes I like to crawl around in the little crevices of the arroyos that are too small for a horse. He's OK? You brought him in to the barn?"

"Who is Raven?" asked Jacob and Fray Alonso told him about the magical stallion that only María and her mother before her could ride. "I am lucky, he lets me lead him to the shelter of the barn," joked Fray Alonso, and then suggested that, since Jacob would be staying a while; they breed his mare to Raven.

At first María was angry at her husband for presuming to make such a suggestion without consulting her first but he told her that he was simply looking out for their grandchildren and María understood then that he knew Raven would take care of her and that Raven's offspring would take care of her child, the child that he knew she would have with the stranger who had traveled so far and shared their faith. This excited María but she was also worried because if her husband wanted her to be with this man, then he must be getting ready to die. He had often told her of his dream and that he would not die until her intended had arrived and he could see him with his own eyes and know she would be protected, because he knew he would know the man when he saw him.

Now María was afraid that her husband would die and she knew that she would miss him for the rest of her own life. He was close to his seventieth winter now. As if reading her mind, Alonso whispered to her "not yet, not yet, we'll wait for spring when the mare has her foal and we will all have a warm winter together telling stories by the fire, listening to the stories of the wind. I'll mind the cold less knowing it is my last." and then, seeing the tears fill her eyes, "don't cry. At the end we all welcome our rest." and María remembered that her mother had said the same thing before going into the mountains never to be seen again.

María didn't know if her mother had died, her bones picked clean by dogs and birds of prey or if she wandered there still following the wild horses, themselves the abandoned companions of far-wandering Spaniards. Sometimes María thought she heard her mother calling when she walked the land alone in the wind or the rain when the earth and sky camouflaged her high and distant voice. At first she had looked for her mother coming home by the light of the stars but her husband whom she trusted told her that her mother did not wish to be found, not even by María.

"You must not meddle with the destiny that she has chosen for herself. You would thwart her freedom if you found her and brought her home." He had dreamed this he told her and she believed him.

So the two horses were bred and Jacob settled in with Alonso and María to spend the winter. He was given his own room with a fireplace and a bed and table and chair in what had once been a small monastery in the desert west of Taos at the foot of a red mesa that hid a deep arroyo that deepened further into caves and springs and a pool that swirled around a rock that spun around and around, deepening the natural well.

María showed Jacob how to read the secrets of the earth, where to find water, where to find edible plants and where to find a place to hide from the weather or groups of strange men who sometimes rode through the land looking for gold, or horses or Indian women. The wind blew so strong that sometimes it threatened to carry off María in her wide skirts and capes and they reveled in the brilliant, clear blue skies, the sun that shone down hot until clouds were blown across it giving the land a magical moment of darkness as if preparing the scene for some great revelation.

"On such a day, the Messiah will come" Jacob told her. And María thought quietly to herself that on such a day, her beloved Alonso couldn't possibly die. The world had energy enough to spare even for the old man who grew weaker and weaker before their eyes. She would run back to the house to get him, insist that a walk in the air would be good for him, make him feel so much better, but he would not leave the house. He sat always by the fire, smiling certainly, but saying good-bye to the world and turning his back on it.

"You said we would listen to the stories of the wind." she reminded him but he shook his head and told her he was out of stories now and content. Slowly she turned to Jacob for the comfort Alonso used to give her and Alonso saw this and was glad.

Then the snow came and María and Jacob no longer ventured out to explore the land but stayed by the fire with Alonso and saw to his needs. In the end he could not sit but lay on a bed of quilts and rugs and María or Jacob would feed him the tiny bit of food he consented to eat. He drank even less, letting go of his body day by day.

"But you wanted to see the foal" María reminded him, and he said he could see the foal in his dreams. And then he stopped talking, letting go finally of words, words that had been his greatest joy in life, and even his dreams were silent now and in his last silent dream, a woman came to him and took his hand and led him up into the mountains where he thinned to a mist and disappeared into the sky.

Jacob found him when he came into the room early to replenish the fire. The old man had turned his face to the wall in death and Jacob closed his eyes reverently, said the Hebrew prayer for the dead and sat for a long time waiting for María. He did not want to wake her; he did not know what to tell her. He would just be there when she found her husband, her father, her friend . . . gone.

In 1595, Juan de Humana organized an expedition to seek the kingdom of "Quivira" about 200 leagues NE of Santa Fe. Once again Spaniards went forth looking for gold. Jacob, hearing this, was inspired to explore unknown lands one more time even though María dreamed that he would be lost and never find his way home again. Jacob had always respected María's wisdom but he desperately wanted to go and simply could not believe the expedition would end in disaster.

María perhaps could have convinced him to stay with her had she told him she was carrying their child but she wasn't sure yet and did not want him to feel trapped. Instead she gave him Raven to ride in the hope that Raven would bring her husband safely home. She began to believe that Raven had godlike powers.

She watched him leave with the men as excited as a child and sent her prayers with him. Even after she received the news that each and every one of the men who had left with de Humana had been murdered at the place called thereafter, *La Matanza,*" the death place, María dreamed that Jacob was alive somewhere, perhaps a slave, and unable to return to her, but still alive.

Chapter Nine
Mother and Daughter
Denver 1990

From the Rocky Mountain News
Tuesday Feb. 6, 1990:

> Indian activist Russell Means' Columbus Day protest
> last October - pouring fake blood over a Denver statue
> commemorating the explorer - is constitutionally
> protected speech, a Denver Judge ruled yesterday.
> . . .
> Means said he would take down the Columbus
> statue himself if it is not gone by 1992 - the 500th
> anniversary of the Indians' discovery of Columbus
> wading onto their shore. . . .
> Columbus Day became a national holiday largely
> through the efforts of an Italian from north Denver,
> Angelo Noce who had emigrated from Columbus'
> hometown of Genoa. He lobbied the legislature in
> 1907 to make Colorado the first state to recognize
> Columbus with a holiday. . . . "

Some mornings when the sky was too overcast to see either
moon or sun, just a gradually lightening gray and a feel of cloud
and damp in the air, Lois dreamed that the ocean waves lapped
at her house just beneath her window and threatened to draw
her under, all traces, all memories of her life just drifting out to
eternity in the undertow. Some days she welcomed it. On those
days, Lois wondered what she worked for every day all those years,
wondered what anyone worked for. She'd made a niche for herself
watching people, listening to their stories, speaking for them when
they got caught in an alien world. She was a translator crossing the
boundaries, from the world of the poor to the world of the entitled,
from the world of the lost to the world of the powerful.

Often she found herself engaged in earnest conversation with strangers wondering who they were, wondering who *she* was, wondering where the hell they *all* were and what they hell they were doing there. But then the day moved out of limbo and she got busy doing what kept her busy from one day to the next, and she got interested in what she was doing, and it all turned out alright in the end like someone used to say, she couldn't remember who, but it seemed wise enough. So by the time the sun was high on the horizon, Lois was out walking to work again.

Motorists on Montview probably thought Lois was in a serious hurry. It was the allegro section of a violin concerto on her Walkman that made her walk so fast. In fact, if it weren't for the motorists on Montview, she would probably be dancing up the street.

The morning sky was full of leaves that blew off the red and golden trees in furious bursts, mingling briefly with the flocks of tiny birds before settling into crackling heaps on the pavement.

The morning sky was washed with clouds that still held the residue of pink and orange, a glorious backdrop of color to the geese and the crows and the magpies and sparrows who never failed to announce the coming of the sun in loud, joyful, raucous voices.

The morning sky was full of music.

Lois was overwhelmed with the beauty of it and sadness as well, a feeling of exile. The mountains were so clear in that high morning sky that she could see the depths and swells, the forests and bare places and she longed to be in them, to find some secret spot and build a house right into the hillside with a sod roof and windows facing east. But meantime she had a fun case coming up: an Indian activist, Harvard Law School grad who taught political science and had worked with her on her amicus brief arguing the illegality of the forced relocation of the Navajo from Big Mountain had called and asked if she could be ready to defend Russell Means if he got arrested when he came to town to protest the Columbus Day parade.

"Russell Means . . . isn't he? . . ."

"Yeah, he's the one."

"Ran for president on the Libertarian ticket? "

"Well you know. They offered. Indians got to take what power they can get."

"So what are we talking here?"

"It'll be some municipal ordinance violation. They haven't decided yet what to arrest him for but we know they plan to arrest him for something. We got a spy at the police department and they're all talking about it, what to arrest him on. They're trying to find out what he's planning to do besides just speak. We need to be sure he isn't held in jail, too many people out there would like to see him assassinated."

"Seriously?"

"Yeah, seriously. Look what they did to Leonard. Shit happens."

"OK so I need to be on call to get him out on bond if they take him to jail and then we'll worry about charges and defenses later. Obviously we're going to have a First Amendment defense. What is he planning to do?"

"Well, he's going to throw blood on the statue of Columbus in the park. Symbolic of what Columbus did to the Indians."

"Real blood?"

"No, we'll mix up some stage blood that looks real and washes off easy."

"I don't know why you don't get folks to come and donate a little blood, dedicate it to the tribes that were extinguished and recite the names of the tribes as they go up, one by one, and pour their blood over the statue. That would be very theatrical don't you think?"

"Too complicated. I think we'll just go with the stage blood."

"What if, instead of removing the statue, the city re-named it in honor of another famous Italian? After all, it is very modern, sort of a generic figure and could be anyone. How about Dante? Then the inscription beneath the statue could read:

BEWARE ALL YE WHO ENTER HERE!"

"Very funny but let's not get too esoteric."

The demonstration went off well, Means made an excellent speech, was arrested, freed on bond, went back to South Dakota, or Arizona or California and returned three months later for the hearing on his case. Lois had prepared a pre-trial motion to dismiss based on the predictable claim of his First Amendment right to free speech and added just for fun another claim of selective prosecution using a case that was nearly 100 years old but still good law if only they could prove that the arrest was planned ahead of time because the police had it out for Means. They couldn't prove it, that didn't matter; the Judge dismissed the charge of defacing a public monument anyway and then asked Means for his autograph. Then Lois, her professor friend and Means all went out to lunch.

Means asked if anyone had heard that Columbus was rumored to have been a *Marrano*, a Crypto Jew, a secret Jew? Lois and Means talked about Jews and Indians and what they had in common. He asked her if she would like to go dancing.

"Well, I'd love to but I live with a cowboy and we wouldn't want to start that old mess all over again would we?" His face broke out in a million laugh lines. He told her he dated a Jewish woman once and the woman had wanted to marry him but he didn't think he fit in with her social set, doctors and lawyers, he said with a sidelong glance at Lois. It was her turn to laugh at herself. He was OK even if he was full of himself. On the more serious side he told her he admired the Jews for keeping their culture alive such a long time. Her friend, the professor, said it was time to develop a five hundred year plan and Means said they'd be lucky to keep the Indian ways alive for another century because the young people didn't care and Lois was entitled to put her two cents worth in because her people had lasted so long and she said it goes back and forth, the young people rebel first one way then the other: if the traditional ways are repressed by some foreign government, the kids will fight to keep them alive, if their own elders become too repressive, the young people will fight for "progress" . . . " there are always rebels" she said and they all nodded, and then fell into an abrupt silence. They'd talked the day away and were suddenly talked out and tired.

§§§§§

Once a week, Lois visited her mother. Usually they talked about politics, the news, sometimes Lois told her mother about her cases, and sometimes they watched a movie. Then her mother found the photographs. They were in a box she had taken from her own mother's closet when she was going through her things after the funeral. She had brought the box home and moved it from her house to one apartment and then another. It had been twenty years she had stored that box, the size of a large shoe box with a lid, boots maybe had come in it. It was tied closed with a string, easy enough to open and reopen, but for some reason, Rose had to forget about the box and find it again as something new, something unknown, before she could bring herself to open it for the first time after all those years.

That box, which had moved from one place to another over the years, turned up one day while Rose was looking for something else. Almost without thinking, she opened it and there it was: her past, spread before her in the hundreds of photographs that had been thrown into the box over the years, the decades, a lifetime. There were pictures of her mother as a young woman and the beauty of that young woman surprised Rose. There were pictures of her father as a young man except that he had always looked older than his years and sorrowful, but beautiful too, he was, with his black eyes and black curly hair and carefully trimmed mustache. They were a beautiful couple and seeing them together, apparently in love, made Rose cry. She cried a lot at first and decided to get rid of those inevitable tears before she called Lois to help her sort the pictures. She didn't want Lois to see her cry.

"Did you see the paper this morning?"

"Not yet."

"You're on page two. Your messhugganeh client is all over the first page. I think they should have put in a picture of you. They've got a couple of him and he isn't as pretty."

"He's famous. He'll sell papers."

"He sells himself."

"So? Somebody has to tell folks it's not over."

"What? What the U.S did to the Indians? What can anybody do about it now? They can't give them the land back, where would everyone go? You can't turn back progress."

"What's bugging you mom?"

"I'm just irritated you did all that work for free and he gets all the glory. A lawyer friend of mine said you did very good work."

"I always do good work. So what?"

"So maybe people should appreciate it a little better, pay you maybe."

"I was having a nice morning mom."

"I'm sorry. I really am proud of you."

"Thanks."

"And your grandfather would be proud too, I know it."

"Which grandfather?"

"Well both of course, but I was thinking of my father."

"I thought you hated him."

"I never hated him. I missed him. I was angry."

"But not now?"

"Not now."

"I didn't know. I grew up with your anger. Do you think grandma ever forgave him?"

"I know she did. When we are dying all we crave is forgiveness."

"For whom? Ourselves? Or the people who hurt us?"

"Everyone. It's just easier."

"How do you know? Are you dying?"

"Not imminently but at my age it could be anytime."

"You could live to be a hundred. You're in better shape than I am."

"Would you want me to?"

"Of course. But I'd want you to play right up to the end."

"Play what?"

"Oh, I don't know, the trumpet? Tennis? Maybe some poor younger guy who was madly in love with you? It does happen you know."

"By the way, how is your Dad doing?"

"Well. Still smokes and drinks and eats meat but maybe he'll live to be a hundred anyway, just to show everyone. If he wants to of course. I hope he'll want to."

"He always was stubborn."

"And cute too. Are we going to do pictures today?"

"Sure, get the box." She said it like she might be telling a visiting grandchild to find toys. For Lois it was a treasure hunt; for Rose it was an excavation, sometimes painful. Lois began to sort through the photos and souvenirs in the box while her mother made tea and she found the old pages of music with the penciled comments before her mother had had a chance to see and hide them.

"Who played the piano?"

"I did."

"I never knew that. Why did you stop?"

"I wasn't really ready to talk about this with you now. But I guess it came up for a reason. Of course you want to know everything about your parents and your grandparents, that only makes sense. We took secrets for granted when we were growing up but now everyone is into genealogy, oral history, roots."

"So?"

Rose waited a while to get herself under control. She had looked through so many pictures and cried so many private tears, always putting on a good, cheerful face for her daughter and she didn't want to blow it now, didn't want her child to see her vulnerable. They didn't do that, the mothers, let their children see them vulnerable. Then she said it low and hoped Lois wouldn't ask any more questions.

"I was quite good at the piano. My father insisted that I take lessons and to me it was pure magic. Other kids complained about having to practice but I loved nothing more. He sang with me when I played. He had a beautiful voice. He sent away for special music, most in a minor mode, Jewish songs, sad songs. When he left us mother sold the piano. She said we needed the money but you know we had always needed money."

Lois said nothing, put the pages of music back, and took out the photographs.

At first they sorted the pictures into piles, brusquely, not paying much attention to anything but who was in them, what cousins, what old friends and were they still alive? Did they have children who might want the pictures? Rose didn't want all of them of course. But then, she began to remember things about all the people she thought she had forgotten who came to mind again, as she searched her memory to figure out who the tiny faded faces belonged to.

Most were small snapshots taken in the mountains on holidays, some with horses or in front of tourist shops: The Garden of the Gods, Estes Park, Central City, the top of Mt. Evans. There was a man standing in the snow among the others dressed in their hiking clothes who wore business shoes and coat and hat, just as if he expected to go to the Brown Palace for dinner and Rose exclaimed in sudden recognition of this friend of her parents from a happier past. After her uncle's store in New Mexico had gone bust, many of the family came up to Denver to look for government jobs, but try as he might, Isaac had not been able to stick with anything. They put on a cheerful front for visitors from back home but it never occurred to Isaac to put on a cheerful front for his wife and daughter.

And it had wounded him that Dolores refused to have any more children after Rose was born. She said she was waiting until they could afford to give their children a better life but of course things got worse not better and they never gave Rose the sister she longed for. She didn't talk to them about it much after she was of school age, but she dreamed of a little sister, a little girl with curly hair who held her hand and she could take everywhere with her and teach and protect. Lois wondered if that was why she was an only child also, because to her mother she was the little sister she had always wanted.

The pictures of Rose fascinated Lois just as the pictures of Dolores fascinated Rose. To think of one's own mother being so young! They both exclaimed. There were some portraits on hard cardboard, tinted brown, the fashions of the twenties looking so elegant; the cars looking so elegant, the stained glass in the windows of the houses in the background, but of course they hadn't seemed elegant at the time. They had seemed shabby, worn and crowded. Lois remembered the smells of the old buildings she passed by when she walked to work. She felt as if she could remember it herself, the smells of the cooking, the dust, the coal dust and leaking gas, the mice in the walls, a litany of urban life bereft of magic. Stale air, garish colors fading to simply ugly, music played off key somewhere close by and everything too close, too crowded, overhearing other people's fights and love-making; other people practicing a piano, scales up and down and over and over . . . it haunted Lois as if she had been there. No wonder she craved light and the clarity of a running mountain stream. She thought that she could overcome any tragedy but not the lack of magic. She could not bear to live in a place bereft of magic and she wondered truly how so many had survived it, but of course what choice did they have? They made their own magic as she knew she would too if she had to, finding it in the few scraggly leaves of a plant in the window of a basement apartment, the sound of the geese which she still waited for every morning, keeping her own eyes closed in order to pretend that she was still in the forest, imagining the scent of the forest in the sound of the birds.

"What was it like moving to the city after living in a small town? It must have felt crowded. No wonder you were always going off into the mountains for the weekends. You never told me you went horseback riding. Did it feel awful for you?"

"No, not really. I liked the excitement of the city. I didn't mind being crowded. It always felt so vast at home. That little town with so few people, you knew all of them right from the start and if you didn't like them much you were stuck. There was never anybody new to meet, at least not very often and when someone new did move to town the family, my father's family was not always friendly. But they weren't really friendly to him either. They said his mother was a *bruja*. You know what that is?"

"Of course. I know that much. Was she?"

"Of course not."

"Of course not because you don't believe in that stuff or of course not because she wasn't?"

"Look at this picture of you as a baby and then look at this one of me. It could be the same child couldn't it?"

"Why don't you answer my question?"

"I never used to believe in that stuff but now I'm not sure if I do or not. I guess I don't believe in *brujas* but I think I do believe in the power of the *curanderas* and I think my grandmother was a *curandera* or else just a very wise and independent woman, a woman out of her time. So of course people called her bad names. When I divorced your father I was called some names too. You wouldn't remember that."

But Lois did remember, not names, nothing blatantly disrespectful but something subtle: a look of pity she detected on the faces of teachers and some of the mothers of friends, as if somehow she were being deprived of love and attention, as if she were being neglected and she knew that wasn't the case, and she resented their misplaced concern. At home, she had respect and Rose listened to her and she grew up bookish and thoughtful, bored with the frivolities of childhood. She was content with her memories of childhood and content with the person she was. She only wondered sometimes how life might have been different, sweeter perhaps, if the fathers had been part of it: her grandfather, her own father who lived back east and whom she saw only occasionally. She missed what those memories might have been, in a vague way because she couldn't really imagine what they might have been. It was a sadness and an independence that bordered often on loneliness that she saw in her mother and in herself as well.

"So you preferred the city then?"

"Oh yes definitely."

At first Lois had to ask questions but soon her mother began to tell stories that she remembered as she remembered the people in the pictures and Lois was surprised at the number of stories she had never heard before. And they talked about maybe recording the stories, but whenever Lois brought a little recorder and turned it on, her mother found she couldn't talk, so they abandoned that idea and Rose just talked, Sunday after Sunday and Lois remembered, learned the stories, tried to write them down later and sometimes felt she'd caught her mother's voice and the stories piled up.

As fascinated as Lois was by the stories, little stories that added up to an entire life with all the gamut of emotions and thoughts, she was sad too because she realized that her mother was preparing to die. Rose was healthy but seemed tired of life. She'd done all the things she wanted to do, gone all the places she had wanted to go, been married three times for gods-sakes, she told her daughter and her daughter had no choice but to believe it and to listen carefully and remember all the stories.

The last story Rose told was the story of her father leaving, going to the train station and her sense that he was never coming back. She remembered that last good-bye kiss and her father murmuring to her "my little princess" even though she had attained her full height by then and felt way too big. She remembered that her mother had not looked at him or kissed him good-bye and she thought about the guilt her mother must have felt later.

"A lot of men left then because of the depression. If only he had waited." Lois mused.

"What? What if he had waited? He could have seen the end of the depression and the holocaust in Europe. That would have killed him for sure."

"Literally? It would *actually* have killed him?"

"Your grandfather carried a darkness in him, a painful knowledge of how evil the world could be. He was very interested in the Inquisition and the Jews who fled to Mexico. He told me he was Jewish. He was very open about it. Interesting that I was raised in the Catholic Church but I married a Jew. Three times in fact. So, will you tell me that I was looking for my father?"

"I won't tell you that. Apparently someone has."

Lois told her mother about Orlando and her mother said everything happens for a reason; she truly believed that and there were no real coincidences, but connections, important connections and then they had some tea and talked about the movies because they didn't yet know what was going to happen.

Chapter Ten
Le Dor V'dor
(From generation to generation)
Taos, 1595-1639

"Él ke se kasa por amor, vive kon dolor"
Marry for love, live with sorrow
Old Ladino proverb

María lived a silent and solitary life immersed in her work with the clay which she dug in a wilderness that was awesome and austere. Rosaria went with her everywhere, to dig the clay and to find the plants with which María made the glaze for the pots and pitchers that she sold to the Spanish settlers, first as an infant strapped to her mother's back, and later, running circles around her mother, imitating the birds who at least answered back. The little speech that she learned was sprinkled with the singsong Hebrew words of mourning that her mother chanted as she made her pots, lost in dreams, caressing her young husband's body in the clay.

Only when Rosaria was old enough to go to the missionaries to learn a little and work a lot, did María realize she had grown attached to her daughter and missed her. Only then did she make a conscious effort to break the silence in which her soul found refuge and teach her daughter many things: to forage and hunt for food, to cook and sew and sing.

When it came time to find a stallion to sire a foal with that mare that had begun its life only shortly before Rosaria herself and shared her name, María took Rosaria with her into the mountains to find and tame a wild Stallion to bring home to continue what María hoped would be a fine herd to pass on to her daughter. "It has to be a wild stallion from the mountains" she told her daughter, "such a horse will not have lost its magic." and when Rosaria asked her what magic, María remembered to pass on the stories.

When the time was right, María told Rosaria that she was a Jewess and how to observe the Sabbath ritual, the new year and the day of atonement and the Fast of Esther, the patron saint of the hidden Jews, and how to pray over the dead which they did together, once a year, for Rosaria's father, but Rosaria knew that her mother prayed for him daily by herself.

Rosaria learned also that she was not to speak of any of this to the missionaries and that she should confess small sins to the priest so that he would not suspect she was not a completely faithful Catholic. Sometimes Rosaria confessed that she had stolen small amounts of food even though in fact she disdained to do such a thing. This satisfied the priest who was old and barely noticed the little half breed girl who swept and helped the cook, took home the dirty linens and brought them back clean and sweet smelling. He had come to Taos to replace Fray Alonso Salazar when he died, and waited daily for yet another, younger replacement, writing often to the Bishop that he was too old for the climate of such extreme heat and cold. He dreamed of the sea and died waiting, never having fully unpacked all his few belongings, books and little statues and dolls he had collected over the years.

In this way, waiting, he passed ten years and neglected to get to know any of the people, who likewise did not get to know him. When he died and the new younger priest came and moved into his quarters, the young man found his papers full of sorrowful poems and carefully crafted lamentations as well as the books, and the dolls, which he gave to Rosaria.

Rosaria was then nearly twelve years old, nearly a woman her mother told her. Soon she would be thinking of marriage and her mother seemed worried about that. Rosaria, in her innocence, never doubted that she would marry with the priest who was young and handsome and played beautiful music on the organ in the church. Rosaria neglected her duties to go and listen to him, standing hidden against uncomfortably cold stone for hours while he played the music. As time went on she learned the music by heart and could sing it and sometimes did for her mother when she returned home at night, riding the old mare, the one they called simply "old mother" who carried her in the dark while she dozed, the reins held loose in her hands or sometimes simply dropped over the mare's neck.

"The priest will not marry with you" María told her daughter who wondered how her mother had unearthed her secret dream. "I would go myself to find you a husband but you should know that the men never stay and it is better if you learn to take care of yourself. That is what I have had to do and my mother before me. You should learn to make pots and then you can sell these and not have to toil cooking and cleaning for people until you are old."

But Rosaria only pretended to pay attention to this good advice being so sure that her mother was wrong and the priest would marry with her. She knew that the priests who came here so far away from the authority of the Catholic Church often lived with native women as their wives even though the Pope in Rome forbade this practice.

Rosaria had noticed the young priest looking at her in a certain way and she was sure it meant that he secretly loved her and all it would take was some word to get him to confess his love for her. But what word? Words came hard enough to her and to confess her feelings, her wishful suspicions, were not something she could do even though she practiced every day as she rode into the town in search of music and inspiration and a chance to make her dream happen.

Finally it was the music that brought them together. She hadn't even planned it, but couldn't help singing along with the organ and, carried away with emotion, she was not careful to keep her voice low so the priest heard her voice, beautiful and in perfect tune with the organ and he stopped and called out to her, recognizing her voice (so she knew that he had noticed her for sure and that it wasn't simply her imagination as her mother had insisted).

He began to give her music lessons so that she too could play the organ and that was what they did together. About his love he never spoke and whenever Rosaria felt compelled to simply confess her feelings, he felt it coming and brought up some other subject, clearly avoiding what she knew he knew.

As the days grew colder and darker, his need for her deepened. He dreamed of her voice at night, not singing, but whispering, one word at a time, slowly. He fantasized that she told him a story of a man and a woman and in his fantasy; he let the dawning come slowly. He savored the dawning on him that the woman was herself and he was the man. He allowed a slow-growing joy to take hold of his heart. He let the words of love be in her mouth, not his, the sin be hers, not his. But it was a slow burn those words, those constant unspoken words in his soul and he felt himself scorched, branded by the lustful thoughts, deeply, secretly scarred forever. By his fire during the long winter nights, he felt himself burn to ash, he felt the slow steady death of his soul.

When the solstice turned the season around and the light lengthened his daily time on earth, he drew strength from the landscape and resolved to walk, singing his way alone until her voice was merely an echo, fainter and farther away, less than a dream, less than that dark and wintry dream that had become more than reality.

He resolved to walk south in search of endless light as he had heard from the Indians there was such a place. He consecrated his soul to the new god who would purify it for he knew that the old god would be satisfied with nothing less than a terrible suffering in penance for his thoughts. He resolved to travel south, on foot, and seek the god of this new world. He would let his black hair grow long and the suns redden his skin and hide from the old god, become an apache and find a new life. Having made the plan he knew he must act quickly and he left with a warm March wind, alone because the new god would guide him and carrying no supplies because the new god would provide for him. The voice of the wind had told him this.

When he returned a month later, thrown over a mule by a group of Pueblo Indians who had been sent to look for him, he was more than half dead and totally crazed. He pointed to Rosaria and declared her a witch, sent by Satan to lure him from god. He was kept in chains, because he had attacked his rescuers, and sent back to Spain with soldiers.

When she heard he was to be sent away, she went to him, not in the light that terrified him or in the dark in which he lost himself and wandered a world she could not see, but at dusk. She said simply this: "Our love was pure and your god would have favored it." In his brief moment of lucidity between the blinding light and the darkness, he responded to her: "If I believed that, it would be the worse for me." Then he hung his head a long time and didn't speak until she began to leave and then he said: "I forgive you." and he embraced her and blessed her and that tender touch left her with a terrible longing.

It was Rosaria's time to take refuge in silence. The days were longer but winter was not gone in the land. Another snow fell on the land. It fell on the adobe house and the oven where María fired her pots. The snow fell on the Cottonwood trees around them and drifted into the arroyos. The snow fell on the breeze, stifling it and the snow fell on the music, muffling it, burying it deeply in the heart of Rosaria's home. When the snow melted and made rivers run through the land, Rosaria would hear the music, the voices singing, his and her own as she remembered them, but she listened silently, she didn't sing. Sometimes she would get up on the old mother's back and simply ride, let the mare carry her where she would and back home again when she was ready. Sometimes the old horse would lower herself to the ground and Rosaria would slide off her back and go sleep within the crusty arms of tree roots, listening to the sound of mountain creeks, feeling enfolded and nurtured on the breast of the mountain.

When the winter was gone and summer was certain, Rosaria learned to make pots and she asked her mother to teach her, as they worked side by side, the three religions: the religion of the missionaries, not what to do, for she had learned that already, but why, and the religion of the patriarchs, the religion of the Jews to whom her mother so fervently insisted they belonged, needing to belong to a tribe and to a father, and the old religion of the corn mothers, a religion she had heard about from the Indians who harbored their secrets even as María kept hers.

María told Rosaria that in the beginning the father Uchtsiti made the world by throwing a clot of his own blood into space and by his power it grew into the earth. He then planted within the earth two females and these two sisters were nursed in total darkness by Tsichtinako, Thought Woman, and Thought Woman taught them language and gave them baskets that their father had sent for them containing the seeds and fetishes of all the plants and animals. First the sisters planted the four pine tree seeds in their baskets and then they climbed the pine trees from the underworld to the light, pushing a hole in the earth. Then Thought Woman taught the sisters how to praise the sun with prayer and song. Every morning as the Sun rose, they would thank him for bringing them light and offer sacred corn meal and pollen with outstretched hands and blow their offering to the sky as they sang the creation song, asking for long life, happiness and success in their endeavors.

"Why don't we do that?" Rosaria wanted to know.

"Because the priests taught us different rituals and didn't want us to do the sun worship rituals. But then Fray Salazar taught me his way and that felt right to me and he told me that it was good to praise God's works, including the sun, but not to worship the sun as if it were a god, or any earthly thing as if it were a god, for there was only one God and that felt right to me too and really it wasn't so very different from the religion of the corn mothers for the corn mothers were created by one God-father, Uchtsiti, just as Adam and Eve and all the things in the Garden of Eden were created by the God-father Adonay and perhaps they are the same with different names. There are many ways to call the one God. Fray Salazar taught me that we do not bow down nor bend the knee to false gods or to images of God for God is beyond our power to imagine."

"But he did bow and bend his knee to pray to the Spanish family of gods."

"If it was discovered he was a Jew in Spain he would have been killed so he pretended to be Catholic and whenever he practiced the Catholic rituals he asked god's forgiveness for he did these things only in order to survive and he survived only in order that his knowledge could be passed on to others because that is how knowledge survives."

"But why then are we Jews, why did you choose to be something it is dangerous to be?"

"It is already dangerous to be a woman and an Indian here in our own home. There are always men who want to conquer. And I had no father. I looked to Fray Salazar to be my father and I worshipped his God so I would have a father and I don't know if it was right or not. I have simply done these things now for so long and it gives me comfort to speak to my father through his God."

"What about the mothers?"

"The corn mothers know the magic that is in the earth, in trees and mountains and clouds. To the Jews magic is contained, perhaps trapped, in numbers and words and the Jews are forbidden to look for magic in rocks and trees for they call that 'idol worship' and that is forbidden. But I believe there is magic in all these things, the mountains, the trees and the dreams of men and women and the words they choose to tell about them. And I also believe that the one god of the Jews, the father, the king had a mother. All men have mothers and all things on earth are mothered by the earth, so god must have a mother."

"And the Catholic Lord Jesus?"

"Men fight wars over whether Jesus was the son of god or not but no one disputes that he was the son of his mother Mary."

"This is too complicated. We all live secret lives in order to survive. Why can we not simply live our lives in the open and still survive?"

"Because men like to fight each other and they look for reasons to feel good about killing each other. It is because of the serpents. There was a serpent in the Garden of Eden and another, or perhaps the same, snake in the land of the corn mothers, the snake called Pishuni who caused the sisters to become competitive and selfish with one another. I have wondered that both the Jews and the Indians blame the first women and a snake for the evil that is in the world. Fray Salazar and I had many discussions about this before your father came. Then we stopped talking so much about the old stories. I was too busy watching your father. I still don't understand that love that I felt."

Rosaria felt a pang then that made her dizzy and the women fell silent and looked down at their work and not at each other until it was time to stop working and prepare for the night, build their fire and cook their food. Even then, they did not look at each other unless by accident and then not for long, for they shared a secret now as two women but were not yet finished with being mother and child.

§§§§§

The years passed and each spring María rejoiced in the thawing of the land, cultivating her garden, digging her clay to make her pots and to work on the statues that she had begun to create, larger and larger and more and more life-like until she was able to recreate a life-size statue of Jacob that she kept hidden in the cave where she had once long ago stood and watched him riding through the mist.

Rosaria for herself rejoiced rather in the first snow of winter, riding out always that first time in the wondrous white night on the old mother, wandering the mystical land until dawn when they paused to watch, breathless and chilled, as the sun took over the sky, turning the clouds to a brilliant orange and pink that reflected on the snow and ice all around them. Then they would walk back home where María would rub down the horse while Rosaria stripped off her snow dampened clothes and sat wrapped in sheepskins by the fire, drinking the hot soup that María had waiting for her.

When Rosaria passed her thirty-fifth year, two important things happened: her hair began to turn gray although her face remained youthful and very beautiful, and María dreamed of Jacob after many years of not seeing him at all. He showed up in her dream old and bent and spoke to her. He told her he missed her, she told him she would come as soon as she could.

First María went out to find some plants that would restore the deep brown and bright coppery tints to her daughter's hair for she could not bear to see her daughter become an old woman. She showed Rosaria how to color her hair by herself but Rosaria did not take an interest in this and it was her mother who would notice when the gray came back and remind her it was time to rinse her long thick hair in the special herbs.

María waited, at first she didn't know what she was waiting for, but she knew that something was about to happen and that she needed to be there with Rosaria. Then she felt something from the old mare, some weariness in her and she knew that the horse would soon be done with this life and its toils. When the old mother died, they discussed how best to honor her remains and decided to take her body to the foot of the mountains from whence she had come. To do this they built a sled and harnessed the younger horse to pull it and they walked slowly, a full day to the foot of the mountains and said prayers over the beloved horse. Then they built a fire around her, not being able to lift her on high, and they prayed all the way home, watching the flames in the night, finding their way by the moon, knowing old mother's ashes would feed the plants and the trees. By morning the fire had died out, overcome by the heaviness of its task and there were chunks of meat left smoldering which were eaten by vultures and coyotes. From their house the two women could see the vultures circling, disappearing into the scrub to feast on old mother.

Each day thereafter María rose with the sun and walked toward the mountains to the northeast farther away. She walked until the sun was at its zenith and then turned back and followed its declining light into the west and south. Each day the sun rose a little earlier and María walked a little faster and farther before turning back and then, one day after the summer solstice, María did not turn back but disappeared into the mountains of her long silent yearning. She did not tell Rosaria. Rosaria was a woman of middle age by then and it was time for her to let go of her mother. But María had said more than her usual goodnight the night before she left. She told Rosaria that she loved her and to have faith in god and reminded her to dye her hair, so Rosaria knew.

María took only the knife that Jacob had given her to skin small stewing animals and a small stone to sharpen it. She left wrapped in her sheepskin robe waxed to keep out rain. She walked during the chilly nights and was warmed by her exertion. By day, she slept in the sun on top of the woolly side of her robe. She learned to move so slowly and quietly that she could sneak up on small prey in the moonlight and catch rabbits and squirrels in her powerful potter's hands. She slit their throats and drained their blood while she said the prayers that Alonso had taught her and then she cooked them over small fires that sweetened the air with their sage smoke. By sunrise she had eaten and stood facing east to make a silent prayer in her heart, a prayer of gratitude for the beauty of the day and a prayer of supplication that she would find Jacob who had called to her in her dream. Then she would walk in a leisurely way enjoying the wild flowers and the clouds until the sun was high and the day was hot and she would find a comfortable spot to sleep until dusk.

Sometimes while she walked she talked to god, saying that she had learned to live with her loneliness but the loneliness of her daughter broke her heart and asked god to relieve the loneliness of Rosaria, thinking if she could return with Jacob, whom she was sure was alive and lost in the mountains far to the northwest, that she could bring delight to the somber face of her child. Then she remembered that this child was a woman and old enough to find her own companionship but this thought gave her no respite from her aching mother's love.

When María had been gone a week, Rosaria went into town for the first time in many years by herself to trade her pots for supplies. Because she was alone, she attracted the attention of some young Spanish soldiers although in a respectful way, for Rosaria had a look about her that inspired awe. One especially caught her eye because he looked like the young priest she had loved in her youth. She thought she was old enough to be his mother by now and the thought that she was nobody's mother made her sad and even lonelier than ever. She did not flirt with the young man. She went right up to him and asked him to carry her load to her house and she would cook him a fine meal for his trouble. Rosaria realized only then that she was beautiful for the young man blushed and was very eager to assist her.

The young man stayed that night with Rosaria and came back every night thereafter. He was clearly very much in love with her and wanted to marry her. He talked all the time about taking her to Spain with him. Rosaria never said a word but let him spin his stories and dreams and then, when the moon had thinned to a sliver and come back full again and thinned again and come back full again three times, and she had not bled during all that time, Rosaria told him not to come to her anymore. He cried and begged but she was firm and told him kindly but without any feeling, that she didn't want to leave her home to go to Spain, and when he cried and begged some more and told her he would stay with her then in the new world, she told him she was too old for him and pointed out her gray hair for she had never again dyed it after her mother had left her.

"If I didn't make you leave now, you would leave on your own later anyway," she told him and he denied it, said he would stay by her side forever but she, of course, knew better. He came back every night for a month and every night she made him leave again without so much as a kiss. Finally he stopped coming to see her, to cry at her feet and beg her to let him stay. She found out later in the town that he had gone back to Spain, and she was sad, thinking she might have made a mistake.

§§§§§

María threw herself down on the mountain letting it embrace her in a hollow of sun warmed earth but in her dream she grew huge and embraced the mountain. In her dream she felt her long braided hair gently unwind and fan out over smooth and mossy stones in the meandering flow of a sweet water stream. In her dream María stretched up her arms to test the coolness of the air and her arms smelled of pine and birds flocked to her and she spoke to the birds, asking where she could find her beloved Jacob.

She began slowly to rise, unfolding the lengths of her tall body and she began to move. But in her dream, María was frozen mid stride, arms outstretched and birds nested in her leafy arms and fluttered in the long unfurled coils of her hair and she understood that she was rooted in the mountain and could not wander beyond its shadow and Jacob would return to her as streams coursing through the land on their way to the eternity of the vast sea.

Waking, María recalled her dream and it seemed familiar to her like one of Fray Salazar's stories. "I have become a story" María whispered in the gathering wind and far away the wind rustled the pines, the box elders and the cotton woods, the scrub oaks, the willows and the grasses and cried in a nearly human voice:

"She . . . kin . . . na . . . She . . . kin . . . na . . . aa" over and over, farther and farther away and fainter and fainter, until the cry of the wind disappeared into the dusk and María began her journey back home.

As she walked, María prayed to find another magic mountain stallion that she could tame and ride back home for it was becoming increasingly cold, too cold for her old bones and she needed rest and because it was time to mate the younger mare before she was too old. That very day, as she awoke from sleep she thought she heard the sounds of horses and she began to sniff the air for the smell of them, following the smell and looking for tracks.

Tracking the horses, María lost track of time and no longer felt the cold as she ran and concentrated. She found some grasses that she knew the wild horses particularly loved and she burned the grasses, standing in the smoke so that she would smell like the grasses and the horses would come to her and she whispered to them the words that her mother had taught her, the words she said aloud to no human, so as not to diminish their magical strength.

She had woven ropes from the long sweet smelling grasses and with these savory ropes she tied a mare and a stallion to low growing oaks standing in the shade of tall pines. She took first one, then the other and trained them there in the mountains, hypnotizing them with words so they would not be distracted by the smell and sound of their herd as it moved further south. Then she led the two horses to a large boulder that she could stand on and from there mount the mare as she was too old now to jump up on its back the way she used to when she was a girl. Climbing onto the mare's back she kept hold of the rope that she had tied around the ears and muzzle of the stallion to lead him even though he would have followed the mare in any case, as the mare was coming into heat.

She rode and ponied her horses slowly back home, too old now to be galloping across the land as she had done as a girl, her bones felt brittle and she knew they would crumble into dust if she tried to fly like the wind on her new horse, Rosaria's new horse. She had gotten old during her wanderings, in her dreams and now, being an old woman, she no longer yearned for Jacob. She felt like she was ready to die, but she wanted to give her daughter the new horses, her legacy.

When María finally arrived at home she realized that she would need to live longer still because Rosaria was already big in her belly and María was glad for her but worried too and did not want to leave her alone until she had helped to deliver the child for she knew that it was dangerous for a woman Rosaria's age to be bearing her first child.

She saw immediately that Rosaria was too thin and she went out to hunt for small animals to make a thick stew for her daughter, before she even spoke to her or touched her. She simply handed her astonished child the sweet grass ropes to lead the horses where she wanted and went into the woods to find meat. Rosaria almost panicked thinking that her mother was leaving her again but her mother, feeling her daughter's cry before it was uttered, turned and made a reassuring motion with her hand and then, finding her lost voice (for she had not spoken aloud for many months) she called to her that she would be back with some rabbits for the pot.

Rosaria simply stood there on numb legs, the ropes hanging from her numb hands, and cried mightily until the mare began to nuzzle her and the stallion began to rear its head, wanting to move about, wanting to graze. So Rosaria finished her crying until she was empty of tears and then she tended to the horses feeling contented now, almost joyous, being emptied, as well, of all her long hoarded sorrows.

When her time came, Rosaria was calm, knowing that her mother had helped the horses to foal and would give her a brew to help her bear her pain. María made her walk back and forth and back and forth and sing. . . . "Sing loud!" she commanded her daughter and then "breathe!" and then "Push!" and sometimes her mother let her lay down a while and massaged her belly, gently working the body of the baby down, down, down and then she made her get up and squat down, straddling a small ditch that they had dug in preparation for the delivery and then María reached under her and caught the baby as it pushed out of her body. Rosaria felt such a relief that she simply lay back and let María cut and tie off the cord which she would later bury under a sapling by the house. María washed the child and then put the little girl to her mother's breast and softly stroked the little head. "Luisa" she crooned over and over and Rosaria knew that her daughter was named. "Why Luisa?" She asked her mother.

"To honor a courageous man named Luis. It will be an honor for this child to bear that name and will give her courage which she will need in this life."

"Why didn't you name me Luisa then?"

"I gave you the name my grandfather called my grandmother. That was also an honorable name"

María grew young again, mothering her granddaughter and Rosaria felt more like she had a little sister than a daughter even though she was already middle-aged when she gave birth to her. She resented the attention that María gave the infant, remembering the silence of her own earliest years. Sometimes she wished that María would go off again on one of her journeys. And, as if reading her mind, María told her daughter, "When Luisa is old enough to take care of you and keep you from loneliness I think I will go to the mountains again for I feel more at home in the wild than inside our house."

"Why not leave now? You don't think I can handle loneliness? You don't have to stay for me."

"Don't be angry. I *want* to stay with you and watch you with your child. It makes me happy. I should not have said anything."

But María's eyes would wander to the north, to the mountains, whenever she thought her daughter and granddaughter were asleep, and every day she took a long walk, sometimes going back to the cave in the arroyo where she had first seen Jacob, not because she wanted to think about Jacob anymore but because she liked that spot, had always liked that spot, and she would think mostly of her own mother and of Alonso Salazar and the Stallion called Raven. She stopped talking, only nodding or giving brief replies when Luisa, who began to talk early, asked her something. She no longer made pottery but preferred to hunt for small game and gather wild herbs and roots and berries. She let Rosaria make the pottery and take it into town to trade for wine and flour and fabrics to make their clothes and she let Rosaria make their clothes. Then, when Luisa was nearly eight years old, she left again, and Rosaria who had been watching her mother and feeling her longing, was not surprised. She left in early summer and Rosaria did not expect her back until the weather turned cold again.

Then Rosaria had a dream. She dreamed that something thick and sluggish ran through her body weighing her down and she felt such a terrible pain that it woke her, but when she was fully awake the pain was gone and she realized that she wasn't yet sick but perhaps might become so and she drank lots of clear spring water in the hopes of ridding her body of whatever bad thing was growing in her. The dream had felt almost as if her body were rotting like a fruit.

The autumn was long and warm and the winter was mild, almost like the fall but for an occasional snow storm. María did not come back that winter and Rosaria began to worry that her mother had died in the mountains. She herself always felt cold, no matter how warm the sun, and Luisa would tell her often that her eyes looked funny, she didn't know how exactly, just different. Rosaria would be tired earlier and earlier each day until she was always tired, woke up tired, and she was afraid she was dying and that she would have to send Luisa off to find another home, all without María. She would have been angry then at her mother for leaving them, but she had no energy for anger and she resigned herself to doing what needed to be done.

Every day, Rosaria dug a little more of her grave, as much as her strength would allow and while she dug she talked to Luisa and taught her everything her mother had taught her, even though Luisa was too young and it was too much for a child to remember. She told her little daughter about the Jews and the inquisition in Spain and about the three religions and about Alonso Salazar and she chanted prayers and got Luisa to chant them with her and they harmonized and made wonderful songs of all the strange words. And the singing made it easier for Rosaria to dig and she forgot to be tired until her body couldn't keep going any longer and she would fall into a deep sleep leaving the child alone with the night. Luisa would go then to the horses and talk to them until she too was tired enough to sleep soundly through the night, strangely at peace for all that she faced. María had been right that it would be Luisa who would mother Rosaria.

Luisa would drag her covers outside on mild nights and sleep under the stars, sometimes waking up just to look at them, fighting to keep her eyes open for she could not get enough of beholding the wonder of the stars. But finally her eyes would close and she would sleep soundly until dawn and then the sun would wake her and she would go inside to the house which always seemed too warm to her and she would watch her mother and be there when her mother awoke. As soon as her mother opened her eyes, Luisa would bring her some tea that María had taught her to make and she would sit and watch Rosaria drink and slip back into sleep and in this way the winter passed like a long sleepy night.

Rosaria was glad that she had finished digging the grave before the ground had frozen for she was too weak to wrestle with the earth in winter. By the spring solstice, Rosaria was so thin, her skin stretched transparently over her bones and her bones ached with a pain that made her cry out loud. She could not eat but threw up her food and she knew that she could linger no more.

Rosaria had hoped that María would yet come back and take care of Luisa, but Luisa, seeing that her mother was worried about her and in pain, told her mother that she would ride the old mare who would know where to take her and that she had dreamed that the mare had carried her to María. Luisa lied to her mother about that dream because she knew her mother had great faith in dreams, but, in fact, Luisa had not dreamt at all about her grandmother. She had dreamt about animals, all kinds of animals, some she had seen and some her mother had read to her about, like camels. The animals welcomed her and took care of her and she was not afraid of being left all alone, not afraid at all. She knew that she had to set her mother free.

> Yit-ga-dal ve-yit-ka-dash she-mei ra-ba
> be-al-ma di-ve-ra chi-re-u-tei,
> ve-yam-lich mal-chu-tei
> be-cha-yei-chon
> u-ve-yo-mei-chon u-ve-cha-yei
> de-chol beit Yis-ra-eil,
> be-a-ga-la u-vi-ze-man ka-riv,
> ve-i-me-ru: a-mein.

They chanted the prayer together as Rosaria carefully climbed down into the grave after first touching the mound of earth beside it to make sure that the dirt was thawed enough for Luisa to be able to shove it back into the grave. They chanted the prayer together until Rosaria died and then Luisa chanted it alone for a long time, waiting to make sure that her mother was really and truly dead, feeling more pity for her mother's pain than grief for herself.

Luisa was indeed a courageous child. She looked a long time at her mother to make sure she didn't forget what her mother looked like. Luisa waited until birds flew down and sat on her mother's breast before she began to throw handfuls of the dirt into the grave. She threw handful after handful until her mother's face and body were covered and then she went to the back of the house to get the shovel which was too big for her to handle easily but she did the best she could, using the shovel to push the dirt into the grave rather than lifting and flinging it, so it took her a long time and her muscles ached before she was done but she didn't stop to rest until she was done and then her arms ached so much she couldn't even lift her arms above her head. Luisa sat down and would have cried but the mare walked over to her and nudged her shoulder and then when Luisa didn't move because she was too sore and tired to move, the mare lowered herself to the ground so Luisa could climb on her back and then she stood up and walked toward the north, taking gentle strides while Luisa entwined her little hands in the mane and lay across the horse's neck to sleep at long last, grateful to be moving so she wouldn't have to wake up by the empty house.

It was late in the day when Luisa and the mare started their northward journey. They were guided by the shafts of lowering sunlight that pierced the towers of clouds to their left. And then the clouds settled down along the landscape and they walked through a mist, quiet and thick. Luisa could not see her own hand outstretched before her. But the mare marched on straight and sure into the night. She wound her way through the mountains higher and higher until they were above the clouds and Luisa awoke to see the stars bright in the sky and reflected in the slow, clear water of a creek. She thought they walked above the stars but the earth was solid beneath them and she was glad to burrow into it next to the warm, back of the mare and to cover herself with the horse's long thick mane when they lay down together in the pre-dawn chill to sleep and dream.

Luisa was awakened when the horse whinnied softly and moved her legs in the unfinished intention of a stride, dreaming that she was running down the old home mountain to her herd and her own mother. Luisa climbed back up on her back, leaning low into her warmth as the sun was still low in the sky and the air was chilly and damp. The mare carried the child due north past the mysterious shadowy mountains of the Sangre De Cristo range and across a broad flat valley to the single mountain called the White Lady because its high and isolated peak was usually covered with snow or immense white clouds. This mountain stood all alone in the middle of the flat Valley, not part of any range, a sacred mountain to the sheep herders who wandered at her feet and watched her moods and sometimes climbed into her mists to find visions.

The mare carried the child up and up a winding path to the top where the trees and animals all appeared as ghosts emerging from and disappearing back into the clouds that circled the peak, protecting her mysteries. At the top of Mt. Blanca, Luisa shivered with cold and looked around for dry twigs to build a fire. She was hungry too and enticed a squirrel with berries and soft words, but then she found she did not want to kill the small animal for food and simply played with it instead and she went hungry through her second night, nor did she sleep, so fragile was her fire it would go cold if she did not tend it constantly. By dawn she could not wake to this work but lay half-awake enough to feel the cold but too sleepy to revive the dying flames. She slept until the sun was high and warmed her and only when it was too hot to bear did she rise and walk about. A bird fell dead from the sky and Luisa plucked it and found a sharp stick to pierce its breast and once again she built her fire and cooked the bird. She never thought to cry. She knew her mother was safe and she was happy on the mountain. She knew the bird was a sign that god would look after her.

Luisa stayed on the mountain in a small cave where bears had come and gone, until the last spring snow fell and then she climbed on top of the mare and they walked slowly and carefully down a steep and rocky path, not the same of their ascent and down into the clouds and further down out of the clouds onto a broad flat valley on another side of the mountain where an old woman stood still as a statue watching them. All around the woman wandered goats and sheep, grazing what scraps of grass they could find among the sage.

It was sage tea the woman gave Luisa to warm her and sage smoke she blew about to purify herself and her home and her guest who had come down to her from the sacred mountain. When Luisa slept, the woman went out to feed the mare some precious oats she got from a trader a hundred miles away, and to lovingly brush her thick winter coat and her long beautiful mane.

The woman was so old she had no teeth and her face was wrinkled like a dried plum but her long gray hair was still thick and beautiful as the mare's mane. Her people feared and revered her because she could find water wherever she went so they kept a respectful distance and always brought gifts when they came to draw water from her well. They called her Water Woman.

Water Woman kept Luisa with her and raised her as her own daughter for Water Woman had never had children of her own. When Luisa was eight years old by her own reckoning she asked to be taught to weave. She had been watching Water Woman and already knew a lot and wanted to try her hand at it.

"I thought you would never ask" Water Woman said to Luisa and smiled her rare quiet smile.

So when she wasn't climbing about on the rocks following the goats and making sure the newborns didn't fall into the deep crevasses that opened so suddenly and unexpectedly in that dry, cracked land, Luisa would sit at her loom. She took pleasure in the perfection of the warp, laying her palm flat against its tight surface. Then she would pluck the alternate threads like a harp in her fingers and slide a flat stick through them and turn it sideways to hold the threads apart while she pushed another flat stick wrapped in black or brown or gray wool through the space. With each pass of the weft she would carefully push the wool down tight against its predecessor, lingering to caress the wool, the seductive softness of the black, the pleasant coarseness of the brown or the gray, picking out little flecks of dried grasses, savoring the feel and smell of the lanolin. When her design began to emerge, she would sit and stare at it for long periods of time. Water Woman didn't nag her to work more quickly for she understood how much the child loved her weaving.

§§§§§

When María returned from the mountains, her long hair completely white and even her black eyes gone gray and almost blind, she found only the mound of her daughter's grave. She searched silently for Luisa, being too old now to call out loudly, barely able to whisper her granddaughter's name. When she found the small herd of horses wandering about in the hills and arroyos searching for sweet grass and realized that Luisa's special mare was missing from among them, she knew that Luisa must have ridden off and she mounted her own horse to follow her. She let her horse sniff the wind to determine the right direction and then they took off, flying into the islands of clouds in the ocean of sky, riding so fast that María could feel her bones disintegrate and become other things: hail stones and agates, turquoise and silver, and all things hard and bright.

Chapter Eleven
The Darkness
Northern New Mexico, 1990

Many commentators have seen in 'The Storm' the last work of Breugel and indeed it has the appearance of a sort of last will rather like 'The Dream' that was the final work of Durer or that picture of the crows in the corn which Van Gogh left as a last farewell before perishing. In the course of his long initiatory voyage of discovery, is this all that the painter found at the end of the road - this dark desperate territory, a vast variation on the different themes of black? And yet this darkened lowering sky is crisscrossed by great white birds. Are they not sheltered from the misfortunes of the hour by their very grace and lightness? Or have they been driven mad by the harshness of the elements which enfold them and tear them to shreds?" Claude Mettra, *Bruegel, The Man and His Paintings*, Excalibur Books, New York, 1980

It was a five hour drive, four and a half if you knew where it was safe to speed. They left after work so they followed the sunset into New Mexico. It was a glorious sunset, striations of bright pink and orange reflected off the clouds and Lois dozed and woke still seeing the colors and hearing the ballad that she had recorded on both sides of a tape she had made of their favorite songs. It seemed every time she woke, it was to that ballad, a sad Scottish sounding ballad that inspired visions, both horrible and beautiful at the same time like the paintings of Bosch or of Breugel. Lois fell in and out of dreams, while Juan Carlos drove her through the sunset toward the darkness.

They drove through a valley intermittently covered with *Piñón* trees and Ponderosa Pine, the isolated buildings on large ranches surrounded by Cottonwoods and more Cottonwoods growing where hidden streams twisted through the dry landscape in deep arroyos. Driving into Cimarron, they passed the Pendleton bottled gas office and warehouse on the right and the lumber mill on the left. At each place, Juan Carlos honked the horn of his truck in case he caught one of his brothers working late.

The houses were mostly small and dilapidated, many of them built onto the sides of trailers, the more opulent homes being double-wide with redwood decks. Very few houses were the old fashioned adobe, either very old and showing patches of brick where the walls needed re-mudding or very new and neat, built by newcomers looking for a special kind of life in New Mexico. One house had six foot high Kachinas painted on the roadside wall.

Out-of-staters were buying old buildings that had been empty for years, putting in art galleries and craft and antique shops. But the overall feel of the town was still old western: dirt poor and dusty, bleak if the truth be told.

The folks with money lived out of town on ranches, some downright luxurious. They kept the town alive economically year round and the Philmont Scout Ranch kept it on the map and booming in the summer. What was best about Cimarron had to be hunted down and it could take years. As she looked around at the government houses all painted alike under the streetlights (incongruous with the unpaved roads), Lois yearned for the mountains that ringed the vast, grassy valley.

Meeting Juan Carlos' father was like meeting the Pope. In his mid-eighties, he still rode his horse every day and led the annual Fourth of July Parade in his silver studded vest and chaps on his magnificent saddle, his one glory.

When the rest of the family gathered to eat, he was still at the stable, feeding and grooming his mare for the next day's ride from one end of the small town to the other. The main street was in fact the main highway and they would stop traffic for the parade but tourists and travelers on their way to Taos or Raton never minded, they would get out of their cars and take photos and videos of the real old west spectacle.

Juan Carlos took Lois to each of the many aunts and uncles and cousins and introduced her and paid courteous and gallant compliments to all the *comadres*. They went from house to house, tiny houses, lining the dirt road, each the same. Each living room was crowded with statues and pictures of saints, photographs of many generations as they were baptized, graduated, married, toys strewn about, furnishings covered in crocheted shawls and afghans in all the colors of the rainbow. In each living room sat a large old television set, largely ignored, but left on lest one of the children, who came and went from one house to the other, might want to watch cartoons or sports. Tables were laid with pastries and candies, *piñón* and beef jerky and the coffee mugs were constantly re-filled with strong "cowboy coffee" (that means you can walk on it Juan Carlos told her). There was so much food Lois was amazed when it came time to sit around the dining table for a formal meal. How could anyone think of eating anymore? Rice and beans and mashed potatoes, fried chicken and *carnitas*, *pozole* and plenty of green chili. There was some quiet anxious conversation in Spanish before Lois was offered menudo and then much smiling when she said she liked it *really*, she assured the unbelieving Juan Carlos, who was raised to love everything made by the hand of woman. They had sweet rice and *sopapillas* dipped in honey for dessert. "Wait until Xmas" Juan Carlos whispered to her when she groaned in appreciation.

His father came in late, carrying his silver studded saddle and still wearing his chaps and spurs. If anyone dared tell him to take them off for dinner he would grumble so no one did. After eating very little he got up and began to polish and oil his tack right there in the living room and all the children were admonished not to get in his way. He hummed and whistled while he worked. When he wasn't riding or caring for his horse or tack, he liked to watch westerns on the television. By refusing to speak English he maintained his identity and protected himself from frivolous conversation. He apparently liked Lois as he attempted a few words in English for her but very few. Then he talked about her in Spanish so fast she barely caught a word here, a word there, and his sly laughter made her uncomfortable, despite Juan Carlos' happy grin.

"He likes you" he assured her. Cousins came and went as they saw Juan Carlos' truck outside to say hello and plan to meet later in the evening for a beer. Then she and Juan Carlos went to the St. James Hotel Bar where Juan Carlos complained about all the fancy new renovations. The hotel boasted the ghost of an old gun fighter and had been featured on a national television show about such mysterious goings on. Now tourists came for murder mystery weekends and edged out the locals. But Juan Carlos had moved away and this was his chance to catch up with old school buddies and rodeo pals who had also moved away, to Denver, Albuquerque,

Amarillo and Dallas.

Lois quickly found out who all his old girlfriends were, who had married, and how many children, who divorced, moved away, moved back, who had gained or lost weight, gotten sick, gotten well, aged poorly or improved: no detail went un-remarked. Later, after introducing her to what seemed like hundreds of people, Juan Carlos would ask "you remember that tall guy in the lavender shirt?" and give her some important background data she should know but could never connect to the right person. Once she danced with a stranger, making Juan Carlos jealous, because she assumed he was a cousin. They laughed about it later. Yet everyone remembered her and she realized that coming home with Juan Carlos made her the talk, the envy, the hated or the beloved of everyone in town.

They left a day early in order to have time to visit Orlando and Viola in San Luis. There was a bed and breakfast now in the old convent and his brothers teased him about spending the night in a nunnery and told Lois nasty names in Spanish to call him, laughing, when she did, thinking *"cabrón"* was a term of endearment. Then they loaded the back of his truck with seasoned *piñón* for her fireplace back home. She didn't understand; she hadn't asked for firewood. As time went on Lois would learn that she didn't have to ask, Juan Carlos would anticipate her needs and desires and take care of them. It was a heady feeling but she knew she could trust him to care for her.

They weren't expected until morning so Lois and Juan Carlos took their time driving to the Inn in San Luis, stopping to walk in the woods and sit by the River.

"How long do you think it takes this water, this very water we are watching right now, to get to the ocean?" she asked and Juan Carlos pretended to ponder the question. It was getting dark and he suggested they get back but when they got back to the road the traffic was backed up with nowhere to go. There had been an accident; a motorcyclist had gone over the edge. There were two of them, the rider and his girlfriend. People were talking; no one knew who it was. Juan Carlos and Lois went back down to the river and finally at dusk the bodies were carried off in the ambulance, both dead they heard, and the traffic began to move again slowly. They played tapes of the Texas Tornadoes and Al Hurricane to liven the time in the car. When they got to the Bed & Breakfast it was already on the news, the names were not being released until the family was informed.

On the little desk in their room, under a window that looked out on an ominous sky, were some art books and, while Juan Carlos showered, Lois looked through a book of reproductions of the paintings of Breugel, her favorite artist. She could immerse herself in these paintings that seemed to bring back memories as if she had lived in those places in those times. But sometimes the pictures frightened her as if she had witnessed terrible things in those places and times. In fact, she knew that religious wars and the Inquisition were happening during Breugel's life. There was so much killing, pain, starvation and brutality. That kind of madness was the story of civilization right along with the glories of art. Perhaps these paintings appealed to her because she had lived then, she wasn't sure but thought the concept of reincarnation was worthy of consideration. She didn't really remember of course but where did her dreams come from? The ones that she couldn't connect to her real life in the here and now. She wondered if she'd always been incarnated as a Jew, as a woman, as a human being, if she'd been subjected to torture, how she'd borne up under it or worse, if she'd inflicted it.

Lois was relieved when her lover emerged from the bathroom warm and joyful. It seemed the older she got the more afraid she was of the dark, or was it simply the darkness getting closer?

§§§§§

"What exactly is the nature of darkness?"

"What kind of question is that to ask at breakfast? Eat your enchiladas, they're wonderful."

"It's OK. Orlando understands. We have these kinds of conversations all the time. Right Orlando?"

"Well, I don't know if I understand the exact nature of darkness but yes I understand why you might ask."

"You know my grandfather never even knew who or if I would be, didn't care I guess and yet somehow you got word from him. What does that mean?"

"Nothing more than that you were meant to come here, probably to meet Juan Carlos. If we decide we believe in a spiritual afterlife I guess we could say that your grandfather was looking out for you from some other place."

"Maybe I was meant to learn the nature of his darkness."

"His darkness or darkness in general?"

"Whose darkness? I thought I was your sunshine."

"We are talking about my grandfather."

"Well then I am going out for a smoke. Excuse me please. Breakfast was so good. Let me help you, Viola. We can do the dishes while they talk about darkness."

"Why are you so bothered by this now?"

"Because my whole life is fighting for lost causes. What can you tell me about him? I'm ready to hear it now. Why didn't he ever come back? How did he die? Why? When? Whatever you know."

"Something terrible occurred to someone he loved and he didn't want to live in a world where such things could happen, and actually did come about. He reached for the lightening."

"Someone he loved in the catacombs beneath Seattle?"

"Is that so terrible?"

"He was supposed to love us."

"He didn't even know about you, that you would ever be."

"How hard would it have been to guess that his daughter might someday have a daughter or a son? Didn't he know abandonment is hereditary?"

"Probably not. He thought his family didn't need him, even that they would be better off without him. That was what Philemon thought too when he left his family."

"But he came back."

"I can't answer your questions more than I have. People are different. They all do the best they can, most do anyway."

"My mother has forgiven him."

"Your mother is a wise woman."

"She thinks she might die soon. It scares me. I'm not ready to let her go."

"But all of life is a journey toward death, a preparation."

"What I can't forgive is that I think I might be like him."

"Because you think you are a fighter for lost causes?"

"Exactly."

"Rocky Hernandez didn't think so."

"Oh Rocky is worse than I am. He really thinks he can live and hunt in the mountains forever, or else he doesn't worry about what he'll do when all that land is subdivided and developed until there is nowhere left in his grandmother's heart where he can crouch down and be invisible."

"Maybe it won't happen. Maybe it won't matter."

"This sounds familiar."

"Maybe that's the nature of darkness, familiarity."

"And that sounds hopeless."

"But restful don't you think?"

"You mean just give up fighting?"

"No, of course not, but be patient, wait and see sometimes. Pay attention and you will find justice happening and sometimes it will even be because of something you did."

"What I do is always on the most mundane level."

"Exactly where it is needed most. I'm sure defending a famous Indian activist and being in the paper was fun, but it's the poor and the anonymous that need you, and need him too for that matter. There were far more important things for him to be doing. He should have been down here fighting the mine. Is he going to lead that parade every year now? By the way, did you know that Columbus was a Jew?"

"Actually yes. When I was a little girl, I won a book in a contest. It was about famous Jews in history and there were pictures on the right hand side and a little paragraph about each one on the left hand side, in big letters because the book was for third graders and that's what they thought third graders read. I remember there were pictures of Karl Marx and Sigmund Freud, can you imagine writing one liners for third graders about Freud? And of course Christopher Columbus which truly surprised me and an actress with only one name: Rachel. I was most intrigued by Rachel and searched and searched for more information about her. So I guess I just grew up taking for granted that Christopher Columbus was Jewish and never stopped to think about how strange it was for Jews to name a son Christopher or that a Jew would be sent on an expensive expedition by Ferdinand and Isabella of Spain. I learned all of history piecemeal and didn't connect any of it until recently."

"Well, that's exactly why the human race just keeps going from one frying pan into another. Nobody connects history to the present, nobody learns anything from it. Everyone thinks all of history just happened to get us to the here and now, and the only important here and now is twentieth century honky America."

"God, you sound like me."

"If you want to consider piecemeal history you should read this book, I've got it here somewhere . . ." and Orlando got up to find the book but couldn't and sat down again, ". . . well it's in the shop, I found it and set it aside for you, a history of the *Marranos* by Joachim Prinz. Anyway, the author tells of another scholar who went searching for hidden Jews in Spain and Portugal. He discovered some very interesting traditions among them.

As an example, let me tell you just one, but you really should read the book, of course. Anyway, on the island of Majorca there was a small community of crypto Jews and part of their traditional observance of Rosh Hoshana and Yom Kippur involved a card game. Several men would sit outside the house where the prayer services were being held and play cards. They did this in the days of the Inquisition to avoid suspicion and they were doing it still in the thirties when this man found them. You see the fear itself had become a tradition."

"Why not? The 1930s was not a safe time for Jews in Europe."

"There really has never been a safe time for Jews since the Diaspora, not even now, not even here."

"So why is that do you think?"

"Of course, I can't know that, but I've often wondered what the term 'chosen' meant. Chosen' for what? Maybe the constant and universal persecution of the Jews and the persistent survival of the Jews is a metaphor for mankind's' constant struggle for justice. Every terrible thing that has ever been done to men and women in history has been done to Jews everywhere at some time and always at some place, and yet, Jews have been the longest running ethnic show in the history of civilization."

"So what does that mean? If you live long enough you'll suffer everything?"

"If you live long enough, you'll survive everything."

"What's the difference?"

"I'll have to think about that one."

"These dialogues never go anywhere."

"It's not our privilege to see the end of the show."

"If it's a cycle, there is no end. We live, we die but the world goes on, rolling aimlessly around and around somebody's psychic universe. We could say we were a figment of God's imagination if we understood God."

"Well at least we understand imagination."

"Only our own."

"Around and around. When are you going to marry Juan Carlos?"

"What?"

"I had to break this cycle. Seriously you should marry him. He's a good man.

"Columbus Day."

"You are going to marry him on Columbus Day?"

"You read my mind."

When Juan Carlos and Lois got back home there was a message on the voice mail. His nephew had been killed in a motor-cycle accident the day before. They called, they packed, they went back for the funeral and, within one week of meeting his family, Lois found herself a part of it, feeling awkward amidst such sorrow and such love for everyone treated her as a sister already. Dozens of cousins dug the grave deep enough to bury his bike along with the deceased and there were plenty of murmurs that the bike was worth several thousand dollars and the family could have used the money, but the bike got buried in the twelve foot grave in front of hundreds of mourners.

Lois found herself wondering what future archaeologists would assume about this culture when they found the bike buried with the bones. Maybe they would assume that the young man was someone very powerful and prestigious in the community. Maybe they would assume that he came from a wealthy family, a dynastic family maybe. Maybe someone would write a book about it and the bones and the bike would become part of a traveling museum show. After the funeral she wandered with Juan Carlos in the graveyard, reading the names and dates, listening to him tell her about the people, most of whose families, at least, he had known. Lots of little anecdotes, some funny, mostly tragic.

§§§§§

"Why did you name me Luisa Rosaria? I mean that is a pretty heavy name for a kid."

"Well you know I was named Rosaria Viola for my father's mother and my mother's mother but when I was a little, little girl, playing with dolls, my papa asked me a favor, it was the only thing he ever asked of me actually. He said 'Rose, when you are grown and have a little girl as pretty as you are, please name her Rosaria Luisa.' His mother's name was Rosaria and his grandmother's name was Luisa and he told me that those two names had been handed down for generations in his family. I was too little to know from generations. I just asked him if I could name her Luisa Rosaria instead because it sounded better and he laughed and laughed. I hardly ever heard him laugh so of course I never forgot that and when you were born I named you Luisa Rosaria."

"Were you mad when I changed it?"

"Well, I wasn't thrilled but I figured you were being a modern liberated woman making up your own name."

"I may change it back."

"Oh my, you'll have to get new business cards printed up."

"Well, I'll have to have new cards printed up anyway. I've decided to marry Juan Carlos."

"That's funny."

"You bet it's funny. I'll have more last names than first names. I know I have to make some choices. Luisa Rosaria Mendoza Goldberg Gonzales wouldn't fit on a business card, or a driver's license or a credit card. . . . Maybe I should become an acronym . . . how does LUROMEGO sound?"

"Like an eastern European appliance manufacturer . . . you know what else struck me funny? I was raised Catholic and married three Jews and you were raised Jewish, in a manner of speaking, and you're marrying a Catholic."

"How do you know he's Catholic?"

"Juan Carlos Gonzales? Are you kidding?"

"How do you know he isn't Jewish, or Buddhist or Seventh Day Adventist or even a Jehovah's Witness or something like that?"

"Is he?"

"No, but he could have been."

"Well one thing I do know is you would never marry a man who took the bible literally."

"How do you know he doesn't?"

"Because you're marrying him. And because he's Catholic. Catholics can't take the bible literally. Doesn't it say in there somewhere that its easier for an elephant to pass through the eye of a needle than for a rich man to get into heaven?"

"A camel mom, a camel."

"Whatever. Where does that leave the Pope?"

"Good question."

"You see the Catholics play with words just like the Jews do. That's why they get along so well, now anyway."

"I thought it was being raised on guilt. That Catholics and Jews have guilt as a common bond."

"Whatever. It's just strikes me funny you marrying a Catholic."

"Well you will like him I guarantee. By the way, how come you never converted?"

"I ignored the Catholic religion I was raised in so why would I convert just to ignore another religion? Your father considered himself a humanist and so did I. That was the one thing we had in common and we were young enough to confuse it with love. We were both different I guess."

"Why did you divorce him? You still like him."

"He wasn't romantic. As soon as we were married the romance was over. I wanted romance."

"Like in the movies?"

"The movies were based on real life."

"Not then. The movies of the postwar forties were based on dreams that never came true. The movies of those days were supposed to be an escape from reality."

"Well, my life was like a movie."

"I got one more question mom and then I gotta go."

"I always thought you should be a lawyer you know? You were always asking questions and catching people up. You loved it."

"I'm not trying to catch you up. I just wondered why you didn't speak Spanish to me when I was little. I've tried several times to learn it and this business of taking a class once a week at the adult-ed isn't working. I could have been bi-lingual."

"You want to ask me a question or give me a lecture?"

"OK, just tell me why."

"I made a mistake."

"But why?"

"See what I mean? You're trying to force a confession out of me."

"I'm a defense attorney mom, not a prosecutor."

"I was mad at my mother. I blamed her for driving my father away. Whatever she wanted, I did something else. I wanted you to be modern, assimilated. It was a mistake. I think every generation probably makes it."

"Really? Then how is it that all these old traditions that we rebel against got to be so old in the first place? I mean, if every generation rebelled we wouldn't have any traditions left to rebel against, right?"

"Didn't you say you had to go?"

§§§§§

Rose remembered Dolores as strong and practical. She was the parent who disciplined and criticized her but also, occasionally, showed her grave respect. Isaac was sweet to her but in an absent sort of way and had a way of burying himself in books whenever he was home. She struggled to learn to play the piano well to get his attention and, sometimes, that worked but she found it wasn't enough. Sometimes she wanted to talk to him with words instead of with music. She quit playing when he left. So did Dolores. That was the real reason the piano was sold.

Dolores brought her up in the Catholic faith and when she was a little girl she didn't understand why her father didn't participate in any of the festive social milestones celebrated at the Spanish speaking church they attended, the two of them, Rosaria and Dolores. He prayed privately in his study in a language she never heard anywhere else until she married. His few friends were not the Mexicans who had moved up from New Mexico with his family but the Jews who also lived on the west side, serious men who wore skull caps and would not ride in a car on Saturdays. Her mother, who taught tolerance, nonetheless avoided them. It was if she was jealous or afraid of her husband's different religion.

Rose looked at the photos of Dolores, amazingly young and lovely, almost soft in the earlier ones, then growing sterner and stouter in the succeeding years. Rose separated the annual portraits and then piled all the other haphazard, candid photos under the formal dated portrait that they seemed to match in time. Seeing this transformation of her mother made her sad. It appeared to be a shrinking of the spirit. All her life she had endeavored to avoid it. It seemed to Rose that instead of growing wiser with age, Dolores had allowed her mind to be consumed with an accumulation of petty anxieties. Just when wisdom and experience would have enhanced her ideals, she gave them up and gave herself up wholeheartedly to daily banalities, thereby diminishing her heart. Anger perhaps, anger against her husband's mysticism.

Year after year, Rose had tried to get her father's attention, had tried to cheer him up, to talk to him about her own needs as well as to discover his secret sorrows so she could comfort him and in comforting him, comfort herself for she was a lonely child. Just when she thought she was making progress, he left. They waited, never expecting him to be able to make it in the world without them, that's what Dolores told her, a cold comfort to the child Rose was.

It was more than a year before they found out that he had died in Seattle, struck by lightning his friend told them, his head down, not wanting to look into the eyes of the woman he had heard too much about.

He had had some of Isaac's books and asked if they would like them but Dolores said no, angrily, then apologized to Mr. Sánchez and told him that they had lost Isaac to books years before he had physically left them. Again, the man, a stranger, knew more than he wanted to about these proud and hurting people. Still, it seemed strange to Philemon Sánchez that this woman, who was a teacher, would not have wanted the books. He didn't know how she had hated Isaac's obsession with Judaism. He offered again, to keep the books for them, in case they changed their minds, always including the little girl, on the verge of womanhood but shy and withdrawn, in his gaze.

"We will not change our minds" said Dolores without even looking at Rosaria. Rosaria would like to have had the books, not to read, for she could not read Hebrew, but to touch, just to touch. Years later, after she had been married and divorced and married again and widowed, she went looking for Philemon Sánchez and she finally found him and asked if, by chance, he still had the books of Isaac Mendoza and he told her sadly that he had given them away to different people, people he thought might read them, mostly Jews he told her, who could understand and appreciate the Hebrew and the prayers for he was sure they were books of prayers.

Then she married again, and her new husband told her to forget it, forget the past he said, let go of it and live in the moment which was what she had been doing most of her life. It was her second husband's funeral that made her dwell on the past, the thought of oblivion being so close at such times. It made her remember that she had for a moment wanted to touch something that her father had touched and of course she had quite forgotten that she had rarely been able to touch or be touched by him. But she wondered sometimes if he had been trying to communicate to her in some secret code, a language developed by people who didn't really belong anywhere in the world. She felt so guilty then that she had not asserted herself in time and taken the gift that her father's friend had tried to give her. She became morose and aged overnight and the third husband left her then, looking for a better time on his Saturday nights. That marriage lasted less than a year. She barely noticed it until it was over.

"I feel like some kind of undercover agent when I go to court" Lois had once told Rose. Lois was funny but so many of her joking remarks made her mother want to cry.

Rose opened the sealed envelope that had been at the bottom of the boot box, knowing what would be inside, photos of her father, portraits or photos of him with male friends, photos that did not include Dolores. These were the photos that Dolores had hidden away even deeper than the photos of the two of them together that she had put away in the box, sealing them in an envelope that perhaps she sometimes thought of burning, but did not, thank goodness for that, thought Rose. She looked a long time at the photos of her father and seemed to see her daughter in his face. He might have sought oblivion but he couldn't completely disappeared from the world. Rose had passed him on.

Chapter Twelve
Exile
Northern New Mexico 1903

"Kara vemos, Korazones no konosemos"
Even though we see the face, we cannot know what
is in the heart
Old Ladino proverb

The wind blew like a dirge of the angels, and Isaac's half-brothers all cried with it. Isaac stood silently listening to the wind. He didn't resent his stepmother the way he used to when he was younger, but he had no feelings for her at all. He couldn't cry but it was easy to look sad because his father's presence always made him sad. He was a little worried that his father would make him stay with him after the funeral to greet friends and relatives who would be coming to the ranch with food and condolences.

It was Friday and Isaac always went to his mother on Friday nights. This Friday night he would sneak out so as to avoid any problem. His father wouldn't miss him if he was quiet about it.

For as long as he could remember Isaac had gone to his mother's cabin at the far end of his father's property on Fridays before sunset. When he arrived he and his mother would watch the sunset together and sing songs, not in the Spanish that his father spoke but a slightly different Spanish with strange words and phrases mixed in that she only began to teach him a few months ago when he turned thirteen. Until then he merely memorized the words and melodies which were strangely joyful. These were songs that were meant to be sung by many voices, but Rosaria and Isaac did their best, just the two of them.

After all the color had faded from the sky, they would go inside and he would watch his mother light candles and recite a prayer. Then they washed their hands while she said another prayer that sounded like the first one but with a different ending while he poured the water from the pitcher over first his left hand and then his right and when they were cleansed, she would share with him the tortillas she had baked that morning and the sparkling wine that she hoarded so carefully to last each Friday night and some special holidays besides. Over each she said another prayer. Isaac easily learned the first part of each of the prayers because the first part was always the same: Baruch Ata Adonay Eloheinu Melech O'olam . . . Then each ended differently, like a song with different verses but the same refrain.

After the ritual of prayer and bread and wine which always reminded Isaac of holy communion, they had a wonderful meal and then sang songs again before Rosaria put Isaac to bed and sat over him to watch her son, growing ever longer in the bed, until the time came he would sit up late with her and they would talk of many things. When she realized the time was right, she told him about his heritage, about her own life and about the history, as much as she knew of it, of the Jewish people.

During the next day, they would rise early to watch the sunrise and then explore the mountains at the edge of his father's land. There were dark woods there that his brothers never entered and they found many beautiful things. Even death was beautiful here. Trees that fell in the woods slowly transformed into mosses and lichens and soft spongy mushrooms, into soil from whence grew tiny versions of themselves. Isaac marveled at the intricacies of these tiny worlds growing between the ridges of decaying bark. Sometimes they would sit silently watching the deer standing still and watching them back. In the winters they would stay near the creek that grew wider and stronger each year and watch the water bubble beneath thin layers of ice, examine the delicate grasses and flowers, frozen in graceful, linear shapes inside transparent cocoons of silver and white.

They always watched the second sun set until the last streaks of gold and pink had disappeared, reluctant to go inside but even then they ended their time together with beautiful ceremony. As soon as his mother could see three stars in the night sky she would light another candle and hold it in her hand while she said the last prayer of the Sabbath. They would sniff some sage that she had gathered and then put the candle out in a bowl of wine. Isaac's mother dipped her fingers in the fragrant, steaming wine and touched them to his forehead as she blessed him. At last they would walk out into the darkness together and she would guide him back to his father's house by moonlight or the gleam from the creek that meandered now through the land.

§§§§§

Guillermo Mendoza had discovered Isaac's mother in a cave on his property where she had dragged herself to die. She had been left by her people, a band of nomadic sheepherders because her disease was contagious and they already had horrific memories of smallpox and couldn't afford to lose any more of their dwindling numbers to another epidemic. She had been left with a knife to skin small game or protect herself as needed and a small pony. She had turned the pony back to find the people when she found the cave and prepared to die there.

She had built a small fire to be warm and threw upon it the leaves of a plant known to cause a deep sleep and numb pain. She also brewed some of the leaves in water from a spring that had opened up by the cave at her arrival, in order to drink its medicine and sink into oblivion all the faster. She of course did not expect to awake from this sleep and prayed that the disease that marked her body with red spots and heated her skin and weakened her bones would finally be done with her and take her body, leaving her spirit free to find its way home.

But Guillermo, riding fence, saw smoke coming from the cave and went to investigate. He shook the woman to see if she was sleeping or dead and she murmured but did not awake. She looked vaguely Indian but had sharper, bonier features than the Dineh who moved with their sheep and goats all around this area. Guillermo often cursed them and believed that they stole his lambs in the spring to increase their own herds. He guessed correctly that she had been left by these people because of sickness and he thought he could take her home and nurse her back to health. Then he would let her work for him on his ranch.

Guillermo shook the woman awake. He was a Catholic and did not hold with the godless ways of the Indians who often took such matters as death into their own hands. She was hard to wake, grumbling and turning away when he held her face and tried to revive her with wine from his goatskin pouch. He spoke to her in Spanish mixed with the few Dineh words that he had learned over the years.

"Dine?" he asked and she responded by nodding her head, her tongue to fuzzy yet for use. "Adopted" he thought to himself, for hers was not the round face of the Dineh but a face more like his own, a Spanish face. "Or kidnapped?" he wondered. It was important to him what she was for he was already considering how to put her to use after he'd cured her. He was certain she was too weak to walk so he left the wine and rode back to the ranch stables to get another horse for her. Guillermo was not about to walk and he knew she couldn't.

He was astonished when he returned, ponying a saddled mare, to find her gone.

"A *Bruja*?" he wondered. "A vision?" And he noticed for the first time the tiny, almost hidden spring that seeped into the pasture by the opening of the cave. He couldn't remember ever seeing it before. Riding back along the fence line that he hadn't yet checked he caught sight of her staggering further up the mountain and he ran to catch her up. He dismounted and approached her carefully believing she was afraid of him and therefore he was afraid of what she would do to protect herself. But Rosaria was disdainful. He was interfering with her plan for a peaceful and dignified death.

When he was close enough to reach for her, she glanced at his hand in contempt, and then, realizing the reason for the second horse, she gathered her strength to climb into the saddle without his help, gracefully and expertly for she was a superb horsewoman as was her mother before her and her mother's mother and her line was famous among the Dineh for this skill. She then galloped off away from Guillermo planning to lose him. But Guillermo kept pace with her and she turned to see him laughing with admiration and awe and then she fainted.

So at home was Rosaria on horseback that she did not fall off but merely slumped forward and then, feeling the saddle horn, awoke and mumbled to Guillermo to unsaddle the horse so she could lay along the horse's neck in comfort and sleep for she was weak she admitted and he, not quite trusting her, told her they were close to the ranch house where she could sleep comfortably in a bed and no point in wasting time with unsaddling the horse. She rode on, keeping her eyes ahead and expressionless.

Rosaria awoke later in a large carved oak bed unable to remember how she had gotten there. She didn't remember climbing down from the saddle with an automatic grace nor walking with a straight and dignified posture to this room, walking too quickly in fact for Guillermo to catch her up and carry her for she would not allow such a thing and she knew he couldn't carry her anyway. The Mexican was too small a man.

In the beginning Guillermo was awed by Rosaria and believed he was in love with her. He did not think of marrying her because she was Indian, or claimed to be, and his neighbors would look down on her and also on him were he to marry her. But neither could he simply go to her bed as if she were a slave for she would never allow it and he knew that she would find ways to resist, put a spell on him perhaps for he was certain she had such powers.

In his way, Guillermo courted Rosaria. First he brought the Doctor from the town of Trinidad to see to her and the Doctor brought medicines and gave Guillermo instructions for her care which the haughty rancher faithfully and tenderly carried out. Then he brought beautiful fabrics and had his foreman's wife make Rosaria three dresses; one for every day, one for celebrations and one for holy days for he was determined to make a Christian of this heathen woman. And to that end, and so he himself could converse with her more easily, he hired a teacher to come out to the ranch and tutor Rosaria in Spanish, never realizing that she only pretended not to speak it in order not to have to speak to him.

Once Rosaria was well enough to wander around the large house she discovered that Guillermo owned a pianoforte but when she asked him to play it, he admitted that he couldn't. She asked why he didn't hire someone to teach him and he told her he would get a teacher for *her* since *he* had no time for such things himself.

"Then why own a pianoforte?"

"A man owed me money but couldn't pay so I agreed to take his furniture and it was among the other pieces."

Rosaria felt sorry for the man who perhaps had played music on the beautiful instrument and would have missed it. She played sad songs of her own invention even before the teacher arrived.

"A natural musician your wife" said the teacher who was fired on the spot.

Then Guillermo came to Rosaria's bed offering his love and she permitted him, seeing that he had a capacity for extreme kindness as well as a capacity for extreme cruelty, and it seemed little enough to her to ensure his kindness. She had already abandoned her body in the cave.

Shortly thereafter Guillermo moved back into his room for it was his bed he had given Rosaria while he had slept in the bunk house with the hands. He treated her like his wife though they both knew he would never marry her and why.

After the Spanish teacher had done his job, marveling at how quickly Rosaria learned, he was replaced by a bible teacher and this teacher was amazed by Rosaria's knowledge of the Old Testament and asked where she had acquired this knowledge. "I learned from my grandmother, Luisa," she told him as if he would know who "Luisa" was but he was gratified, thinking at first that this Luisa must have learned from one of the missionaries. Then, when Rosaria knew absolutely nothing of the New Testament, he was first mystified then suspicious.

"There are rumors there were Jews here over two hundred years ago" he mentioned to Guillermo one evening after supper, after Rosaria had left the men to their cigars and brandy.

"What is your point?"

"How much do you know about this woman?" the teacher asked with a touch of condescension.

"What business is that of yours? And what are you trying to say?"

"Nada, nothing. It doesn't matter. No one minds about the Jews anymore and it's probably not true. There are a few Jews in Trinidad and a Jewish family in Raton, from Germany or Russia, just came here in the last ten years. I don't believe that story that there were Jews who came with Coronado, do you?"

"Why should I even think about it?"

"Rosaria knows all about the Hebraic religion, says her mother taught her. She knows nothing whatsoever about Catholicism."

"That's what you're here to teach her. You wouldn't be worth your pay if she did."

"They say the Jews were witches but I don't believe in witches. It's a crazy idea born of prejudice. Don't you think so?" But he asked the question without looking at his employer.

Guillermo said no more to the Anglo tutor but the next morning a servant brought the man his wages and told him his services were no longer needed.

By this time Rosaria knew that she was carrying a child. She did not mind that the father was a man she despised but she worried that Guillermo would not allow her to raise her child in her faith. For generations, the women of her family, descended from a half breed Pueblo woman and the lost and wandering survivor of a doomed Spanish expedition, had passed on the Judaic identity and ritual to their daughters with or without the knowledge and consent of the fathers.

The Dineh respected women in a way that Guillermo could

not be expected to understand and sometimes Rosaria thought of running away and trying to find her people. Every day she rode out looking for a sign of them and every day Guillermo would ride out after her, puzzled and hurt that she preferred the company of his horses to himself. Finally he forbade her to ride at all and was surprised when she didn't object or simply disobey his order.

Then winter set in early and she began to grow big and bulky and Guillermo could see that he was going to be a father. He spoke always of "his son" irritating Rosaria because of course the child was hers and, more likely, a daughter. She expected a daughter but then she began to dream of her child and in her dreams the child was always a boy. In that way, Rosaria knew that she was going to give birth to a male child for Rosaria never questioned the truth of dreams.

As the boy child grew inside Rosaria, the little spring by the cave grew and gave birth to a stream that widened into a creek that meandered all through Guillermo's property, much to his amazement and joy for now it was easy to water his sheep and irrigate his fields.

Guillermo treated Rosaria very respectfully throughout her pregnancy, not wanting to do anything that might jeopardize the baby and he was grateful to her when the child was born. He even allowed her to choose the child's name, approving of Isaac as a respectable biblical name, albeit from the Old Testament. He expected his patience to be rewarded so he was angry when Rosaria was not happy to receive him back into their bed after the birth. And he felt hurt that she paid so much attention to the baby that she neglected the baby's father. He could afford nurses to care for the precious baby. In fact such a precious child *deserved* the care of many servants and the father deserved the attention of the mother after all those months of abstinence.

Guillermo had not been completely abstinent but had made trips into town on business and concluded these trips with visits to whores, careful to visit only the women he trusted to keep themselves healthy and clean for he was a fastidious man. He had consulted the Doctor about this, knowing that the Doctor would know who was safe and who was sick and should be avoided.

It was not Guillermo's intention to continue these visits after Rosaria had given birth to his son and he began to think that perhaps he should marry a woman of his own kind and have a more normal family life. At first he conceived the idea in a mood of anger and vindictiveness but then the idea made sense to him for, after all, he had never promised to marry her and Rosaria had never indicated she would even want such an arrangement.

In his mind he imagined asking her to be his wife and in his mind he rehearsed her disdainful rejection until he made himself angry with her. The fact was, had Rosaria wanted him, pressed him to marry her, he would have done so: he had also rehearsed, many times, a variety of haughty responses to the insults of his neighbors until they would be cowed into respecting his Indian wife. But there was a subtle but constant and strong defiance about her that made it impossible for him to talk calmly to her about anything. He could only make demands, ensuring her refusal by his rudeness.

Rosaria, for her part, knew that she was treading on dangerous ground for, as much as he seemed to adore this child, the child was illegitimate and could easily be replaced when and if Guillermo decided to marry. She knew she could have him if she could convince him she loved him, but Rosaria was too proud to pretend that she loved Guillermo even though she had allowed him the use of her body. Now that she had a son and therefore a future, she found she could not tolerate that intimacy anymore.

She became used to his tantrums and he could not rile her, even when he deliberately destroyed the pianoforte and then used the splintered pieces, so carefully planned and pieced together, to start fires in the cook-stove. But Rosaria's heart went cold when Guillermo stopped fighting to conquer her and began leaving her alone more and more often, many nights at a time. She realized then that she had given up her son's security. She made up her mind that if Guillermo would come to her at night one more time, she would stifle her selfish pride for the sake of the child and welcome the father into her arms. He never did. He knew if he came to her completely unprotected, got down on his knees and poured out his soul, told her plainly about his love and his need for her and the grief that he felt for having set them both on the wrong path, if he told her all that and she rejected him even then, he knew, he feared, he would kill her.

The next time Guillermo returned from town, he brought with him his new bride. Of course, he expected Isaac to live with him and his wife. Rosaria could live with the servants and work for Guillermo if she wanted to see her son. Understanding how humiliated she would feel and understanding that she would endure it for the sake of the her child, Guillermo was glad, finally, to have his revenge on this woman who had hurt him so many times with her contempt, with her indifference, this woman he had never been able to truly touch until now.

For a year Isaac lived with his father and stepmother who took no interest in him and Rosaria held him and sang to him secretly when the bride and groom were gone to visit other ranchers in the county and left the baby with the cook. This cook was herself a Pueblo woman and sympathetic to Rosaria. Then the happily married couple both became ill with diphtheria and the young bride died before she could give Guillermo the legitimate son he wished for. Guillermo was certain that it was Rosaria who had set a curse upon him and his bride. When he felt death approach he sent for her and accused her of putting a curse upon him and his bride out of a desire for revenge.

He watched her face while he told her he was sorry for many things and wished he had behaved differently but he saw no change in her expression that told him they might yet live together again. So, believing he needed her intervention to get well, he promised her she could have her son at the end of every week. He told her that he would build her a cabin of her own wherever she might choose as long as it was not within sight of his house, if she would cure him.

Rosaria did not deny his accusation since his belief made him fear her and fear was as close as the man could ever get to respect. She told him she wanted a Hogan built by the cave where he had found her and that she would come for Isaac every Friday two hours before dusk and return him every Saturday two hours after three stars appeared in the sky. She told him these things in case he lived, but she was not sure she could cure him and planned to simply run away with her child if he died.

She did not pray for his death and was diligent in her care of him for she feared God would punish her for such a prayer or for negligence. Guillermo lived. Perhaps he would have lived in any case or perhaps Rosaria really did save his life, but the important thing was he kept his promise to her. Later he married a second wife who gave him four more sons whom he treated more kindly than he ever treated Isaac. Guillermo knew that her child's pain was his best revenge against the woman who would not love him.

§§§§§

Rosaria taught Isaac the prayers she wanted him to know: the

She 'ma which was the most important and never to be forgotten or forsaken. All the Baruchas over the candles and the wine and bread and the Kadush, the prayer said in memory of the dead because as she said, "death has loved our family well".

She taught him also his genealogy which had been carefully passed on from mother to daughter for it was the daughters who had been taught Jewish rituals and family names until Rosaria gave birth to her only child, a son.

"Not even your father can trace his ancestors back so far" she told him proudly. "The first of our mothers was the wild horse woman and no one ever knew her name for she would allow no one to utter it. Her father was a Jew who had been lost on an expedition when the Spanish ships wrecked on a shore far to the east over three hundred years ago. He was already old when wild horse woman was born and he died when she was still a very young girl but he taught her the secret ways of the Jewish people, even her own mother did not know these secrets. He also taught her everything he knew about horses. About this her mother knew something as well. From her father she learned to ride and work them. From her mother she learned how to talk to, tame and care for them.

Wild Horse Woman had a daughter whom she named María with a man named Elijah who appeared and disappeared as mysteriously as the prophet. María married Jacob who had come here with one of the governors of New Spain as they called Mexico in those days. Jacob died in another expedition in a place called La Matanza somewhere in what is now called Kansas and this happened before their daughter, Rosaria was born. She was known as Rosaria Tristessa and it was her daughter Luisa named after the Jewish Martyr Luis de Carvajal, who was adopted by the Dine with whom we stayed until I came here. Luisa was known for her ability as a horsewoman and also her weaving. She was married three times but had only one child. She divorced her first husband when he objected to her raising their daughter in the Jewish ways. Her second husband died and her third husband was twenty years younger than she and cared for her until she died. Her daughter had many names, one in the Dine language, one in Spanish and one in Hebrew but she became known simply as Many Names.

There were also many stories of Many Names because she had the most children and they each had different memories of her. To each of her eleven children she gave a special gift by observing which characteristic of each child could most successfully be cultivated.

The kind child was taught to be a healer, the wisest to be a teacher, the strongest to be a leader and so on. This was her wisdom. The first child, a son, was raised in the Catholic religion and became a priest to protect his family from trouble with the church. The oldest daughter learned the secret Jewish ways to be passed on until the day it would be once again safe to practice this religion in the open. All the other children were raised in the Dine religion. This was how it was done in those days.

This Jewish daughter of Many Names was named also Luisa and her daughter Esther grew to be very beautiful and was known as Esther Bonita Espirita because she was as beautiful in spirit as in body. Esther's daughter, another Rosaria, was very serious and not given to smiles but was observant and thoughtful. She named her daughter Luisa also to honor her grandmother. This last Luisa was known as Luisa the Learned for she could speak and read many languages and translated for the different people who had come to live in her land. She remembered the war between the United States and Mexico. She taught me because my own mother Esther the Dreamer seemed to live in another world and died very young when I was still an infant. To this day I don't know if my memories of my mother are my own or my grandmother's because Luisa wanted to be sure not a single one of us was forgotten and she talked daily of her daughter, my mother, who lived among ghosts and then went to join them. She drowned herself in the river, Isaac, but we say Kadush for her anyway. Luisa told me it was not a sin what my mother did, that she was only going to a place where she felt more at home. I understand this and don't blame her but I grieve for her anyway. Because of her I often dream of death. And you know I almost did die before you were born but god wanted you to be in the world and my life was saved by your father. I sometimes think that my time has come and gone and I could go any day."

When, in fact, her own time did come, Rosaria dreamed of it. She became quite suddenly ill and in her delirium she saw vultures and wild dogs circling her Hogan. She felt fully awake and very frightened to see these visions, wondering if they could smell her illness and were waiting for her to die. She counted the days and fought to make it until Friday when her son would come to visit her and he could bury her body intact, chanting the proper prayers. Had she not been so weak with fever, she would have begun digging her grave herself. It was her wish to be buried in the cave where once she had expected to leave this world.

Isaac and Guillermo also both dreamed of vultures and both woke in a cold sweat, Guillermo moaning, Isaac silent as he had made a habit of keeping himself out of his father's notice. When he had washed and dressed, Isaac began walking to his mother's house, pretending he did not hear his father who called after him in a voice more pleading than commanding. He would like to have taken one of the horses to get him there faster but expected this would anger his father and he had no desire to have to deal with his father at this time.

He ran, thinking to be relieved of an unreasonable fear for he did not yet believe in dreams and premonitions. When he arrived his mother's fever had abated and she lay relieved and cool in her bed, but so pale and exhausted that it was clear she had been ill. Always dignified, Rosaria greeted Isaac politely, got up and asked him to brush her hair for her, apologizing for not being up and properly groomed. She said nothing about the timing of his visit. She had faith in these things and she sensed that her son already knew what she had to tell him.

Isaac gathered the hair that hung to her knees in his hand slightly up from the ends and brushed down until the brush went smoothly through it, then he gathered it higher up and brushed down to the ends and then higher and higher until he could run the brush all the way from the top of her head down to the ends and then he offered to braid it for her and she allowed him to do this.

While Isaac brushed and braided her hair she was thinking that, had she not become ill so many years before with such a dangerous disease, it might have been her lover from long ago, doing this for her. She had not allowed herself to think of him since she had prepared to die in the cave. He would be aged now from the hard life and she imagined him handsome still with gray hair and wrinkles. She remembered his friends dragging him away from her while he cried and called out and she had not responded or cried herself even though it was she who was being abandoned, because she understood the necessity of it and didn't want it to be even harder for him. She had not allowed herself to think of this all these years so now it was a relief to simply look at him in her mind while her son brushed her long hair. She could hear him crying still, but of course it was Isaac who was crying, convinced now that he really was going to lose her.

"I will show you where I want to be buried, Isaac. I think I will live to spend another Sabbath with you but I want you to dig my grave before then. You know the prayers?"

"Si, Madre."

"You must go to David the old vaquero who never speaks, you know him? All the others go to him for help with the horses, he speaks to the horses."

"I know him."

"Tell him I am dying. He will come back with you and help you to dig the grave. He will bring shovels and you can ride back here on horses and pony one back for me to ride to the grave site. David will know which one. I will stay there until it is time. I do not wish to be carried there. I want to ride there on a black stallion I have sometimes dreamed of. It will be a dignified death my son. You can take comfort in that."

Although he was only fourteen years old, Isaac knew not to burden his mother with his thoughts: "how can you die now Madre when I need you? I have no one else." He thought but did not utter aloud because he knew she could not stop death and he didn't want to ruin her last days with guilt. Instead he told her that he loved her and that he would remember everything she had taught him, forget nothing, pray for her and someday name a daughter after her.

It was easy then to be noble and selfless because he still nursed the small hope that it would not really happen. He continued to pray in his mind that he would come back with the old vaquero and the horses and the shovels and she would be better, laughing at her close encounter with death. He wanted to make bargains with God but he knew he could not bargain without betraying his mother. He had nothing to withhold if his prayers were not answered for he had promised her to be faithful.

It was still two days before the Sabbath and when Isaac returned with old David, the black stallion, the shovels they moved the candles and wine to the cave along with Rosaria. David had thought to bring tortillas for he knew the ritual, and he knew the prayers. He did not know their meaning or their origin but he knew the strange words learned by heart from his own mother now so long dead.

David stayed to help Isaac dig the grave, letting the tears flow freely down his wizened cheeks. "*Ah, mi hijita*" he muttered under his breath wishing God would take him in his old age instead of this woman in her prime. For David, getting up each dawn was the hardest task in his hard working day. When the grave was dug, he left with a promise to return the next evening. Isaac stayed in the cave with his mother and at nightfall they lit the candles, drank the wine, recited the prayers and sang together, making beautiful harmonies that lingered in the night. Rosaria slept peacefully throughout the next day, the Sabbath and by the time three stars appeared in the sky she was dead. It seemed she smiled and Isaac at first thought she had awakened and began to speak to her but then he realized she was gone from him and he cried and felt abandoned. David found him lying next to his mother, his arms thrown over her body, sobbing like a baby.

"Come *hijito*, we must bury her before the coyotes come. Hard work will help you sleep." And so they did and when Isaac's mind wandered, David helped him remember the words of mourning and helped him mount the horse he had brought back with him and took him to the bunkhouse where the hands slept and put him to sleep in his own bunk, knowing Isaac was not ready to return to his father's house.

The next morning Guillermo went looking for Isaac and found him in the bunkhouse still asleep and shook him awake. "Tell me, tell me what is going on?" and only half awake, Isaac said "she's dead" and both were silent. Guillermo had no idea what to say and so said nothing. He got up and walked back to the main house where he sat a while remembering every word he wished he hadn't said, remembering every thought he wished he had expressed. He resolved to be kinder to his son. He had loved his first child but his anger at the mother had made him hurt the child deeply and now he sought frantically to think of ways to make amends. Meantime, Isaac could not speak for his heart was full of anger at God and he felt completely alone in the vast universe. He slept a lot that first week and Guillermo did not disturb him but made sure that breakfast was taken to him in his room every morning. Isaac was surprised and touched by this. He began to feel sorry for his father. In his own way, his father was lonely too.

Every night until the next Sabbath he went back to his mother's empty Hogan. He took the candles and the wine to the cave and there he whispered the prayers, whispered songs and slept there next to the grave. The last day he slept late, not hearing the morning birds. It was overcast and the birds had not begun to sing at dawn as they always did, waiting, Isaac thought, for the pink and golden light to loosen their tongues. But Isaac sang, in a whisper still and then he thought he heard them, the morning birds. He stopped to hear them better and there was only silence but when he began to sing again he was certain the birds sang with him and he sang louder and the birds sang louder and then they flew up and out of the surrounding trees calling to the sun that appeared briefly out of the grayness.

After a while Guillermo made tentative attempts to speak gently to his first son, the illegitimate one, the one he had ignored except to criticize or command. Isaac seemed lost in another world and didn't hear the softened tone of his father's voice and Guillermo feared the son was like the mother and would never love him. Too old and tired now for rage, Guillermo succumbed to sadness.

Chapter Thirteen
Flight
Brabant 1600/Seattle 1931

". . . In fact, the bird has always a metaphysical
function here. In it the human and the divine meet.
. . . They are the fire bearers. But they also steal fire
like every living creature that longs to live out his
adventure to the end. And it is the tragedy of the
beggars and the blind that the infirmities of their
bodies which match the infirmities of their minds
should forever prevent them from flying like birds
up into the sky to steal thence that fire which is
nourishment."
Claude Metra: *Bruegel, The Man and His Paintings*,
p. 11

When Mayken was younger she was always in a frenzy to paint
and her dreams were indeed her inspiration but after Jacob left he
took that kind of energy with her and she became quiet and content
to simply enjoy the simplest sensual pleasures. She enjoyed the
smell of herbs on her fingers when she picked them from her garden
for Miriam to use in her delightful and creative concoctions. She
enjoyed watching the stars from her tower until her eyes were heavy
and she even enjoyed the fatigue of her body as she walked back to
her bed. Then, hating to leave the stars, she had Miriam help her
make up a bed in the tower and she loved waking up to watch the
night sky and to listen to the groan of faraway trees bending stiffly in
the night breeze that caressed her own eyelids. And, as always, she
enjoyed the discourse of birds coming and going, sorrowful, joyful,
far away or nearby on her own windowsill, and the inspirations of her
dreams became revelations now she was old enough to understand
them. She began to see a picture of the history of the world, a story
that repeated itself over and over and everywhere essentially the
same: the faces were different, the costumes and landscapes, but

the way that people loved and hated, created and destroyed, this was all the same.

As the two women aged together they began to look alike. Miriam and Mayken were both gray, their hair, their eyes, their skin and dressed all in black, they looked like two large birds of the night. One day Inquisitors came to talk to Mayken about Miriam, find out where she had come from and what she did for Mayken. But Mayken could tell them nothing, lost in some quiet secret madness of which they had heard long ago. Madness was nothing new to the priests of the Inquisition. For centuries they had suspected it, preyed upon it, tortured it, induced it and often succumbed to it. For all that the priests persecuted madness; they were still, at each and every confrontation, afraid of it. When madness took hysterical and noisy form the fear of the priests inspired them to hysterical and noisy reaction. But Mayken's madness was quiet, serene and she simply stared at them, smiling, with old birdlike eyes. On the sill of the window behind her stood a large crow also quiet and staring and so still as to seem dead. But the bird was not dead and let out a single piercing cry before taking off into a lazy flight, riding the warm air currents from the steaming earth and then, cried out to them once more before disappearing into the mist.

The men, all younger than Mayken, young enough to be her sons and grandsons and local young men at that, who remembered her family and lacked the vituperous passion of the Spaniards who returned from time to time to revel in the fires of redemption, these slow Flemings simply watched and spoke warnings to Mayken that it was dangerous to be harboring Jews, if indeed her maidservant was such, and trailed off and inquired as to her health and then her art . . . did she still paint? No? . . . a shame . . . and then good day and they turned to go the way of the crow, looking up at the sky, speculating to one another on coming storms, peasants yet beneath their Jesuit robes.

Mayken walked as if in a daze to her tower and watched the retreat of the priests until they disappeared from her vision and then she stared at the road out of town until it too disappeared into dusk and dream. When the last evening light seemed to lift all forms from their roots in the earth and float them softly like feathers in the early autumn air, Mayken saw an old man dressed in simple white cotton and dancing into town as he vigorously played with a bow upon a fiddle and soon she could hear the plaintive call of the violin. It seemed to her that the fiddler struggled to keep the instrument from flying out of his hands as it cried louder and louder with some feeling that wasn't grief, no, but made her cry over some long forgotten loss. It wasn't Jacob she cried over, or her husband, or the hordes of refugees who fled through her dreams. Rational still, she worked to remember what it was that tugged at her heart, pulling it down, down to the ground, the earth, she remembered, she remembered the earth, the smell of haystacks in the noonday sun, the scent of water on ferns that grew in the woods beside the running streams, the silver streams that ran through a green-black forest, places where the sun came through the trees and lit up the water, caressing its banks and the roots of trees as it ran over and around rocks tirelessly, and the breeze that always blew off the cool racing creek, no matter how hot and still the day outside that secret dark leafy place . . . she remembered.

Mayken walked slowly down the stone steps, quietly past Miriam who had fallen asleep in her chair, some mending still in her lap, out the large carved oak door into the moonlit night. She listened for the sound of the violin but the fiddler had gone into a tavern where travelers paid him to assuage the loneliness of the road. Mayken followed the road the music had come in on and she followed it until dawn brought her to rest at a farm like the one she remembered from her childhood. She slept a while in the hay piled in the center of a field, lulled by the rising sun and then, when it got too hot for her, she got up and picked some apples in the orchard. She carried them in her long apron that she held up by its corners to make a sack.

Everything seemed so familiar, even after all those years, and she found the creek, listening and sniffing the air for it in the woods. There she found a large tree root that curved out over the creek and she could sit with her back against the tree trunk and watch the water ripple beneath her as she ate her apples slowly and completely one after the other.

Mayken was startled then by a sharp intake of breath that had to be human and turned to see a small boy with a frightened look staring at her. He began to back away as if hoping she wouldn't notice him if he remained very quiet and nearly still.

"What are you afraid of?" she asked him. "I wouldn't hurt you if I could."

Then he turned and ran. Mayken paid no more attention and continued to watch the mesmerizing water and dozed.

When she awoke it was because of voices that sounded so near she thought at first she was in her own bedroom and could hear Miriam and Pieter who always visited her dreams, talking about her, worried about her. But she was still in the woods, sleeping in the curl of an ancient tree root and it was a strange young couple who were talking about her in such worried tones.

"She is such an old woman. How could she have gotten here?"

"She must belong to a family nearby but I can't think of which one."

Then they noticed that she was awake and watching them and they both knelt to speak to her the way they might speak to a small child and indeed, there, hovering between them was the little boy, their son.

She had to explain herself to them. There was no way out of it. She told them about the fiddler and how she had come out on the road from town in the hope of hearing more music and she tried to describe the music to them and how it reminded her of her old childhood home, this farm, or another just like it. They only perked up their ears when they heard she had come from town so now they knew where she belonged and they insisted on taking her back.

They walked her back to their house behind the apple orchard and hitched a horse to a small wagon. The young husband, the boy's father, would drive her to town and hoped she'd recognize her home. Mayken told him it was near the Cathedral, the large house with the tower and he knew the house, knew a painter had lived there many years before. On the way back to town the young man apologized for his young son's behavior.

"He thought you were a ghost because there are stories of ghosts that live in a cave behind the hay field up ahead. When I was a child a dead family was found there and it was pretty terrible, I remember. The woman had a dead baby still in her arms and she had had her throat cut. The young man, a priest if you can imagine, must have cut her throat and then fallen on the knife. There was blood all over them and the baby was not formed right. Some of the local people called it a monster but you know I don't believe in that stuff, that the devil begets such children. The Spanish priests burned the bodies, said they had run away from the Inquisition in Seville. Such stories. I was only a little boy myself but even then I didn't believe any of it. I believe in what I can see and touch. Of course I don't usually talk about what I believe and don't believe. Whatever you believe, that's the story and there's none around here that hasn't heard it and I guess my boy does believe in ghosts because you sure scared him."

The young man laughed and Mayken said not a word. In fact the friendly young man talked all the way and then talked to Miriam like he knew her and Miriam thanked him over and over for bringing back her mistress and gave him some fresh baked bread to take to his wife and son. It seemed Miriam had helped bring the boy into the world. It seemed to Mayken that there was a lot in the world she had somehow missed. But she could hear the gulls from a faraway sea when no one else could. Next time she would walk all the way to the sea. In her dreams she heard the soothing sound of it but when she woke it was only wind in the trees.

> "Ye-hei she-mei ra-ba me-va-rach le-a-lum u-le-al-ma-ya. Yit-ba-rach ve-yish-ta-bach, ve-yit-pa-ar ve-yit-ro-mam
> ve-yit-nasei, ve-yit-ha-dar ve-yit-a-leh ve-yit-ha-lal . . . "

Mayken heard Miriam chanting her strange prayers as she had for so many years and paid no heed as it was understood that these were secret prayers that no one overheard. But this prayer had the rhythm Mayken recognized from the anniversary of Pieter's death and Miriam chanted each year when they visited the grave and she laid a small stone on top of the larger carved gravestone, to let him know they'd been there to visit him, she told Mayken. Now Miriam sang it in the privacy of her home for no one but herself. Miriam knew it was time to die and she was ready and at peace but for her worry over Mayken. Mayken had a boundless energy and wanderlust and Miriam was afraid she would wander off again into the midst of some battle somewhere: there was always some battle somewhere, and Mayken could walk long distances without tiring. She often talked about going to look for the old widow-woman and the preacher she remembered from a time before she knew Miriam, or finding a ship to take her to Jacob across the sea, across the world. At those times Miriam would give Mayken something hot to drink that would make her drowsy and when she awoke they would talk about the garden or ideas for the paintings that Mayken planned to do one day.

Mayken dreamed of being very tall and striding throughout the land right through the fires of death and hell on earth, going somewhere with a purpose, but she could never glimpse the destination in the distance and sometimes it felt as though the earth moved backwards beneath her feet even as she moved forward with longer and faster strides. She tried, at Miriam's urging to make a painting of this but could never get it right. "I have to get there first" she would tell Miriam, "before I can paint it." She tried painting storms and she was especially fascinated by the lightning storms that broke the sky in the summer months. She would run outside to chase them and Miriam would wake and go looking for her. It was a worry to Miriam when she realized it was her time to die, but after one hundred years in that time and place, she was tired and gave up her responsibility for Mayken to god.

When Mayken was in a period of lucidity, Miriam talked to her about death. She did not want a Christian burial, of course, but not to bury her within the dictates of the church would have put Mayken under suspicion again, so Miriam suggested that she be sealed up in the secret room where she had practiced her Jewish rituals for so many Sabbaths. There were no openings to the outside and the large oak door fit tightly. She and Mayken together moved a large and heavy tapestry from another part of the house to hang there over the door and the two women went into the room together. Mayken sat with Miriam who reclined on pillows they had laid out on the floor. Mayken ate and drank at Miriam's request but Miriam ate nothing, drank nothing and within a few days and nights, Miriam was first delirious with dreams, then dead. When Mayken was absolutely certain that Miriam would never wake again, she left the room, locked the door and pulled the tapestry across it the way they had practiced and never went back. Even when Mayken's mind wandered, she never returned to that room. At the end, Miriam had said prayers and asked Mayken to lay out the lace tablecloth, the silver candleholders, the silver wine cup and the silver plate for bread, as if ready for the Sabbath service and so they would be found centuries later in the secret room with the mysterious skeleton by archaeologists in the year 1931.

§§§§§

Isaac Mendoza rode the train as far as it went and as far as his money would take him which was San Francisco. He was lucky to be approached immediately by a panhandler, a *Mejicano*, who looked him up and down and took in the aura of respectability from the shoes to the briefcase and the hat, along with the dark complexion and the black mustache and asked Isaac, in Spanish, if he cared to share a little something with a brother. Isaac explained he had no money and that his life was ended, he wasn't sure where, but somewhere in the city that very day, his misery would be over. Philemon Sánchez asked what he carried in the briefcase and Isaac explained that he carried books with him wherever he went, whereupon Philemon laughed thinking it funny that a man bent on suicide would bring something to read on the trip. He took Isaac's arm and suggested they go get drunk and promised to cheer Isaac up. Isaac's ache was so deep and overwhelming that he was grateful for the friendship and followed the penniless drunk, literally putting his life (worthless as it was) in the man's hands.

He allowed himself to be led to the bar where Philemon found friends to buy them both a few drinks and Isaac, who never drank, was lifted out of the miserable world quickly and cheaply. He sat quietly, drifting about now and then around the overhead light-bulb, and listened and watched while Philemon socialized with his friends from the street and by dark he was part of a small group of men who had decided to hop a freight to Seattle.

One of the men knew a railroad guard who would look the other way while they boarded the train before it began moving so there be no danger to their new friend in his leftover fancy clothes, the kind that at one time or another each of them had worn, to a funeral perhaps, to a wedding or a baptism. They called him "the gentleman" and were already concocting ways to take advantage of Isaac's appearance of affluence and respectability when they got to Seattle.

He never asked why they were so eager to go to Seattle but Philemon explained anyway that there were catacombs beneath the city where the homeless could set up fairly comfortable households and there was gambling going on there where a man might get lucky and various kinds of entertainment establishments where he might spend his winnings. Although Isaac had grown up in New Mexico and lived a while in Denver and was therefore used to sunlight, he had been ready to throw himself into eternal darkness so the catacombs sounded OK for the meantime. It was Philemon who remembered to grab Isaac's briefcase full of books as they left.

§§§§§

The bark of the geese reminded Mayken of the gulls by the sea and she could smell the tart sea air carried on the morning breeze.

A walk to the sea would soothe her restlessness. She went back to the farm of the family who had found her before and told them that Miriam had gone and not come back for many days and that she was looking for her. She told them she thought Miriam had said she was going to the sea and would they take her to look. On foot it was a week-long journey for an old woman, maybe longer as she tired more quickly these days. Their harvest was in and now they were gathering wood and the dried manure of the cattle for the winter hearth. They could take a day to ride to the sea to look for their friend Miriam. The young man had a brother who was a fisherman and they could stay with him while they searched. Before they set off on their journey, they stopped at their own village church for mass and Mayken noticed the priest looking at her, not so young anymore but younger by far than Mayken, and still both suspicious and cautious. She looked through him with no expression as if daring him to accuse her of something. She took communion and suffered his touch with serenity.

After the mass he followed them out into the autumn air, so cool and soothing yet ominous, a hint of storm coming, a warning of winter, it seemed to the priest that storms followed Mayken. He asked the young man where they were going and why and the young man, not quite as trusting of priests as he seemed, told the story of a visit to his brother before the winter weather set in and the roads would be too wet. The priest, not trusting Mayken, arranged for the little family with their guest to be followed.

§§§§§

Isaac and Philemon were welcomed to Seattle's netherworld by a slender fiddler named Jake and a large bulky man named Benjamin who followed Jake everywhere. Benjamin seemed to Isaac to be in love with Jake and to Philemon to be soft in his mind. They were both right. Jake although well into his thirties, perhaps older, had a childlike look to him, the barest blond fuzz on smooth cheeks and large innocent blue eyes. He was medium height and extremely slender. Benjamin walking behind or beside him always seemed to engulf him in the embrace of his large bear-like shadow.

Jake introduced the bigger man, ironically, as his "husband". Isaac and Philemon were embarrassed by Jake's candor but he didn't give them time to flounder, just went right on talking about the life in the catacombs, who was there, what to watch out for, how to act.

"Just be polite" he told them. He made more money than most of the men in the catacombs who did day labor when they could get it. He played the violin like an angel and dressed up respectably in a white tuxedo left over from better days, to perform in the early afternoons. Some restaurants allowed him to stroll through to entertain their lunch patrons for tips, and dusk would bring him back to the shelter and safety of the catacombs with pockets full of cash. In the evenings Jake serenaded his friends in low places as he laughingly called them.

Soon Isaac also had a special function in the underground community. He became the designated Justice of the Peace. All disputes were taken to him for his Solomonic resolution and he was amazed that, with no procedure for enforcement, he was able by simple dignity and common sense to lay down the law for rough men who clearly respected him. Perhaps they were awed to see a man with his education among them. Although there were plenty who had read history and philosophy and literature and loved to banter ideas back and forth, usually when drunk, none had achieved such a high station in life as they believed he had when he admitted to having graduated from college.

§§§§§

Mayken lay awake all night at the Inn. She rarely slept anymore. And she heard the priest's messenger with a young serving boy come in after midnight and ask about her and her companions. He didn't stay but she heard him go outside to their wagon and watched through a window as he put something in it. She could see him clearly in the moonlight. She waited until dawn and then dressed and went outside to sniff the air and look for what had been left in the wagon. She found it beneath the seat in a place intended to be secret. The moon was still high in the clear blue sky and there was a light frost covering everything. Mayken retrieved what turned out to be a book and opened it carefully as it was frosted close. The book was a Lutheran bible and they could be arrested for carrying it. She knew the priest had had it planted there for a reason and she wanted to be rid of it but knew it wouldn't be safe to leave it at the Inn or try to discard it while the priest's spy might still be watching.

Mayken wrapped the book in her most intimate undergarments in her little bag and waited for a message to know what to do.

Sometimes Miriam talked to her, sometimes others. Eventually she would hear a voice and follow instructions. Perhaps the birds would tell her. Soon her companions were awake and got ready quickly to continue their journey while Mayken walked around in wide circles, hugging herself for warmth and watching the moon fade from the morning sky. They knew she was listening for birds. Old as she was, she would still insist on helping to harness the horses and talked soothing nonsense to the animals that were always calm with her. "What do you think I should do?" she asked the horses and some children nearby stifled laughter.

§§§§§

As the weather warmed and it stayed light longer on top, Jake came home later and later from his concerts and often Bennie would get tired and bored and return to the catacombs earlier without him. He didn't like to, but Jake would urge him to go home, promising to follow soon thereafter. Problem was, he didn't always come home at all and Bennie would be up at dawn, sensing the hour by the sound of the birds, and go searching for Jake. Oft-times he would find Jake hung over with some lover of the night and, broken hearted, Bennie would carry him to their home underground looking for all the world like a gigantic troll in a tale kidnapping the fair-haired princess.

§§§§§

They reached the seaside village of Ostende at dusk and went directly to the brother's home. When all had eaten an evening meal of fish soup and potatoes they went to a local tavern to hear a wandering fiddler who had arrived that selfsame night. Mayken recognized the fiddler she had tried to follow once before and he was still wearing his simple peasant outfit of white cotton pants and tunic. He danced while he played. Mayken also recognized the priest's spy among the villagers and she grew afraid and told the young man about the book in the wagon. The young man told her he had an idea and would explain later as the spy was watching them that very moment. He then left Mayken to mingle among the villagers and she watched him engage in brief animated conversations with one after the other.

After the revelry in the tavern there was a ruckus when the

spy found a heretic Lutheran bible among the fiddler's things. At first Mayken thought her friend had put the book from their wagon where suspicion would be diverted away from them and she worried about the fate of the fiddler. Then she realized she must be wrong when someone else from the crowd yelled that they had found another one of the blasphemous bibles among their traveling clothes. Soon all the villagers were producing bibles and shouting that some stranger amongst them must be planting the evil books. They called to one another to burn the books and find the cursed heretic who had done the terrible thing, contaminating their righteous community. Naturally suspicion fell first on the strangers among them, the priest's messenger and his companion. Then some of them confronted the spy with such ferocity, such righteous and holy indignation that he decided to abandon his mission.

"Burn the books and burn the heretic that brought them here!" someone shouted and soon the Jesuit spy and his companion were seen galloping out of town at breakneck speed leaving their wagon behind. When Mayken asked the young man where he had found so many of the wrong kind of bible, he asked her if she had seen anyone actually read any of the books that had been brandished at the spies. The people asked the fiddler to play again and he played through the night, while the people laughed and danced and enjoyed themselves and he was well paid in the morning. Then the little family left to return to the care of their home and livestock and take Mayken back to her home.

§§§§§

Jake was gone all summer, living several weeks at a time with different lovers, reveling in the sunshine and warmth, reveling as well in the drama of romance and broken hearts, a drama he played out in cycles like his alcoholic binges. Bennie never stopped looking for him and when he did encounter Jake, whether in a dive or some fancier accommodation, he would plead with Jake to come home and Jake was always kind to Bennie and promised to return and sometimes he did, for a night or two. Bennie never became disillusioned with Jake's habit of breaking promises. When Philemon talked to him about it, Jake only laughed. When Isaac tried to talk to him as well he made light of his concern.

"Bennie is simple minded" he told Isaac, "He doesn't even know enough to be jealous."

"Bennie may be too innocent to be jealous of your tawdry affairs. But he has the sense to worry that you expose yourself to danger when you consort with any stranger. He loves you more than himself and you repay him with contempt and indifference. When I first heard you play such beautiful music I thought you had a lofty soul but clearly it is base, unworthy of such a gift. You abuse everything you are given, talent, love, you don't deserve these gifts."

Isaac instantly regretted his harsh words but Jake was gone before Isaac's words were done, let alone recanted. Isaac had chided Jake for breaking such a pure and innocent heart, but it was his own heart that was broken. Isaac had invented a dream of the camaraderie of the catacombs that was as innocent as Bennie's for Isaac truly believed that the camaraderie in this surreal world beneath the city was conscious.

Bennie wandered through the storm of that late summer night to find Jake the last time, still and pale and bloody from numerous stab wounds with a sign on his chest that said FAG in red letters fading fast in the rain. He examined Jake frantically, needing to see everything he couldn't bear to see. Jake's genitals had been cut off and stuck in his mouth and it was that horrific mutilation that caused Bennie's voice to dry up forever. He sat there silent in the rain shivering until someone found him and the body. First it was just a couple of people asking each other what happened, then a crowd formed and all around Bennie and Jake people shouted, calling for an ambulance, shouting that it was too late, get the police, and the police were already there, shouting to be let through, but all the noise came to Bennie's ears as if from very far away and he sat hunched over on the wet pavement in a vacuum of sound, of reality, even the rain stopped falling in that small space that enclosed Bennie and Jake.

§§§§§

Mayken stayed in her tower all the time now. She didn't even walk out to follow the lightning storms that clustered that year around a lingering autumn. She neither ate nor drank but talked incessantly to the birds that flocked to the open window for nothing more than the sound of her voice. She had become the voices she heard. She was trying to die now, to follow Miriam, but it took so long and she prayed for the lightning to take her, lifting her into the sky to fly with the birds. When the last autumn storm broke the afternoon sky, she reached for the lightning flash, leaning far out her window and the lightening reached for her and clasped her hand in its embrace of death.

§§§§§

When Isaac looked upon the hatred and violence that had been done to Jake's body, he remembered why he had left his home and resolved to get it done. A leap from the top of a high building was the easiest way, the journey he had imagined so many times. Before Philemon noticed Isaac had gone, Isaac had a city block head-start on his friend and saw exactly where he was going. Philemon ran through the streets alone calling Isaac's name in a desperate benediction. Bennie still paralyzed with a horrified grief had been lifted up by strangers and walked to a bench inside a building somewhere and there he sat and couldn't help and everyone else was huddled in doorways and telling the police that they didn't know anything, had just come over when they saw the huge man crying loudly over something and no one but Philemon noticed Isaac and poor Philemon was struggling to catch up to his friend when he was stopped by a policeman who thought he must be running away from the scene of the crime and precious minutes were wasted before they realized he was chasing his friend and why. And then they all ran with him but were too late to catch Isaac.

Isaac ran up and up the stairs of a warehouse he found and then out the last exit door that let him out onto the asphalt roof ten stories above the street. He never jumped. A sudden flash of lightning caught his upraised arms and lifted him into the heavens where Philemon could see him, at last, illuminated like a prophet. It seemed like a costume falling and fluttering through the air so lightly with no body inside, but when the crowd ran to the heap of clothes on the sidewalk there was indeed a body inside, broken, shuddering and then still. The clouds broke again and again, raining down on the city, on the people, the living and the dead, and cleansing everything.

§§§§§

Mayken flew awhile, wafting on rising currents of warm air that rose from the earth as it steamed in the rain. She felt herself transform, her arms becoming wings that she moved through the air with strong slow strokes, like swimming in the sea, like she had so often practiced in her dreams. She could see herself below as a woman reaching out for the sky from her tower and the Cathedral tower growing smaller and smaller as she soared higher and higher. The people were tiny like ants and swarmed over the countryside to the sea, running hard and breathlessly, while she rode the waves of air without effort. Mayken flew to find the far off crow of so many mornings and watched a fiery sun explode the sky beneath and around her and fill her own lungs with light until she cried for joy.

She-mei de-ku-de-sha, be-rich hu, le-ei-la

Min kol bi-re-cha-ta ve-shi-ra-ta, tush be-cha-ta

Ve-ne-che-ma-ta da-a-mi-ran

Be-al-ma, ve-i-me-ru: a-mein

Chapter Fourteen
The Wedding

Denver October 1990

"La ora mas eskura es antes del amaneser"
The darkest hour leads to the dawn
Old Ladino proverb

Rose tried to ignore the pain in her groin and sleep in her warm bed but finally she was forced by her nagging, insistent body to get up in the cold dark night and go to the bathroom. She glanced at the luminous numbers of her digital clock: 2:12 a.m. and she knew it would take hours to get back to sleep. She groped in the dark, feeling for the door, having again forgotten to switch on the night light. She felt lost and confused in the dark, as if in a strange house.

During her three marriages and during the times in between, she had lived in six different houses and three more as a child. She never knew anymore which one she would wake up in. She passed too many mirrors in this bathroom and the night-light caste eerie shadows across her face. She frightened herself and decided to switch on the overhead light, bracing herself for the shock. She stared at her face, barely recognizing it. Her face was old in this glare. Her face reminded her of Dolores. Her apartment reminded her of the last place Dolores had lived. Dolores had retired from full-time teaching early and supplemented her pension with occasional substitute teaching jobs around the city. She played cards with friends once a week and walked in the park near her building. She didn't read much in the end because her vision made that too laborious and tedious a task. She had stopped playing the piano when Isaac had disappeared because she felt guilty playing the music that he had so loved when he was not there to hear it. "The end" for Dolores had been years and years of gradual and aggravating decline that Rose had been determined to overcome in her own old age.

Finally Dolores, despite the dictates of the church, had tried to bring the end closer, to avoid surprise and pain, and she took an overdose of various pills she had been collecting. She had called Rose one evening and asked her to come by the next morning, not before ten o'clock she had said and Rose recalled all of these details as if they were yesterday, more vividly even than that, as if they were occurring just as she recalled them one at a time.

When Rose arrived the door was ajar and she knew that something was wrong because Dolores had always locked both the locks on her door, a precaution which Rose had often scoffed at. She called her mother's name and then entered into a palpable silence. She found Dolores on her bed with her dolls that Rose hadn't known she collected. They weren't collectors' dolls but children's' toys, baby dolls and a bride doll and Dolores had made them all clumsy clothes, badly sewn, un-hemmed and pinned together. On the dresser were her papers, some jewelry and the key to her safety deposit box. No note. But Dolores was still breathing and, without thinking, Rose acted in a panic and called an ambulance and burdened her mother with two more months of unwanted life.

After pumping her stomach, the ER Doctor decided to do some tests on the patient who seemed to have little control over her body, falling out of bed and bumping into walls. That was when they found the tumor in her brain that had grown too large to be operable, the cause of the unbearable headaches that her own Doctor had dismissed as the hypochondria of a lonely old woman.

Rose never forgave herself for interfering, for subjecting her mother to more weeks of pain and the humiliation of a nursing home and the unwanted attentions of Doctors who had never seen her as an intelligent and healthy, even beautiful human being. Rose remembered them as hovering vultures that discouraged her daily visits.

"She can't see you. She doesn't even know you are here." one told her, first holding then dropping her mother's limp hand to demonstrate his point.

"She knows I am here." Rose told him, picking up her mother's discarded hand and holding it silently until visiting hours were over.

Rose looked into the mirror and saw that she was crying. So many ways for old women to die she thought, the diseases that bent their backs almost double, suffered alone after the men had escaped the slow and painful, the humiliating, deaths of women by dying suddenly, sometimes spectacularly, often heroically and widely mourned. Old women too often outlived their mourners she mused.

She wasn't sleepy. She put on her robe and slippers and went into the kitchen, turning lights on as she went, and made a cup of mint tea. Mint was good to calm the nerves and still the racing out-of-control brain. She used to meditate, thought she should again, not tonight though: tomorrow, and tomorrow and then again tomorrow, like most things, postponed indefinitely. She fell asleep in her chair and woke up as the sky began to lighten. Luisa would already be out walking. Rose went back to bed and slept soundly, dreamlessly, peacefully in the clear morning light.

"Ma, ma, wake up ma. Its ten o'clock already."

Rose opened her eyes slowly, luxuriating in waking very slowly, stretching her legs a bit.

"I called up but you didn't answer so I used my key. I was worried ma. Are you alright? We were supposed to go shopping for wedding dresses today, remember?"

"I'm alright" Rose said, "go fix a cup of tea while I wake up and dress."

Alone in her room again, Rose finished her recollection: her mother's last words: "I didn't need those last twenty years" was what Dolores had told Rose before slipping into the coma from which she never awoke.

But Rose had a wedding to go to and she was determined to be absolutely beautiful. She and Luisa were going to vintage shops to find exquisite antique dresses.

"It's impossible to get enough lace" Luisa had said, "except in the vintage stores."

§§§§

In the foreground, the bride in an oyster lace dress circa 1930. During that time women of elegant taste and limited means sometimes made fancy frocks out of lace tablecloths left over from better days. This appears to be one of those, in perfect condition. The groom by her side wears black dress wranglers and fine lizard skin boots, a black tuxedo jacket in the style called "cowboy cut" with a silver and lapis bolo and a silver belly Stetson. His gold and silver belt buckle proclaims him the winner of a saddle bronc competition some twenty years earlier. He sports lapis cufflinks and buttons, a gift from the bride, which match her earrings, a gift from him. There is no diamond on her engagement ring because, as she archly reminded him, diamonds come from South Africa and cost too many lives. She eschews gold for similar reasons but she draws the line of her austerity at silver worked with turquoise which she wears in a tasteful display.

In order not to offend any of his brothers, the groom stands alone and all his five brothers stand behind in a half circle that includes her mother, her father and a half-sister and half-brother. The father's current girlfriend and the spouses of the siblings stand beyond them with the groom's many cousins and in-laws and the bride's clients and friends, forming a colorful group on the left side. There are several distinctive portraits among them. On the right side is the band stand where a live local band sets up its equipment, and behind them, a lake, placid beneath a blue autumn sky and reflecting with perfect reciprocity the red and golden trees and lazy, white fluffy clouds above it. In the far background are blue and brown mountains topped with patches and glints of sun-golden snow.

Tucked in corners of the scene, the viewer can find small oddities: A woman on horseback disappears into trees, a priest leans against a rock reading a book. Making her way through the trees toward the wedding party is an extremely old woman with a crow sitting on top of her bent back. She leads a trail of gleaming silver water that has broken through the grassy ground she has trod. Also in the trees stands a young man in boots, breeches and stained smock. He is very still hiding behind an easel on which leans a painting. The painting reproduces the entire scene including the painter.

The short ceremony begins. They have labored carefully over the few discreet lines. Juan Carlos said his family would be disappointed if God wasn't mentioned and Luisa said fine but no, absolutely no mention of Christ, and no gender designations: no God the father or God the king stuff.

"What do you want? God the mother, God the queen?" he'd asked desperately afraid she might say yes.

"No, just God will do fine, it's neutral, everyone can draw their own inferences, and of course none of that stuff about obedience either way, 'obedience' implies an archaic idea of hierarchy that we want no part of." Juan Carlos just said "OK, go for it" and she wrote the rest of the speech.

It emphasizes mutual respect, and no one really listens anyway. When they practiced it with a stop watch and it only took five minutes, ("My family will never understand such a short ceremony" he had told her " They are used to Catholic weddings") they decided to beef up the ceremony with more music. She wanted classical and he wanted George Strait so they compromised on some songs by Kathy Matea. He knew she wouldn't turn down songs written by a modern woman, just none of that Tammy Wynette stuff.

For the dance afterward they agreed that the local Chicano band would have to expand their repertoire of Nashville hits and Mexican Rancheras and learn some Israeli folksongs as well. It is a heady mix that dancing. After the bride and groom walk through the soap bubbles the guests blow at them and cut the cake which is served from a portable picnic table, they open with a traditional waltz which expands to include all the closest family members and then they go right to the money dance before folks have a chance to get tired. Then the band proudly plays the Hora they have just learned and everyone is soon drawn into the circle and they dance around and around, faster and faster, and some boys break from the line and enter the center of the circle to perform some tricky maneuver that looks like break-dancing but is really an old Russian folk dance for men, and finally, the men make two circles and lift the bride and groom on chairs above them.

Her father had brought the chairs along with the glass that Juan Carlos had broken beneath his heel at the end of the service. He told his brothers that this was an ancient Jewish custom that would in no way imperil his soul. While everyone's energy is still up from the circle dancing, they play "*La Bamba*" and then "Hey Baby Qué Paso?" so many times that whoever didn't know the words to sing along the first time around is singing loudly by the fifth. When the band notices folks breathing heavy and sitting down on lakeside benches or the steps of the bandstand to eat second servings of wedding cake, they begin some slow romantic songs and lure everyone back to pay tribute to love.

One of Lois' clients approaches with a dollar for the money dance and they talk a bit.

"So" he says tactfully, "What do you think of that big-shot Means selling out to Hollywood?"

"Oh I don't hold that against him, I suppose some of those stereotypical roles are insulting, but those movies would be made anyway and there's been some bad feeling that non-Indians get to play Indian parts and real Indians can't get parts, you know?"

"So you forgive him?"

"It's not really my place to forgive the guy, he can do what he wants but yes I forgive him for several reasons."

"Like what?"

"Well, to begin with, from the moment we are born we begin our journey toward death and when we are dying and know it, all we crave is forgiveness."

"That's heavy."

"And because like I said, he isn't hurting anyone, at least not by being in the movies. He's human, I'm sure he's hurting someone somewhere."

"Whatever."

"And, you know, he laughed at my jokes."

"Now that I can understand."

"Well, my friend, there's quite a line out there and I got to dance for my dowry."

"Thanks. You guys have a great honeymoon and don't forget my sentencing hearing when you get back."

They part with big grins, feeling good about their lives.

Juan Carlos had given one of Lois' mental health clients a buck to pin on her dress so he could have a dance and he talked all the time about the ducks on the lake and he was just sure some more birds had escaped from the zoo. He was so excited Luisa was afraid he was planning another break from the home and reminded him that if he stayed put she and Juan Carlos would take him out for really good Mexican food when they got back from their honeymoon.

"Don't you worry. I ain't goin' nowhere this time."

Dancing a slow number with one of her brothers in law, Luisa gets the chance to watch her mother dancing with her husband and is gratified to see her so happy, beaming in fact. Each dance gets shorter and shorter as the line gets longer and longer and soon the couple has greenbacks pinned all over them. Juan Carlos is ready to leave then. They had decided, at their age and the second time around, they could skip the traditional kidnapping . . . "If anyone is going to kidnap the bride, it's going to be me and I ain't bringing her back for several weeks so you guys don't hold your breath" was what he told his cousins who were thinking up hiding places.

When the bride and groom get into his pick-up to ride into the sunset, the people dance on and some folks make runs to a liquor store on Colfax. A couple of the brothers get into a half-hearted fight just to make the wedding official. By dark everyone has dispersed to smaller parties around the city. Only a lone guitarist remains playing sad tunes and drawing a crowd of homeless men and women around him. The painter packs up his paints and easel and loads them, along with the painting, into a pickup truck and drives away. The old woman disappears into the trees from whence she had come. As the evening chills and a full moon ascends, a mist rises from the still warm waters of the lake. The lingering image of the reds and yellows gives a sense of homecoming.

18557464R00106

Made in the USA
Charleston, SC
10 April 2013